PRAISE FOR KITTY COOK

"A gratifying romantic and personal adventure."

— *Kirkus Reviews* on *Sleeping Together*

"This genre-bending romantic thriller delivers steamy chemistry, razor-sharp witty banter, and twist after twist."

— BookLife Prize on *Sleeping Together*

"Through her exploration of the dangers of being a woman in a male dominant society, Cook turns a modern-day love triangle into a thought-provoking story about the inner conflict that drives humanity to seek stability while avoiding stagnation. SLEEPING TOGETHER is a marriage between romance and thriller that will leave the reader with questions about the nature of love and a yearning for adventure."

— IndieReader on *Sleeping Together*

Poison Dream

Poison Dream

PERFECT DRUG, BOOK 2

Kitty Cook

BRASS ANVIL BOOKS

SEATTLE

Printed in the United States of America

ISBN-13 (paperback): 9781732998421
ISBN-13 (ebook): 9781732998438

Cover design by Scott Howard

Brass Anvil Books
Seattle, WA

KITTY COOK BOOKS

PERFECT DRUG

Sleeping Together

Poison Dream

TUESDAY, APRIL 16

Why am I still keeping a journal when I'm not taking Morpheum anymore? Probably a valid question. But when you consider all the non-FDA-approved pills I ate over the past few months, I can't really see a downside to keeping track of things—you know, to make sure they actually happened. After watching *some* Morpheum patients (*cough, cough,* Ness, *cough*) exhibit a hard time telling fact from fiction, I worry that my mind will similarly poop the bed—that I'll get confused and (I don't know) throw myself out a window thinking I can fly.

NOTE TO SELF: I CANNOT FLY.

So, I'm going to keep up with my note-taking, and I don't care if it's a little precious. I, Altan Young, am a modern man: I'm allowed to have a diary.

In the interest of establishing a record of sorts, here is what I *think* has gone down so far in regard to this WellCorp debacle, rendered in full, exquisite detail—because Ness wandered off to photograph the back of Notre Dame twenty minutes ago, and now I know enough to guess that she won't be back for at least eight hours, *so I have the time.*

I met Ness two years ago when she joined WellCorp as my fellow medical trial coordinator, a job she was jazzed about as much I was, which is to say not at all. I'd always thought she was cool to have at the office, first because she was capable at her job (which meant I didn't have to do any extra work), and second because she literally gave no shits about me. Some people are dogs that slobber all over you and stick their noses in your crotch and make you pet them. Ness is an especially antisocial cat who thinks you're a dick, which has the effect of making you want to prove that you're *not* a dick—or that you're (at the very least) a dick who has value in that you can make her laugh.

I liked making Ness laugh at work. It really broke up the day.

When June and I split up, I hired Ness's husband to represent me since I didn't know any other divorce lawyers. Hell, I don't know a lot of lawyers in general, so I have no idea if they're all as chill as Pete, who would schedule most of our meetings at this bar near my apartment so I could drink while he illustrated the many ways in which my life was falling apart. When business was over, he'd join me in a beer so I wouldn't have to go immediately home to my (tiny, inhospitable, shitty) apartment. He'd talk about Ness in passing, not a lot, but enough for me to imagine they had a good thing going.

I spent a lot of half-drunk nights in my new bachelor pad, imagining my lawyer going home to my coworker in their tastefully cream apartment, where they cooked dinner and chatted about their days over wine. How does anyone come up with anything to talk about after looking at spreadsheets for eight hours a day? Beats me (clearly), but I guess they figured *something* out. Lucky them.

Or not, because apparently the one thing Ness *didn't* want to talk about was having kids—but Pete wanted to, so eventually the situation ended up inducing some gnarly stress nightmares for her. I did what any good work friend would do: I slipped her a couple of sleeping pills I'd been stealing from our latest pharmaceutical trial to combat my own post-divorce insomnia.

BUT IT TURNS OUT that if you take Morpheum under the right olfactory conditions, you can share dreams with other people. This was discovered in the weirdest way possible when Ness and I accidentally mind-sexed each other in our sleep. Awkward, but then we were like, "I wonder what else we can do while high?" So, *for purely scientific reasons*, we decided to keep dreaming together.

Ness made it clear that she wasn't looking for anything other than some medical experimentation and maybe a little nonsexual mischief, which was fine by me. I wasn't *looking* to fall for her either, but still I did. Like an idiot. What can I say? Chemistry always wins.

SO *THEN* out of the blue, our boss (weapons-grade jerkoff, Malcolm Jacobs) started getting handsy with Ness at work. To up the creep factor, he threatened to fire her if she didn't keep giving meds to one of our patients, who ended up overdosing himself into a coma. Yadda, yadda, yadda: Ness had a breakdown in front of our CEO and confessed to stealing company property and being high on the job, which . . . wasn't the *best* idea? But hey, she got the months-long medical trial thrown out to keep Morpheum away from public consumption—so that was good!

But then we found out torpedoing the trial was what Malcolm wanted all along so he could convince his dad to sell Morpheum to the government since there was no other market for it.

So, that sucked.

After Ness got fired, she stole all the pills I had rightfully stolen from work and treated herself to a weeklong bender, which also sucked because she was *deep* into the dreams to the point where I wasn't sure she'd come back to reality. And if I lost her, even though I never really *had* her in the first place, I would have a hard time living with myself. Or anyone else, for that matter.

The last turd into the fan was when Ness dreamed she was pregnant—only she didn't realize she'd taken the test in a dream.

When she told Pete he was going to get that family he'd always wanted, he accused her of cheating on him, because they hadn't had sex in over a month (side note: *really?*) and Ness was like *Whaaaat?* Pete walked out, and in a blind panic she decided to leave the country, and I just happened to catch her as she was walking out the door, so I came along for the ride.

Now we're in Paris, and even though we've only been here a week, Ness has already taken at least twenty-billion pictures. Surprisingly, only ten of them are of the Eiffel Tower, and (unsurprisingly) only one of them is of me. She prefers subjects that I don't exactly consider "special." Like, I'll watch her snap a photo of a bicycle leaning up against a tree and think, "Why are you documenting something this boring?" But when I see the photos she downloads to her laptop every evening, they're *really* interesting: maybe because they are so boring, but she makes them seem cooler than they actually are. For all the times I've been inside of her head, she still manages to surprise me with the way she sees the world.

Anyway, on Morpheum, Ness and I kind of jumped straight from work banter to trauma resolution without much small talk in between, so it's nice to go on actual dates: no pills, no shortcuts, no gimmicks. We tell stories like normal people do instead of replaying the footage in our minds. At night, instead of exploring Machu Picchu or blowing up the Death Star, we drink wine and watch French TV in bed and dub over the dialogue with fart jokes, which is exhilarating in a different way.

When it's time to sleep, Ness curls her body around mine and drifts off almost immediately. I play with her hair and try not to think about having sex with her. (Even if we've just had sex, I still think about it.) So much of it reminds me of high school, when someone's parents would go out of town and there'd be a party, and by some miracle I'd commandeer the last sofa in the house when everything would be winding down—and even more miraculously there'd be a girl I liked who needed a place to sleep. She'd fold herself into me the way all girls know how to do, and I'd wonder if I was brave enough to try something but wouldn't because the sheer pleasure of her body against mine was the most erotic thing I'd ever experienced at sixteen years old.

It feels like that with Ness, all this mystery and potential. Lying there in the dark with her in my arms, I wonder what she dreams.

I've been asking myself, *Why do I enjoy this woman?* Because as smart as Ness is, she makes some *really* dumb decisions (see the aforementioned drug use)—not to mention the fact that she's *ridiculously* stubborn and (understandably) in need of therapy. But all of this makes her interesting, and challenging, and frustrating, and complicated: things that are completely underrated in relationships. People say they like being happy, but happiness can look a lot like boredom. Personally, I like being entertained.

Before we left Seattle, Ness said she wanted to come to Paris together to figure out—how'd she put it?—if we were "lovers or lab partners." I don't know which way she's leaning, but I'm voting for lovers.

Or, at the very least, lab partners who have sex and travel the world together until they die. That would work for me, too.

THE
SEXIEST PLACE

On my fifth date with Peter Brown (future lawyer, sometime bartender, collector of books, world-class kisser), he takes me to the sexiest place he knows: the central branch of the Seattle Public Library.

"Seriously?" I scoff as we walk up to the doors off of Fifth Avenue—not Fourth, Pete insists, because you can't see the ceiling from that entrance. "*This* is sexy?"

His blue eyes light up in good-natured shock, two electric spots against the paleness of his complexion and the concrete color of winter. "Of course, it is! When was the last time you were here?"

"Grade school."

He slumps his shoulders, relieved. "That explains it. They never show you the sexy stuff in grade school." Here, Pete tries to wink—and fails. Both his eyes flinch.

I can't tell if he *thinks* he's a good winker, or if he knows he's a bad one and does it regardless. Either way, I like how he shakes off the landings he doesn't stick, like being imperfect is no big deal. A high tolerance for flaws is chief among my requirements in a date.

Look at my reflection in the glass door: see what I mean? The perky ponytail I spent thirty minutes fixing in my bathroom mirror has been flattened by rain. I yank the elastic out in case Pete hasn't yet noticed what a complete and melodramatic *train wreck* I am, but this only leaves a tremendous divot in my hair. *Shit.*

As if reading my mind, Pete takes my chilly hand and says with the tiniest hint of blush (maybe it's just the cold), "You look great." When I catch another glimpse of our reflection, I see that he's right: we look good together. He pulls the door open for me.

The library is a behemoth of modern architecture skinned in glass and harlequin-latticed steel—a misshapen box ten stories high that crumples in some parts and protrudes at others, creating fantastic creases on the inside where those gigantic angles meet. "I love this ceiling," says Pete, craning his neck to look up. (I notice, for the tenth time in as many minutes, how much I love his Adam's apple.) "Every time I come here, I spend at least ten minutes looking up. Probably a bit much."

It's not. When the rain is on the *outside*, Seattle under all this glass could pass for mysterious and misty, like those moors Romantics always harp on about. Pete would look great on some moors. He's got the jawline for it, and that aforementioned paleness, and that disheveled hair of his is just begging to be ravaged by wind. I wish I had my camera. I tell him, "Most people don't take enough time to appreciate what's right in front of them."

We ride escalators up to the eighth floor: *Literature.* The architecture up here is function over form: no glass, low ceilings, cramped stacks with bland metal bookshelves. Pete unzips his parka to reveal a blue button-front shirt wrinkled in places but not all over, like he tried to iron it but realized he had no idea how half-way through. *No biggie.* He wanders, pulling books expertly, a cook selecting ingredients for a dish.

At twenty-one years old, I'm old enough to know guys who claim to like poetry are probably tools. But Pete is a real-deal connoisseur of the written word. The shelves in his apartment are bursting with books—novels and essay collections and tomes of poems. Their spines are cracked, pages dog-eared, passages underlined and annotated in his small, academic cursive. I know, because last Tuesday—the morning after we had sex for the first time—when he rushed off to class but told me to stay because he'd be back in an hour, I thumbed through his books to check if he'd even read most of them. He had.

There is much to like about Peter Brown—his playfulness, his encyclopedic knowledge of weird trivia, how he argues for fun the same way wolf pups practice biting each other, and beneath all that a whiff of shy awkwardness he tries so hard to pretend he doesn't have. But when I saw his books, I knew I could *love* him. He is with his library as I am with my camera. I don't know what to call it, but he and I have this same double vision: in one eye, there is the world, and in the other, there is this search for a richer story or a prettier picture—a kind of art overlaid on the mundane you can only see when you're quiet and alone.

With a stack of books in the crook of his arm, Pete takes me back down to the heart of the library to a table for two near the coffee shop (it's Seattle: of course there's a coffee shop). "I'm going to show you how sexy the library is," he tells me when we're seated with our hot chocolates. Opening the book at the top of his stack, he licks the pad of his middle finger and flicks the page.

I am treated to Pablo Neruda and his thirsty milk. Ellen Bass's basket of figs. The filthy letters from James Joyce to Nora Barnacle about how much "cockstand" he gets when she farts, and I shriek so loud into my hands. Pete watches me like it's the greatest thing he's ever seen, my smile—even better than the ceiling we sit under. His eyes widen in proportion to my mouth.

I'm completely smitten with his bookishness, his dedication to reading "dirty little fuckbird" straight-faced, with a crappy Irish accent just to make me giggle. He's funny and patient, and he doesn't push me into anything—not like the other guys I've gone out with. (Or haven't.) I know we've only been dating for a few weeks, but Peter Brown makes me feel safe.

Wait: "safe" is doing him a disservice. I *should* say that Peter Brown doles out peril in doses I can handle, because when he leans over to kiss me like one of his poems, it feels deliciously dangerous, to be snogging in the library. His jaw is smooth beneath my palm. His thumb caresses the spot just below my ear, the four fingers of his right hand cradling the base of my skull. I imagine them trailing down my back, along the outside of my hip until they take the hairpin turn of my knee and go north again. "Let's get out of here," I purr into his ear.

A voice, low and lazy, replies, "For sure. Lunch is almost over, and Malcolm will shit if we're late."

Who?

When I pull back, Pete is gone. In his place is another man: dark-haired instead of blonde, gold-skinned instead of pale, bearded instead of clean-shaven. He wears a nondescript flannel open over a nondescript T-shirt, and his posture is *the worst*, like even his bones are too lazy to stand up straight. "Did you find those books on Wiccan dream magic?" he asks, tossing his chin to swing an errant lock of straight black hair out of his eyes.

"Um, what?"

"Hello? We're supposed to be *researching?*" He slaps an open book shut and pounds it on top of a stack.

"I'm sorry," I stammer. "I don't know who you are."

"Of course, you do. I'm your boyfriend."

"No, *Pete* is my boyfriend."

Another toss of hair, this time toward whatever is going on behind me. "Not for long."

I turn—and there's my date, bound to a leather armchair about twenty yards away. He's gagged with a white handkerchief, arms tied behind him: basic victim pose. Stacks of oil drums surround him in tipsy-looking columns. "You better hurry," bearded dude says as he holds up a detonator with comically large digits. "Once I press this, you got thirty seconds till *boom.*"

Every muscle in my body coils. "Why are you doing this?"

He treats me to a sinister flash of teeth. "I get bored."

When the clock starts counting, I run: toward Pete, not away. But when I get to him, the armchair is too heavy. The knots are too tight. There's not enough time, and Pete's eyes bulge with fear. 9, 8, 7—

When I pull the gag off, he tells me to run, but instead I stay and kiss him, thinking how *unfair* it is that he and I end like this, without getting married or growing old together. All we got was five dates and some poetry; all we get is each other's mouths and five more seconds, but the way Pete kisses me . . . it's like that's all we need. The energy in the room compresses inward, the paper of the books and the panes of the glass ceiling shimmy as the clock goes 3, 2, 1—

THE
CRASH LANDING

Ding.

The fasten-seatbelt sign on the ceiling panel above me pinged on.

"Errrr, good morning, ladies and gentlemen," a voice crackled from unseen speakers, as my heart threatened to punch a hole in my sternum. "This is yourrrrrr captain speaking. We're making our final descent, so flight attendants, errrrrr, please prepare for arrival."

"Yo!" said Altan as he slung his headphones around his neck. The greeting was suspiciously Platonic, like what he would have said two-ish months ago when we were coworkers with solid psychic barriers and not the mental lovers-*cum*-actual lovers we were now. "You good?"

Sure, I could be good—assuming I had woken to a plane (pun intended) of consciousness that other people could also experience without pharmaceutical help. I blinked against the gray light provided by dozens of small oval windows. This was that plane, right?

Sure, it was. It had to be. The stink was unmistakable: body funk and lavatory chemicals and recycled air. A dream plane wouldn't smell nearly this bad.

I scrubbed my hands up and down my face, trying to wake myself up. "Dude, I just had the most messed-up dream."

Altan had a smirk that was either sexy or terrifying, depending on if you'd recently seen it in in your mind's eye before exploding into a pink mist. "Was I in it? Was I *naked?*" he teased.

"No. You blew up Pete and me in the middle of our fifth date."

The smirk slid right off his face. I was sorry to see it go. "*How?*"

"Remember *The Dark Knight* when Joker kills Rachel Dawes?"

"Barrels of explosives." He nodded like this was a clue to a game I didn't yet know was afoot. Without the clarity of Morpheum, Altan and I had started to psychoanalyze ourselves the old-fashioned way. It was both exhausting and inefficient. "Is your subconscious trying to tell you something?"

"That I made a mistake in running away with you?" I quipped.

He looked unfairly good for the tail end of a transatlantic flight. I'd learned in Paris that Altan's grooming regimen required three different products to make his hair look like he'd just rolled out of bed, though on the plane he came by the mess honestly. (His beard was always scruffy. It required no special maintenance.) The rest of his outfit was disheveled chic: skinny jeans, gray T-shirt, black hoodie, Converse sneakers. The ensemble was pure Seattle, a city whose pragmatic fashion sense could best be described as *outdoor clothes to smoke weed in.* "Did you?" he said.

"Did I what?"

His eye roll clearly stated: *get a grip.* "Make a mistake in running away with me?"

Oh. Right. *That.* I craned my neck, looking for the flight attendant with the coffee cart. No dice. "Can you ask me when I'm not jet-lagged?"

"Nice try. With me, you're always going to be jet-lagged."

"Well, then." My attempt at being coy was marred by a T. rex–size yawn. "I guess I'm always going to be avoiding that question."

Ever since leaving for Paris two weeks ago, Altan and I had been trying to keep things light—things like: our sudden unemployment (his voluntary, mine not). The fact that a man was in a coma due to my professional negligence. How I'd accidentally left my husband. Our tandem recovery from sleeping pill addiction. You know: normal, everyday things that don't warrant any kind of stress—not when you're in Paris and there's *that* much wine.

I took, conservatively, about three thousand pictures of our trip. The champagne we drank beneath the Eiffel Tower on a stolen airplane blanket. The gardens of Versailles on a day so hot we got sunburned. Altan at Père Lachaise Cemetery, mounting the recumbent bronze statue of Victor Noir while I felt myself die of both embarrassment and hysterics. At one of the outdoor kiosks along the Seine, he bought me a stack of sepia photographs tied with a trim velvet ribbon. "I guess these are someone else's memories," he told me, handing over the bundle with a shrug, like even *he* couldn't believe how sappy he was getting. "For inspiration."

The photos I kept on the nightstand of our hotel. If I woke in the middle of the night confused as to where I was (this sometimes happened, but don't tell Altan), I could reach over and feel the velvet and the paper and know the pictures were real, that we were *here* in Paris, and Altan was wonderful, and all my dreams were coming true. In 32 years, I had never felt so light—this as I was hauling my camera everywhere and consuming the densest French cheeses known to man.

Now, Altan and I were jetting back to Jet City to sort out our affairs, so all the heavy stress we'd chucked into the bottom of a closet now had to be addressed. Outside, small snakes of water streamed across the window. Naturally, it was raining.

Le sigh. When returning to a town haunted by student debt and your soon-to-be-ex-husband for the sole reasons of selling your stuff and initiating your divorce, a little sunshine goes a long way in helping you think it's all going to work out. But Seattle isn't the best place to believe in happy endings. Between the drizzle and the rent hikes and the corporatism and the fact that they are now opening restaurants for dogs in storefronts where restaurants for people used to be, this city's motto might as well be *Remember you are screwed.*

If we survived, Altan and I were moving to Bali in a month. Yes, this had technically been *my* idea, but in my defense, I was drunk when I proposed it. (Damn you, Eiffel Tower airplane-blanket picnic!) Before I could sober up and walk it back, Altan had already set a plan in motion, which involved emailing some friend of a friend who was still in contact with the brother of his old boss from the *last* time he was in Bali six years ago to get us some jobs. "What kind of jobs?" I'd asked, hungover, the next morning.

"Surf instructing," he'd replied, to which I'd said, "No, seriously."

But he *was* being serious.

"So, I can't surf . . ." I said.

Altan scoffed in the face of setbacks. And reality. And maybe logic. "Of course, you can surf: you just don't know how to yet."

As much as I loved his optimism and his cryptic Yoda-style life coaching, I did not share his confidence. *Don't worry: we'll figure it out,* he kept telling me, but I didn't even know how to define the "it" he was referring to: a means of income? A knowledge of tides? A sense of comfort in the face of performing a net-less trapeze act with a partner potentially too cavalier to put chalk on his hands?

Living overseas had seemed like a fun idea when I had no chance of doing it, but now that it loomed on the horizon close enough to see, the logistics felt bonkers—especially with Altan at the helm. At WellCorp, he'd been easygoing bordering on comatose, a joke-cracking slacker with dubious life skills and that just-divorced smell. In dreams, he was more multidimensional: thoughtful and loyal and willing to throw himself between me and a Sasquatch.

But now, in the third act of getting to know each other, I saw that when he traveled, Altan was prone to an impulsiveness that stressed me the hell out. Either I didn't quite grasp the difference between carefree and careless, or Altan was a psychopath with no concern for his well-being. Exhibit A: That time he spent months ingesting sleeping pills that he stole from work for funsies.

Exhibit B: He walks barefoot on hotel carpets.

Exhibit C-J: Numerous French pâtés containing unspecified organs that he ate without a second thought.

Exhibit K and L: The two pairs of boxer briefs he'd brought with him, one to wear and one to wash nightly in the bathroom sink with a small bar of soap.

Altan retrieved a breakfast muffin from his seat-back pocket, which everyone knows is the grossest, most germ-ridden part of a plane. (Exhibit M.) "Do you want to talk about your dream?"

"Not really." I said, motioning for him to open the wrapper so I wouldn't have to touch it.

Without even asking why, he complied. "Back to avoiding sensitive topics, are we? How'd that work out for you last time?"

Har har. I slipped the muffin out of the cellophane and took a bite. (Too dry.) "I might be freaking out," I said with my mouth full so Altan wouldn't detect the nervousness in my voice.

He pinched off half my breakfast. "About?"

Mine wasn't a fear of missing out: it was a fear of opting in, a kind of preemptive buyer's remorse fueled by the possibility of karmic retribution and good old-fashioned low self-esteem that made me worry I didn't deserve to be happy. But how was I supposed to translate this existential squeamishness into words, out loud, without Morpheum? Where were my mental DMs when I needed them?

"So, all *this*?" I said, waving my arms as much as I could from a coach seat to denote "the vibe" of my life. "It's everything I ever wanted." (Understatement: I ODed on Morpheum chasing this world-traveling-photographer-who-got-to-have-sex-with-Altan dragon.) "But, now that I have it"—(along with economic uncertainty and a future full of dubiously washed undies)—"I guess I just . . . I feel like . . . like King Midol. Or something."

Altan choked on his portion of the muffin and coughed up a spray of crumbs. "*Who?*"

"You know." (Ugh. *Pete* would have gotten the reference.) "That Greek guy who was like, 'I want everything I touch to turn to gold,' but he forgot to say, 'Except people: duh.' And then he hugged his daughter and she died. King Midol?"

Altan was still pounding on his chest, trying to dislodge the carbs clogging up his trachea. When he finally managed to swallow, he said, "Are you talking about King *Midas*?"

Oh.

Oh no.

Altan *lived* for making fun of me, so I had to twist out of this right or I'd never hear the end of it. As much as I hated being teased, there was something undeniably sexy about Altan's BDSM relationship with my ego. When he found a flaw, he flogged the hell out of it while I begged him to stop. "Yeah, King Midas," I repeated, trying to sound casual. "What did you think I said?"

"You did *not* say King Midas." He was already quivering, like his glee would rip him apart. The lady across the aisle glared at him when he shrieked, "You said King Midol!"

Altan lurched forward in his seat with laughter, making a huge (but completely earnest) scene. "I'm half asleep!" I said, slapping him on his biceps with the back of my hand. (Altan did push-ups every morning when he woke up: you could tell.) "There's no coffee! How am I supposed to get my Greeks straight?"

Altan wasn't listening to my defense. "King Midol is making wishes like, 'I want everyone I touch to have less menstrual pain.'"

"Stop it!" I was laughing.

"And when he touches his daughter—"

"Shut *up*!"

"—her uterus explodes!"

"I hate you so much."

"No, you don't," Altan said through tears. "You enjoy me."

Enjoy. This was the verb we were using in lieu of anything more potent. There's nothing like an impending divorce to make you question all the things you thought you knew about love and its ability to sustain happiness. I imagine Eva Braun entertained similar notions as Hitler put the cyanide capsule in her mouth, like *OK, I love this guy, but does that* really *mean I have to eat this?*

After all, I loved Pete. There was a time in my life that *he* had been everything I'd ever wanted—and before that, all I'd ever wanted was my driver's license, and before that, a Game Boy for Christmas. I used to like ponies. I used to have bangs. I used to think I'd be OK living in Seattle all my life with a nice guy. People evolve. Tastes change—until you get married, and then for some reason everyone expects you to stay frozen to your person forever, like a tongue on a flagpole in winter.

I looked at Altan as he wiped the tears from his eyes, and the words just fell from my mouth: "I'm terrified this is all a bad idea."

He was unfazed, still chuckling weakly as he took my hand across the arm rest. It was a strong, assertive gesture, the kind you might execute right as the roller coaster stops clinking up the slope. "That's OK. You'll get braver."

"But what if this is a mistake? What if I get everything I wanted only to realize I shouldn't have wanted it in the first place?"

"Well, I guess you go back to the way things were."

"But what if I can't?"

"Then you make a new plan."

"I hate planning."

"Yeah, dude. Planning sucks."

One of the things I loved most about Altan was that he didn't minimize. Other people try to make molehills out of mountains so things look more scalable, but Altan stood with me in the shadow of my Fuji-sized fears and said, *Damn, this is a whole heap of angst.*

"It's a big thing to leave someone."

"You're right. It's huge."

"*Anyone* would be freaking out."

"Of course."

"It's not totally about you."

"I know it's not. Besides," he said, finally calming down. "You act like I didn't just go through this same thing. I get it. You're allowed to feel weird. Or scared. Or, like, you're not sure the future will be worth the price you're paying for it. Bird in the hand, two in the bush."

Fair, but also uncomfortable. One likes to feel confident in tremendous life-altering choices. When you take Morpheum, all that guesswork goes away. I'd gotten used to a certainty I didn't have anymore. "I can't tell if my remorse is just garden-variety adulterer's guilt or if it's *actual* regret," I said.

"Garden-variety adulterer's guilt," Altan replied, too quickly, like he hadn't even thought about it. "I'd bet money on it."

"How would you know? Did you ever cheat on June?"

"No."

I noted this with disappointment. Not that I *wanted* Altan to be an adulterer, but if he was, we could room together in hell when we died. "Well, with all due respect, you don't know how this feels."

"You're right. I don't," he agreed. Altan never got caught up in the urge to argue when we talked about important things, which was refreshing after being married to a lawyer who *loved* to object. "I'm sorry you're going through a hard time. Can I take your mind off it?"

"How?"

There were those teeth, the same ones I'd seen in the dream, wicked and sexy. He leaned forward and kissed me greedily. It was a kiss designed to lobotomize me, and for a second (or a hundred), it worked. I felt nothing except Altan's body and his need and his beard against my face (funny: it never tickled in a dream), and his heart going faster *ba-dum ba-dum ba-dum* along with mine. But then, stupidly, I opened my eyes and caught the lady across the aisle glaring at us again. "Altan, stop," I gasped. "People are staring."

His reply against my neck was, "Fuck 'em."

Was that the answer? Seriously? *That* was the thing I was supposed to do with my worries and fears and regrets—with Pete and Malcolm and poor Sam Stevens, who was in a coma because I wouldn't stand up to my garbage boss—*just don't even worry about them?* Sounded irresponsible, but maybe worth a shot.

I kissed Altan again, and I felt our future unspool before us. As we obnoxiously made out through the landing *and* the taxi to the gate, my stomach unclenched. My arms grew loose. This was me, becoming braver, turning into someone who only gave shits for important things, who didn't worry about the cleanliness of hotel rugs or the visual comfort of strangers or "financial security." I ran my fingers through Altan's thick hair and surrendered to whatever came next. I had no say over it anyway.

The pinging of the seatbelt sign brought us back to reality. I was officially free to move about the cabin, gather my baggage *and* my luggage, divorce my husband, and start a new life with someone who scared me in the best way possible. "You ready, King Midol?" Altan said.

"Depends. Are you ever going to stop calling me that?"

He handed me my backpack from the overhead bin. "Not any time soon."

Wedged into the aisle of the plane, we stood there smooshed against hundreds of smelly, disgruntled travelers, shuffling from foot to foot for what felt like ages. Altan was in front of me. "What's the holdup?" I whined as everyone around us asked each other the same thing.

"Don't know," he said, trying to leverage his height to look over the crowd. When we finally got to the gangway, he made a strangled noise as he saw the gate. "Damn. Homeland Security. They're checking papers."

"Don't they know we have sex to have?" I purred, helping myself to Altan's passport from his rear pocket and passing it over his shoulder. Altan had the passport of a real-life Indiana Jones: it was dog-eared and beat up, with the binding almost completely unraveled. He removed the rubber band he kept looped around it to keep all his miscellaneous visas enshrined. By contrast, my passport was so virginal it squeaked when I opened it for the officer after he'd waved Altan through.

"Vanessa Brown," the officer said smoothly, motioning to another person in a uniform who was standing just behind him. "Can you please come with us?"

"That depends," I said as even my pubic hair stood on end in warning. "What's this about?"

"Let's go someplace we can talk."

The officer put his hand beneath my upper arm. It wasn't an uncivil gesture, but since being grabbed by a man against my will tends to stress me out, I instinctively lost my shit. "Let go!"

Altan saw me struggling and attempted to push his way back down the gangway, but two other officers put their hands on his shoulders and shoved him back into the terminal. "Ness!" he shouted. "What's happening?"

"I don't know!" I shrieked. The man with his hand on my arm started pulling me down a hall that forked from the top of gangway. My feet went with him for some reason. Stupid feet.

"Ms. Brown," the officer said to me, tightening his fingers. "You're under arrest. It's easier if you don't make a scene."

"Under arrest?" I repeated uselessly. "For *what?*"

Altan was still scuffling behind me. I heard him shouting, *Where are you taking her? What's going on?* But then I was pushed through a heavy door that slammed shut behind us, and everything went deep-space quiet.

MONDAY, APRIL 29

Pete's not picking up his phone, and he doesn't appear to be at his apartment. I'm sitting on his stoop waiting for him to get home. What good is having a lawyer on speed dial if he won't *take your goddamn calls?*

THE PUBLIC DEFENDER

Sam Stevens died while I was in Paris.

This was the only thing that registered during the ride to the police station. There were words beyond that, and noises, sure—officers talked when they escorted me from the cruiser by my elbows. They asked me questions at intake, raised their eyebrows when they wanted me to nod and frowned when they wanted me to shake, but I didn't hear anything.

It was all indoor lap-pool noise, dripping and echoes, the slow whoosh of water being dragged through other water. A flashbulb went off in my face, and then I was led though locking metal doors with chicken wire windows into increasingly nondescript chambers, until I was told to sit in a small, off-white interrogation room with a round table and four molded-plastic chairs. There was something about it that reminded me of the blank white canvas of a Morpheum dream in neutral: the bleakness was *that* infinite. When I looked down at my hands, there was ink on my fingertips.

Huh. I wondered how that got there.

It would have been inappropriate for me to experience real grief at Sam's passing—especially considering how much I contributed to it by giving him all that Morpheum. After all, we weren't technically friends in that we never drank a coffee together that didn't come from the WellCorp break room, so it didn't feel right to cry the way his (now officially orphaned) daughter was probably doing right now. He deserved better than my tears.

Still, I had liked him. Sam was chattier than most of my trial participants due to his unabashed loneliness, and this had endeared me to him. Pre-Morpheum, Sam was a cheerful former literature professor at U-Dub, so maybe he reminded me a little of Pete. Post-Morpheum Sam only reminded me of myself, so his death was a wake-up call as to just how close I'd come to a more permanent kind of sleep.

I'd been so careless. Maybe I deserved punishment for Sam. Even though it was Malcolm who told me to hand out the pills, I was the one who did it. I'd known what I was doing, enough to feel bad about it at the time. But I'd ignored the guilt in favor of keeping my job and my access to Morpheum, praying that the dumpster fire would just put itself out while I slept. And now, it had. Sam was gone. The problem was over. I'd gotten *exactly* what I'd wished for.

Me and my Midol touch.

I thought of this as two detectives—both white men, one ginger, one bald—came in and out of my interview room, offering me water and then forgetting to bring it, sitting at the table and then getting up again, needing a pencil and leaving to find one. I couldn't tell if they were inept or if this was some psychological warfare to drive me crazy. "Can I get you anything?" they kept saying (and forgetting).

"Coffee?" I begged for the third time. *Also, can you call me a Lyft?*

Just kidding. This was what I really needed:

A time machine, so I could undo all this. A gun, to murder Malcolm Jacobs. A sandwich, ten Americanos, some fresh jeans, the modest contents of my bank account as reparations to Sam's daughter. A priest to forgive me (though I'm not even religious) and a plane ticket to Siberia, where I would live alone since I couldn't be trusted not to hurt anyone.

But what I said (after the fourth failed attempt at a beverage and a face-to-face conversation) was "I'd like a lawyer."

The bald detective asked, "You got one we can call?"

The only lawyer's number I knew by heart was Pete's, and I wasn't too keen on calling my kinda-sorta ex-husband collect from jail when he didn't even know I was back in the country (especially when he kinda-sorta hated me). "Public defender is fine."

"Sure thing," the detective said and left me, thirsty and alone with my thoughts, for a very—

Long—

Time.

This *had* to be one of their tricks. They were stewing me in here, waiting for the confession to sweat itself out—which was wholly unnecessary, considering how sick I was about the situation. All they had to do was ask, "Did you kill Sam Stevens?" And I would have wept and said *yes* a thousand times.

Just to give myself something to think about other than Sam, I replayed Parisian highlights from my trip. On our first night in town, Altan had taken me to his favorite café, on a massive roundabout that was lined with cube-cropped horse chestnut trees in deep, glossy green. The waiter seated us at the back of the terrace, which had rows of tables facing the street (three deep) and the chairs positioned side-by-side so we could both overlook the sidewalk. We would sit in many terraces like this over the course of our trip, but the first time I ate next to, rather than across from, Altan, I felt almost rude to be looking at something other than him. What could possibly more engrossing than the visage of a lover?

Plenty, it turned out. Paris—and maybe even *the world*—was teeming with things to look at: long-limbed women in belted coats, prune-faced grandfathers in tweed, shitty drivers, squabbling pigeons, handsome waiters treating themselves to cigarettes on the curb at the very moment you needed another drink. "Get your camera," Altan said. "I know you want to." So I did, and I took pictures of everything: the occasional rat, beret-wearing tourists drowning in their French, and on that very first evening, a woman surreptitiously rubbing the crotch of her husband under the table (to completion!) as they sat at the table in front of ours drinking wine.

I never would have seen this if only Altan got the view, or vice versa. Without both of us watching this sneaky hand job at the same time, we couldn't have spent twenty minutes elbowing each other in the ribs in a hysteria so high-pitched it was silent as we wiped our eyes with napkins. ("The French call that a *bleu* job," Altan had whispered, and I *died*.)

Why should only one of us get to see, as if life was meant to be enjoyed in turns? Sitting next to Altan in a café felt democratic in a way I hadn't even known I craved. We were equally important when facing the same direction, experiencing life at the same time. And at that moment, I knew with Morpheum-like clarity that I had found what I desired most in life: my camera, the world, and a man who wanted to watch it, too.

And yes, I felt sorry for Sam, but selfishly I also felt sorry for myself, because now I might not get to see anything more.

After what felt like hours, the ginger detective came back, this time with a paper cup of water that he placed on the table. (I didn't deserve coffee.) "Sorry about the wait. Lawyer's here."

Never mind, I almost said. *Nix the lawyer. I'll just go to jail and die.* But before I could, a tall man in a severe-looking suit stepped into the room, and I knew, unequivocally, that I was somehow even more fucked.

Like that, all the air in Seattle was gone. Windows were blowing out all over town trying to equalize the pressure. My lungs collapsed; my heart shuddered to a stop before collapsing on its side like a fainting goat.

The man smiled and said, "Hello, Nessie."

THE KNIGHT IN SHINING UBER

Malcolm Jacobs looked the same as when I last saw him in person on the day he jerked off in front of me at work: same unnecessarily expensive necktie, same hubcap of a watch, same slick *American Psycho* haircut with the salt-and-pepper temples. Same untrustworthy handsomeness, like how the devil must look—nice enough to be tempting, suave enough to be questionable. The way I leapt to my feet and spun around to put the chair I'd been sitting in between Malcolm and me? Pure instinct. They don't teach you that anywhere. I retreated into the corner behind the table for protection, gripping the back of the chair in case I needed a weapon, like a lion tamer would.

Naturally, Malcolm was holding a briefcase, likely as empty as his heart. "Oh, god, Nessie," he said, dropping the case on the table so he could glide toward me with both arms outstretched. "I've been so worried."

It's a dream, I told myself. *It's a very bad dream.* Where was the elevator full of blood? Where were the twin girls holding hands? How the hell did I wake up from this?

"Get back," I snapped, brandishing the chair. "Take one more step, and I'll kill you."

Malcolm paused, like he was truly hurt. His face tastefully arranged into a mask of concern, he took the chair from me and set it gently to the side. His hug was quick and chaste, nothing like the human mammogram he usually passed off on me as an embrace. His aftershave was subtle and spicy. I hope I never smell it again.

"I'm so glad you're home from Paris," he said, holding both my hands. "We were terrified you'd hurt yourself after what happened. Such a tragedy. I'm sick over it. I know you didn't mean to do it. These things happen. But fortunately, now we have the chance to make it right for Steven and his family."

"Sam," I corrected him, dropping his hand. "His name was Sam Stevens."

He tapped himself on the forehead like he'd forgotten to pick up milk. "Yes, of course. What am I saying? I'm just so upset. Here. I've brought someone I'd like you to meet."

Malcolm gestured behind him to a woman standing in the door. She was around my age but eight times more glamorous in a black pencil skirt and matching tailored jacket. A long chestnut side ponytail was slung over one shoulder, like a python. Her nails were filed into points and varnished the same blood red as her lipstick.

"Lady Malcolm," she said, marching into the room with her hand extended. (Just kidding: her name was Victoria Esposito, but she looked every bit like a female supervillain version of my greatest personal enemy.) "I'm WellCorp's legal counsel, here to represent you in this matter." Her eyelashes trembled beneath the weight of her mascara. "I'm better than a public defender."

"How did you know I was here?" I asked. Malcolm was holding out a plastic chair at the table for me to sit in. "And how did *you* know I was in Paris?"

"Let's focus on the matter at hand," said Esposito, pulling out her own seat. When it was clear that I wasn't ever going to put my ass within grabbing distance of his hand, Malcolm shrugged and took the chair he was holding for himself. I remained standing.

Esposito cleared her throat lightly. "What we need to focus on is a strategy for your murder charge. I admit our options are limited since you already confessed—"

"Confessed?" I blinked. "When did that happen?"

Malcolm piped up. "The day we fired you when you had that mental break at work. You said, 'A man is in a coma because of my negligence,' and then you levelled some pretty inflammatory accusations against me, which was how we knew you'd gotten in too deep with the Morpheum."

Was this happening? The whole scene had the surreal aura of a dream. "You didn't fire me," I said. "I quit."

"Then why have you been receiving severance pay?"

"I'm getting severance?" My bank account had been unchecked since leaving for Paris, as I insisted on paying for everything in the cash I had from my photography hustle. Maybe I was heartless enough to accidentally kill someone, but I sure wasn't going to treat myself to a vacation with my lover from my shared marital bank account.

"We thought it best, considering you so clearly needed help. After all, you were high at work when you overdosed Sam. We didn't want anyone to prosecute, but when Sam died, the city insisted." He clucked his tongue. "Such a shame."

If we were alone, I'd know he was full of shit. But that Victoria was nodding along confused me for some reason, as if having someone to corroborate somehow made something true. "I overdosed Sam because you made me," I stammered. "You threatened me. It was *your* idea—"

"Nessie, your name is all over the paperwork," Malcolm said with a calm that made me look even more deranged.

"You said you would fire me! You *made* me poison him! And *then* you tried to make me blow you in exchange for making it all go away. That was real." (Believe me: I wished it wasn't.)

Malcolm sighed at Victoria and raised his eyebrows, a face that clearly said, *See? I told you so.* "Nessie," he said in a voice dripping with concern, "I think those drugs did a number on your memory. If any of that happened, there'd be proof, right?"

Of course, there'd be proof: there'd be emails from Malcolm threatening to let me go if I didn't comply with Sam's dosing, phone calls, video footage, credible witnesses with whom I wasn't romantically involved. There'd be *evidence* of one kind or another. If it was real.

In movies when someone experiences a shock, there's always a guy nearby to tell that person to sit down and put his head between his knees. But is that something you do in real life? And if so, what's the point? Is it to keep your shoes mostly clean in case you barf? Oh my god, was Malcolm's antagonizing just another pregnancy test I dreamed up? When I held the memories in my mind, they *felt* like they'd happened, but I was jet-lagged and starving and caffeine-deprived. Even on my best day, I wouldn't trust my brain under such conditions.

When she saw my shoulders slump, Esposito unscrewed the cap to her pen. "I'm recommending we approach the prosecution for a plea bargain. Settle this *outside* of a courtroom. After all, your confession, like Mr. Jacobs said, is pretty damning, and—"

The door banged open again and in strode two brown wingtips topped by navy suit pants and a matching suit jacket in summer-weight wool. White shirt. No tie. Open collar. A jaw that had been shaven at some point in the morning but now hinted at a reddish stubble. A slim nose. Blonde hair, a mess. Blue eyes, wild. My heart, stopped.

"Malcolm Jacobs," Pete roared. "What the *fuck* are you doing with my wife?"

Try enough drugs in your life and it's easy to think that everything nice in the world—chocolate, aromatherapy, crack—is only a series of chemical reactions telling your brain it's safe to chill. With this in mind, you could believe love is similarly nothing more than a soup of hormones and survival instincts bubbling away in our brains. Like burning sage to kill ghosts or using lavender to calm stress, love could be nothing more than a placebo, a way to trick us into relaxing into the belief that we won't die alone.

But sometimes you come face to face with proof that love is *more*: sharper than attraction, deeper than sex, stronger than pain, more powerful and complex than any combination of atoms, and you find yourself questioning everything cynical you thought was true about the world. This was *that*. When a man—who no longer bears any responsibility or tenderness to a woman who has betrayed him—shows up to his own detriment, of his own free will, to save her in the crisis of her life, it's the kind of miracle you can hang a sombrero on.

I thought of this as Pete charged Malcolm like he was going to throw a punch, and I finally sank into that chair across from Victoria Esposito. I was either asleep or crazy or dead: it was hard to know which. All I knew for sure was that I needed to sit down.

"Mister Brown!" Malcolm stood up with his hands out, trying to ward off Pete. (Wait: how did they know each other? It's not like Malcolm had ever thrown us a Christmas party or anything.) "I can explain!"

"Don't bother. Get out." Pete then let loose a string of artisan-crafted swears so full of acid they practically hissed steam.

How? I mean, *how* had Pete managed to ignore my many treacheries in favor of rocking up like a knight in shining Uber to slay my private dragon? Look at him, bulldozing Malcolm out of here with the man's own briefcase. I didn't know how he'd found the strength, but then again Pete had always been famous for his crackerjack heart and an even better moral compass. It was one of the reasons I'd married him: he always did the best thing.

Once Malcolm and Esposito had been disposed of, Pete slammed the door shut behind them. It made a noise like an explosion—just as it had two weeks ago in our apartment when he left after I swore I never cheated on him, and he (rightfully) didn't believe me. When he went, my heart cracked right up the middle with that loud snap of branches giving way beneath heavy snow. I broke his heart, and then he broke mine by leaving, and for all I knew there were still pieces all over the apartment floor along with the wine corks I'd dropped under the fridge and the wads of my hair that rolled like tumbleweeds from the bathroom because I was a terrible housekeeper. Leave it for the archeologists: I was pretty sure he and I were history.

"Bastard!" Pete spat at the door, raking his hands through his hair. He whirled on me. "What did he say to you?"

"Nothing!" I said. Nothing except *Maybe you fried your brain on Morpheum because you're a loser*, but I didn't feel the need to remind Pete of this fact.

"He's been coming to the apartment looking for you," he snarled. "Every night since you've been gone, he rings the bell after 10 p.m., half drunk. Says you're going to be arrested but that he can help and you should call him. I had no idea what he was talking about, but he kept showing up—like he didn't even care I might be sleeping or that you weren't interested in whatever he had to say. I told him to leave you alone, but here he is again. *Sniffing.*"

He kicked one of the molded plastic chairs, sending it skittering across the linoleum floor. He'd never been so furious. "Pete, calm down," I begged.

"Calm down?" he said, waving his hands. His face was approaching a shade of mauve that clashed with his blonde hair. "You want me to *calm down*? That fucker fucks with my fucking wife and you want me to calm the fuck down?"

And the award for the most F-bombs dropped in a single sentence goes to . . .

"Why didn't you call me?" Pete advanced, his index finger brandished like a dagger. "When you got arrested, you should have called."

My voice was tiny as I shrank back into my chair. "I was afraid you wouldn't come. I thought you'd be mad."

"That you got your ass arrested the second you got back from an international fuck-fest with the man you left me for? Of course, I'm *mad*. I'm fucking *furious*!"

His voice broke on the last word with the slightest whiff of a laugh, like he couldn't believe how cosmically ridiculous all of this was. But then, he bent over where I was sitting and cupped his hands to my face so I'd have to look up and see the pure, clean truth that lit his eyes. "But fuck you if you think I'm going to let you go to prison just because you broke my heart."

This was a weird way to say, "I'm here to help," but I took it. I took it and I cried right into it, like it was a tissue. Now that Pete was here, I could fall apart. How many times had he put me back together? Bad days at work, fights with friends, overdoses: he was the best at gathering up the pieces, so very patient with the glue.

Dragging myself to my feet, I stumbled into his arms and pressed my oily, snotty face against his button-front. Unthinking, I did a quick, nostalgic calculation: it was Monday, and since Pete had for the past five years picked up his shirts from the cleaners on Sundays, he'd have more at home if I ruined this one. They'd be in the third drawer of his dresser, folded, not on hangers, because he hated to waste the plastic.

I sobbed and sobbed. He was so goddamn thoughtful.

"Hey," said Pete quietly, smoothing my hair. "Look, I'm sorry I yelled. I was just worked up about everything."

Altan had been wrong: "garden-variety adulterer's guilt" did not adequately explain why I was having trouble walking away from Peter Brown. My whole adult life was infused with him, had been built on the complex root system of our love. The past few months had been hard and full of hurt, but deep in the earth below the smoking remains of our trunk, there was life. It was growing in my chest, tendrils curling around my bones, blossoms rioting through every vein and capillary, to the point where I thought I heard my ribcage creak beneath the strangling of all that tender green. "Don't be sorry," I choked. "Never be sorry."

"Yeah, well, remember you said that the next time I'm wrong," he grumbled, pulling a chair out for me at the table. I sat in it: I trusted Pete with my ass. For some reason, his knuckles were swollen, but he was still wearing his wedding ring. For all I knew mine was still on the kitchen counter where I left it before Paris.

My sorrow was giving me hiccups as if to punctuate all the crappy things I'd done to Pete (*hic*), to Sam (*hic*), to Altan by getting arrested (*hic*)—even though I didn't exactly volunteer for the incarceration, but he was still probably frantic. Pete passed me the paper cup of water the detective had left for me on the table. "Drink this," he said gently. "Can you calm down for me?"

For Pete? I'd do anything. Even still, it took me three tries to drink before I got even half the cup down. *Hic.*

"I'm trying," I wailed. "Scare me or something."

Pete lurched at me like a bogeyman, hands up next to his face. "Boo! You're pregnant!"

"Jesus," I gasped—but it worked. The hiccups were gone.

Pete chuckled nervously. "Man, you really didn't want kids, did you?"

"What tipped you off?"

"Only the ten times you tried to tell me even though I wouldn't listen." His smile was a baby animal, small and shy and soft, but he didn't elaborate on the fact that he'd just acknowledged that he could have listened better. (Which, trust me, was a big deal coming from him.) Instead, Pete launched into a game plan.

"OK, listen. I have a friend from law school who's a criminal attorney—a good one. I texted her about your case on the way here, and if it's OK with you, I'll bring her to your arraignment tomorrow so she can represent you and negotiate your bail. Does that work?"

I hadn't thought past my next cup of coffee, but Pete had always been three steps ahead of me. This was why we never ran out of toilet paper, why our taxes got filed without penalty, why he set calendar reminders for both of us to schedule our physicals the same time every year—only I put it off until we were four months out of sync but he'd still think to update the invite. His ability to anticipate was always more dashing than dorky to me: that he could be a successful lawyer *and* know our license plate number off the top of his head was proof there was nothing he couldn't do.

"Yeah, it works," I said, grabbing a tissue from the box on the table and howling into it.

Pete usually got flustered when I cried, but today he had on his professionalism. He was probably used to his clients' losing their shit in meetings. "Ness, everything is going to be OK. I'll see you tomorrow. Can you hang out for, like, eighteen hours?"

"Hang out where? *Here*?"

"No, probably jail," he said delicately. "But it's just for tonight. I'm sure we can negotiate bail tomorrow. OK?"

More nodding from me: it was all I could manage aside from hugging/choking him out in a screaming panic—though I did that for good measure as he stood to leave.

He rubbed my back lightly with the palm of his hand. "Try and get some sleep," he said.

If the roles were reversed—if *Pete* had accidentally confessed to quasi-cheating on *me* because he was too high on sleeping pills to keep his facts straight—I would have thrown in a shitty dig for good measure, like, *Try to get some sleep: I know you're good at that.*

But my husband had always been better than me, so he didn't.

TUESDAY, APRIL 30

When Pete came home from work and saw me sitting on the step of his building, he walked right up and punched me in the face—from a standing position. Yeah, I get that I stole his wife, but still: *not cool.* Especially when you consider Pete probably has fifty pounds on me.

But you should see his knuckles! My face *ruined* them.

Anyway, he was halfway through choking me to death when I managed to croak out that Ness got arrested—I didn't even know for what, only that the cops took her off the plane. Pete dropped me right there on the stoop of his building and took off running like a goddamn superhero. I chased him until I caught him on Pine as he was getting into an Uber. I got in with him.

Predictably, that did not go over well. But hey: he's a lawyer, he has connections. If anyone can get me in to see her, he can.

I went with him to the police station, but I had to stay in the waiting room while he went inside the lockup. Or jail. Or prison. I don't really know the difference; they all look the same on TV. All I know is that they put Ness behind actual, literal bars because I grabbed him as he was coming out of the police station and he filled me in. He was so upset he didn't even bother punching me in the face: that's how I knew this was bad.

So now it's dawn, and I'm back in my apartment, and I can't sleep because I hate everything, especially Pete—even though I have no right to hate Pete. But I hate him because he gets to make calls and file motions and *do* things while I sit here and do nothing. I wish I'd gone to law school instead of shitting all those years away overseas because then I'd have some *skills* that would be useful.

But I don't. All I have is a black eye and a backpack full of dirty laundry. And I feel like a gigantic loser because I didn't see this coming and I should have. I should have known better.

I shouldn't have let Ness come back.

THE
GUNSLINGER

After Pete left, the detectives led me to a large communal cell in a room with no windows. The bars were painted the same putty hue as the cinderblock walls, creating an effect that almost passed for seamless in the dim lighting. When the door rolled shut behind me, it landed home with a deafening *clank*—just like you hear in the movies. Only a thousand times more terrifying in real life.

I was still audibly sniveling.

The three other women in the cell had each claimed a hard, backless bench for the evening. I collapsed on the last available one and tried not to completely unravel at the thought of spending the night in here. "Hey, shut up!" one of them barked.

"S-s-sorry," I babbled, then stuffed my fist between my teeth. Inhaling deeply through my nose, I tried to do some breathing I learned that one month I tried yoga. I had to switch to my mouth on the next breath because everything smelled so dankly of piss.

How the hell was I going to sleep in here? My brain was a rave in an abandoned warehouse that the rest of me wasn't cool enough to go to. The inside of my skull had been tagged in neon graffiti and splashed with strobe lights; it thrummed with the deafening noise of techno. Terrible thoughts rubbed up against me like unwanted suitors on a dancefloor I was trying to make my way off of. My friends were gone and my purse was lost and it was 3 a.m. and my head was spinning like I had vertigo even though I was lying down, and this was *awful*. I wanted to leave. I wanted to go home. I wanted quiet. I wanted Altan, wanted Altan, wanted Altan, make it *stop*.

Then, with a *whoosh*, everything went still.

When I opened my eyes, I found myself looking at the pitted foam ceiling of the conference room in WellCorp's Urban Campus, site of many unpleasant work meetings, including the one where I "confessed" to screwing up the Morpheum trial. The buzzing noise of the lights was unmistakable: I'd sat bored enough times in that room to know it like a birdcall.

I was lying on my back autopsy-style on the faux mahogany tabletop of the conference table. When I sat up, everything was just as I remembered it: the fake fichus my plant-loving coworker Diana had bought to cheer up the room. The window into the cube farm, where Altan sat, with his back to me. Malcolm smirking at the head of the table from the "ergonomic" rolling chair he'd purchased only one of and didn't let anyone else sit in, even when he wasn't there.

"Hello, again," he said.

He may as well have dreamed up a shower and then stabbed me through the curtain, because that's exactly how I screamed.

Malcolm flew back in his chair so hard I hoped it would tip. "Oh my god, your face!" he brayed, clutching his stomach. "You had no idea, did you? Oh! Oh, shit. I got you *so* bad!"

"Is this a dream?" I shrieked, scrambling to my feet on the table. "*Did you give me Morpheum?*"

He dabbed the tears from his eyes with the heels of his hands. "Oh, oh my god, I can't. Yes, it's Morpheum. I drugged you at the police station. Oh shit, your face!" Malcolm was definitely the kind of guy who applauded in restaurants when a waiter dropped a tray.

This was the scare I needed to get rid of my hiccups—for eternity—but now that we'd established Malcolm Jacobs was officially the world's biggest dickhead, I was free to get mad. "Well, thanks for drugging me without my permission. I'm just going to wake up now—"

"Wait, don't!" Malcolm said as he finally stopped hyperventilating. "I brought you here for a reason. I have a proposal you might be interested in."

The last time I dreamed with Malcolm, he had tried to put his dream penis in my dream vagina against my very real will. He rolled his eyes as he felt me remember. "Jesus, Ness, it was *one* time. Get over it already."

Malcolm used to have power over me when he was my manager, but now that I didn't work for him anymore, he had a lot of nerve trying to bully me in my *own damn brain*. "I don't think 'attempted dream rape' is something I can forgive and forget, shithead."

Malcolm started giggling again, like my rage was a feather on the soles of his feet. "See?" he said to someone behind me. "I told you she was perfect."

The man at the opposite end of the table was in his early forties and appeared to be crafted entirely out of pizza dough— figuratively, not literally (you have to specify in a dream where anything goes). He wasn't ugly: just completely unexciting looking, with a high forehead and a weak chin and thick black Buddy Holly glasses that looked good on Buddy Holly only because he was cute.

Even in a dream, the man's suit was ill-fitting, which gave him the impression of being someone who *never* quite got the hang of things. Look at the sweat glistening on his upper lip. *Ew.*

"Who's this? Is he real?" I turned to Malcolm and pointed down the table. "Or is he just some gross, nerdy portrait of you decaying in your mental closet?"

"Don't worry about him," Malcolm replied, waving off Dorian Meh and gesturing to the chair I'd been sitting in the day he put his hand on me under the table. "Take a seat."

Hard pass. In fact, now that I was acclimating to the situation, I saw that his attempts at being scary were actually kind of comical. Here we were on a drug that allowed us to manifest any locale or scenario imaginable, and he was trying to intimidate me with the *conference room at work*? "Fuck *this*," I said, sourcing my Big Altan Energy. "Let's go somewhere else."

I tore open the ceiling to change the setting—just as I realized I had no idea where I actually wanted to go. Oh well: too late! In poured a new scene courtesy of my subconscious. It fell like a three-ton cloud of cinnamon and hit the ground with a heavy *floop*. Malcolm gagged on all the dirt. (Good.)

As the dust settled, I hoped we'd find ourselves at a battle site worthy of this meeting between Malcolm and me—someplace authoritative and iconic, like the dueling ground of Aaron Burr and Alexander Hamilton. Or maybe the Supreme Court! (Hell, I'd even take the People's Court.) But instead, I was disappointed to find that my deepest instinct had transported us to what appeared to be a Tex-Mex restaurant at Disney's Frontierland.

The saloon came stocked with a basic cowpoke starter set: off-tune player piano, bandana-wearing outlaws, the skull of a longhorn displayed on the wall. A pair of swinging doors emitted a shuffling stranger, spurs tinkling, hat dipped low over his face. He grumbled, "Howdy," to the bartender, who had a handlebar mustache.

So, this was *mortifying*—and then I looked down at my outfit and saw I was wearing *chaps*! Chaps and a bandolier of bullets slung over my shoulder like Chewbacca. The WellCorp conference table had shrunk to a wobbly four-top surrounded by Dorian Meh (who had a red kerchief around his neck) and Malcolm (dressed all in black, Johnny Cash style) and me, trying to keep a straight face in what felt like a thirty-gallon hat.

Malcolm let his eyes drift over the saloon. "You're right," he deadpanned. "This is much nicer."

"Beats your taste in office furniture. So what's your proposal?"

"Well, Cool Hand Ness," Malcolm said, crooking a finger at the bartender, who deposited a quarter-full bottle of whisky on the table. "I have a question for you."

Malcolm took his time pouring liberal amounts of booze into three (dirty) glasses, if only to build suspense. "What will it take for you to plead guilty to the manslaughter of Sam Stevens?"

He handed me my drink. "Are you trying to buy me?"

"You really *are* just a pretty face, aren't you? Of course, I'm trying to buy you, dipshit. And by the way, your life isn't even that expensive. I can easily afford it."

Me-ow. "I thought only the prosecutor could make deals."

He threw his whisky back and set the glass on the table. "Once I know which one is assigned to your case, I'll know which one to bribe. It shouldn't take very long, so you'll be out of jail in no time."

"I'll be out of jail tomorrow. Pete says I'll make bail."

"You won't," Malcolm said, pouring the end of the whisky bottle into his glass. "To shift the focus away from WellCorp, you need to look threatening enough to keep you off the streets. Fortunately, the judge presiding over your case is a friend of the family. So . . ." He trailed off, allowing me to do the math.

It was suddenly stunningly clear that even though I didn't work for Malcolm anymore, he still had power over me. When it came to clout or cash, I'd never amass enough of either to compete.

"Scheduling a trial could take *months*!" I said, annoyed that my voice went shrill at the end. (So much for being a badass.)

"Sometimes it takes years." He motioned for more whisky— this time from a waitress who was wearing a corset and a black velvet choker. (Pretty sure she was Malcolm's contribution to the dream.) "That's why you should take my deal: plead guilty to manslaughter in exchange for community service and rehab." He threw back a second shot. "I've already picked out the nicest spa for you in California. They have round-the-clock trauma specialists and mud baths for days. Maybe they can help you with those humongous pores of yours."

"Really?" I said. "You think I care about my pores enough to confess to killing someone?"

"Well, you should." He sneered. "They're awful. When you get out of rehab, I'll make sure your bank account has enough in it for you and Altan to make a tidy life someplace far away from here. And you can live out your days never thinking about WellCorp again. How does that sound?"

Even though I hated Malcolm on a level usually reserved for Nazis and people who set off fireworks after ten o'clock at night, for some reason I had a hard time saying *No* to him. Wait: not true. I *did* turn down the opportunity to blow him once, but not with the venom it deserved. My *No* to Malcolm was always halfhearted because I was so afraid of what he could do to me, and *that's* what power was: a landfill with its own gravitational pull, a loathing so massive that it drew you more than it repulsed.

"What happens to Morpheum?" I said.

Malcolm's eyes drifted to the waitress's bosom. "Life's been hard on you," he drawled, like he hadn't had a hand in the pushing of all that downhill-rolling poop. "You deserve the care you need."

"*What happens to Morpheum?*"

He heaved a sigh. "Why do you ask so many questions?"

"Because sometimes I *am* more than just a pretty face."

Malcolm chuckled under his breath, which meant he didn't find this funny at all. "With Sam's death squarely on the shoulders of a rogue employee, Morpheum is free to be sold to the American military for intelligence gathering. Right now, the government won't take it because they think it kills people." He made a face at Dorian Meh, like the military was *so* unreasonable.

"Let me get this straight," I said. "You want me to take the fall for murdering Sam in order to convince the military that Morpheum is safe to take under normal circumstances?"

Dorian Meh nodded along when Malcolm said, "That's right."

My eyes narrowed into suspicious slits. "Didn't you factor this in when you planned to overdose Sam in the first place?"

"I didn't think the government would still be worried about Abu Ghraib stuff! I thought we'd be past that already."

I sighed. The only thing worse than a villain is a stupid villain. "So if I *don't* admit to killing Sam, I go to trial, which means I might win, and you'll lose millions of dollars in a military contract."

"Trust me. You won't win."

"Then why are you even offering me a deal?"

"I don't know! Because I'm *nice*?"

"No, you're not. You suck."

Malcolm took a deep breath and gripped the edge of the table to steady himself. "*Nessie, do you want the deal or not?*"

Just then, one of the nameless cowboy extras in the bar bumped me as he passed my seat. "Pardon, ma'am," he said absentmindedly as I turned just in time to see the pink rosebud pinned to the heart of his dusty vest.

The memory came to me in a flash: Sam had worn a flower like that in the lapel of his jacket once when he came in for one of our WellCorp appointments. Where was he now? Had they buried him yet? Had he found his wife in whatever dream that plays when you're asleep for good?

Did he deserve to have his death swept under a rug?

I popped to my feet, toppling my chair into the piano, which stopped playing immediately. The sundry bandits in the bar turned to watch as my hand went to a big chrome revolver at my hip with a mother-of-pearl grip. Malcolm sat in his chair, legs spread in a V that would have been obnoxious on the bus. Arms crossed in front of his chest, he didn't even flinch.

"You want to know why I ask questions?" I said. "Because you're a smarmy asshole who can't be trusted. There was a point where I just assumed you could be. When it came to Sam, I thought, even as I was killing him with pills, that you were human enough to have another human's most basic interests at heart. But you're a soulless loser, and Morpheum is too dangerous to be used anywhere by anyone for anything whatsoever. So, fuck your deal, and fuck you."

And *that* was the *No* I'd been waiting so long to give Malcolm.

I drew my pistol and trained it down and across the table at right where Malcolm's heart should have been. "Don't bother," he said, utterly blasé. "You know I won't die in real life."

"But you'll die in here, and that's the closest you'll ever get to giving me an orgasm."

Now he looked concerned. "Seriously, Ness, don't—"

Bang. I shot him. Oh my god, I'd shot him! So then why was Malcolm still sitting there manspreading? There should have been a cantaloupe-sized hole in his ribcage, but he didn't even drop his eyes to inspect the damage. He knew there was none.

I moved the gun up to his forehead and pulled the trigger again. The noise was tremendous but ineffectual: no brain matter fell into our whisky glasses. No blood splattered across Dorian Meh's face. I fired again. And again. I aimed for his crotch to mix things up and shot until my hand went numb from the recoil and my wrist felt weak and my ears rang from the sound of Roman candles going off in my brain, but Malcolm just *refused to die*. Which was unexpected. And annoying. And terrifying. Because if he was invincible in here that meant . . .

I threw the gun on the table, reared back, and punched him in his stupid, probably cosmetically enhanced face. His head snapped to the side under the blow so I knew he felt it. (My hand hurt like hell, so feeling was possible.) "*Ow*," he complained. Slowly, he turned back to face me, rubbing his jaw. "You done?"

My breath came in gasps. "I guess." Short of running him over with a panzer tank, I wasn't sure what my options were. "This isn't the same Morpheum we were using before."

"No," said Malcolm. He was enjoying himself, watching me figure it out, a fly struggling against the silk strand of a web. "It's a new formula."

That last part echoed in the pit of my empty stomach. *A new formula.*

Like a government-strength formula?

An Abu Ghraib kind of formula?

Had it been tested? Was it safe? Were the rules the same in here as they were when Altan and I took whatever watered-down infant-strength Morpheum we were giving our patients in the trial?

All these questions, and yet the one I asked for some reason was, "How did you drug me with it?"

"Confidential," said Malcolm. "As is the fact that we made the sedative stronger. It's more like anesthesia now. You can't wake up until it wears off."

Terror, cold and eel-like, slimed up my spine. "How long does that take?"

"About eight hours." Malcolm retrieved a pocket watch from his vest. (The man loved a good timepiece.) "By my count, you have seven and a half hours left. I wonder what we can do with so much *time*."

Like this was the signal they were waiting for, the bandits all scraped their chairs from their tables and formed a posse behind Malcolm. Even Dorian Meh, who in real life wouldn't have looked scary to anyone except maybe an entire box of donuts, got ominously to his feet. The bandits were figments of Malcolm's imagination, but I'd fought enough imaginary pirates in my other Morpheum dreams to know I should still be afraid, especially in a setting where you could still feel pain but couldn't die.

Groping behind me through the sea of tables, I made for the swinging half doors of the saloon. "Oh my god, ten naked women!" I shouted, pointing toward the back of the room.

The bandits, all being stupid, spun to look (even Dorian! What a loser). But Malcolm kept his eyes trained on me as I turned and ran like hell.

WEDNESDAY, MAY 1

I couldn't sleep at all last night, so at 3 a.m. I decided to burn off some energy by deep cleaning my apartment. Do I want it to be nice in case Ness gets out of jail? Yes. Was I also looking for Morpheum I may have carelessly dropped before Ness made off with my whole stash that one day we had a fight? Well, I wasn't—until I found one under the stove and realized a second one would get me somewhere.

So, I doubled down until I found another straggler behind my mattress as I was moving it out of the loft and into the living area so Ness and I will have more room to sleep when she comes home.

Once I had two, that's when I got a *really* bad idea.

THE NEW
MORPHEUM

While I had spent the last two weeks boning Altan in Paris, Malcolm had clearly been boning up on his dream-weaving skills. All night, he chased me—on wings, with fins, on foot, through cities and jungles and desserts and space. Even with Dorian Meh (who clearly did not know what he was doing) in tow, Malcolm kept pace, sometimes letting me get a bit of a head start so he could explain what he was doing.

"Yes, she's very quick," Malcolm told his dumpy little shadow: in *Russian*. I was hiding out in the forest of Altan's and my Sasquatch dream, reminding myself that this was where we learned you couldn't die in your own mind. *Yay*, I thought, balled up in the boughs of a tremendous pine, trying to catch my breath, dirty and scratched from running through the woods. It was the darkest night I could muster while still being able to track the two men on the trail below my tree. "Ness is uncommonly fast because she's taken Morpheum before."

All of this was being translated mentally in real time. It had to be, because I didn't speak Russian—and I was pretty sure Malcolm didn't either—and yet I understood Dorian Meh perfectly when he said, "So most people wouldn't be this good at evading?"

"*Nyet*," Malcolm assured. "Your average person wouldn't even know how—or why—to put up a fight. But I wanted to show you someone who could maneuver so you could get a sense of what you might expect from the closest thing I have on hand to professional counterintelligence. Though *intelligence* when it comes to Ness is . . ." He held out his hand, palm facing the ground, and rocked it side to side.

Dick.

Either he heard me think this, or he knew he was standing beneath me the entire time, because Malcolm then tilted his head back so I could see the spooky green shine of his eyes in the moonlight. "There you are."

Crap.

"I can make it stop," he called, making his voice singsong at the end. "Just agree to the deal."

"Agree to *this*!"

Crashing through the underbrush, the Sasquatch who lived in the woods attacked the two men at my behest. He was flanked by a thousand bald eagles with iron claws, a cavalry of mutant bucks with swords for antlers, and two battalions of tiny little chipmunks with razor blades strapped to their ankles. Every murderous forest creature I could imagine bore down on Malcolm and Dorian Meh, but they blinked out of the scene without so much as a drop of blood shed.

The thought of Morpheum Classic being used by the U.S. Army was enough to give me the heebie-jeebies. But if Malcolm was cooking up a more powerful formula (a.k.a. New Morpheum) with deeper mind-reading capabilities and an equine-strength sedative that could be delivered without anyone's noticing . . . *and* he was demonstrating it to Russian-speaking parties? This was *bad* in ways I didn't have the time or energy to comprehend. Dream fleeing makes you tired. I was running out of ideas.

At the six-hour mark, Malcolm cornered me in the white room of a dream in neutral. I didn't know he had access to that room. I didn't even know that room *had* corners. But somehow I'd gotten trapped in there, limping across endless blank miles, Malcolm and Dorian casually strolling twenty feet behind me, just waiting for me to surrender. The moment I knew I couldn't keep running—not when it was so completely useless—a wall formed out of nothing to catch me as I gave up.

Malcolm was still narrating his actions in Russian. I couldn't tell if his step-by-step commentary for Dorian was comforting because I knew what he was doing—or horrifying for the exact same reason. "Now I'm accessing her memory," he explained. My brain tingled, hot and itchy. "Now I'm finding the worst moment of her life." In my skull there was a pulling sensation, like a soft pretzel being ripped in half.

"Now," I heard Malcolm say. My eyes were squeezed shut. "We scare her to death."

This was how I found myself in the memory of that goddamn college dorm room, where my life had taken such a stupendously shitty turn at that stupendously shitty frat party all those years ago. *It's a dream, it's a dream, it's a dream*, I said to myself as I paced the small space between the single bed and the particle board desk, pulling on windows that would not open and door knobs that came off in my hands. Malcolm had conjured the scent of those boys perfectly. Foamy beer and Camel lights. Axe Body Spray. Wodka and Irish Spring. Their stench was so chokingly close, close enough for me to know they were on their way. That smell was hardwired into a terror I didn't even know I carried.

53

Malcolm and Dorian were nearby watching; I couldn't see them, but I heard Malcolm say in Russian, "If you find the right scenario, the subject will be too scared to find a way out."

Dorian replied, "Impressive."

I raked my nails at my throat, trying to make a hole for the air to get in. Maybe you *could* die in a Morpheum dream, but not by a gun or a knife or a Sasquatch. Maybe your mind could snap beneath its own tonnage. Maybe Malcolm had learned this. Maybe a stronger brain could withstand this kind of torture, but mine was creaking like an old house, beams splintering beneath the weight.

"It's good to practice on someone with a similar age and gender as your target," Malcolm told Dorian with a slight, sexual pant. He was getting off on this, on killing me.

The demolition in my head grew louder as I heard Dorian Meh reply, "But don't you need her alive to confess?"

"Shit!" Malcolm's voice was a mixture of panic and regret, the kind of tone you might use for a fumbled phone falling into an open toilet.

And then: the air was back. My eyes were open. I was leaping from a bench into a room I didn't recognize. *Where was I? Was Malcolm here? Was I dead?*

I exhaled shakily as I focused and found the putty-colored bars. Oh, right!

Jail.

What a relief.

THE
ARRAIGNMENT

The rest of the morning was kind of a blur, but in my defense, I had, you know, *almost died.* So, I felt like I was entitled to a few hours of staring blankly into the middle distance. (Besides, there wasn't much else to do in lockup.)

But even after I grappled with my own mortality over a granola bar in the van to the King County District Court, there was still the horror of achieving said mortality at the hands (or chemicals) of a weaponized Morpheum. Would anyone even believe me if I told them? No. No one, except Altan.

If I could get him alone for five minutes, I could tell him everything: about New Morpheum, and Malcolm's Russian-speaking associate, and how much I missed Paris. Those croissants we ate for breakfast in bed last Wednesday that I was still thinking about. The Ming-vase fragility of my mind. How I didn't know what the seasons were like in Bali. How scared I was that I wouldn't survive what came next.

Altan was literally a part of me: his fingerprints were all over my cerebral cortex. I needed him to soak in all of this with me, to *understand* without my having to explain. I needed him to tell me that Malcolm was just another Sasquatch, and all we had to do was figure out how to get free.

But there was no freedom now. I couldn't just text him or shoot a joke over the cubicle wall or hop a plane to Paris with Altan anymore. Our once constant connection was now severed, and to not have him close was to lose a limb and still feel it tingle when it rained. And Seattle, as we all know, is famous for the rain.

In a movie, the King County courtroom would have been paneled entirely in mahogany—but Seattle is too practical and eco-conscious for such extravagance. The dais at the front of the room where the judge would sit looked like it was built out of bamboo at best and Ikea bookcases at worst. The wood was flimsy and unimpressive. The carpet was balding. The bailiff was rough; he pinched my arm too hard as he marched me toward the defense encampment, which was a folding table. Pete sat by himself, poring over papers. He didn't see me come in.

Folding chairs were positioned in rows at the back of the room for a handful of spectators—an entry-level court reporter, some senior citizens who looked like they enjoyed live entertainment, and a homeless woman probably here for the air conditioning. The gallery wasn't demarcated by any kind of bannister or anything—just a wide swath of chairless space. And there, in the front row, slouched Altan, gnawing on a cuticle.

Touchingly, he looked like shit—just the way you'd want someone to look when they were being tortured by your absence. He looked like he'd spent his evening exorcising his grief over losing me in a number of underground fight clubs. (How else could you explain the shiner staining one of his eyes?)

Altan straightened in his chair when I approached the defense table, and when his gaze locked with mine, the world paused, almost politely, for the length of a single breath. In that moment, I was light enough to float out of the courtroom, beyond

Washington State, into the great white north of Canada where Altan and I would live among the smell of pines. I stepped toward him, the words *Let's get out of here* on my lips like snow—but that damn bailiff jerked me toward where Pete sat. I sank all three hundred tons of my heart in my chair.

"Hey—" Pete said, then stopped. Awkwardly. He'd not so smoothly swallowed a pet name for the sake of professionalism. Or decency. Or whatever it was when you found yourself almost within hearing distance of your not-yet-ex-wife's new lover.

"Hey," I said.

"So, um . . . how was jail?"

Nothing was funny right now, but still I fought the urge to laugh, because he was serious. This was Pete's idea of small talk between him and his estranged, incarcerated wife. My life had achieved Salvador Dali levels of surrealism: everything was hilarious. "Jail was the *worst*," I said. "I'm leaving them a horrible Yelp review when I get out of here."

Pete seemed relieved that I was at least trying to joke, like my talent for sarcasm was a crocus poking its head through March snow. "I haven't heard good things about the service," he replied.

"Tell me about it."

Instead of adding to the game, he slipped his arm across the back of my chair. To a casual observer, it would have looked harmless, a professional confidence boost between client and counsel—reassurance that this was all insanely fixable in a professional's hands. But as Pete's fingertips grazed my shoulder so slightly, the enormity of the past ten years flooded my senses. Like a magnet, my body bowed imperceptibly into his for comfort—again, too slight to be conspicuous to the casual observer, but enough for him to know I was grateful for whatever small comfort he was trying to lend.

Altan was surely cracking his knuckles behind me, but how could I fight a decade of conditioning? Pete touched me, and I unfurled. It had been that way for as long as I could remember.

Finally, my lawyer took his hand back so he could square a stack of papers in front of him. *Back to business.* "Janet's on her way."

"Who?"

"My friend from law school? Your criminal attorney?"

Oh, right. Guess it slipped my mind—you know, because I'd spent the whole night trying not to die.

"I confirmed with her when we met last night: since this is your first offense, she's pretty sure you'll get bail—"

"I'm not getting bail," I blurted before realizing I had no idea how to explain what followed: "Malcolm said I wouldn't."

Pete stiffened, senses on high alert, like Malcolm might leap out from behind the witness stand and attack. "Wait: Malcolm came back to jail after I left?"

"No—"

"So when did you talk to him?"

Ummmmmmmmmmm . . . in a dream?

No. That wasn't the way to drop the bomb. Information of this magnitude had to be fed slowly lest Pete think I had *completely* (instead of just mostly) lost my mind when I told him my former boss had drugged me with the same mind-melding sleeping pill that (by the way) caused Altan and me to fall in love—oh, and he's trying to sell it to governments.

So on one hand, thirty seconds before my arraignment was *not* the time to broach this subject. But on the other, when was I going to get another chance to talk to Pete alone?

And who else was going to help me defeat Malcolm?

The courtroom was humming efficiently; people shuffling papers, bailiffs chatting, the stenographer adjusting her weird little typewriter. Everyone was waiting for the judge to arrive, so I leaned into Pete and whispered in his ear, "I have something to tell you. It's going to sound crazy"—(most things sound crazy when you whisper them)—"but Morpheum has a side effect."

Pete narrowed his eyes. I couldn't tell if he was concerned or intrigued. (Please let it be intrigued!) "What are you talking about?"

"It's impossible to explain. I'd— I'd have to show you."

He actually recoiled so I could see the look of horror on his face, but I went on both stupid and desperate: "In my closet, in one of my Doc Martens boots, there's a Ziploc bag full of pink pills. If you could bring one—"

Pete was already shaking his head, his eyes trained on the front of the room so it wouldn't look like we were arguing. "Listen to yourself," he whispered. "You're asking me to risk my career—"

"Pete, I know what this sounds like but just listen—"

"Don't." He cut me off, his eyes darting around the room, trying to find anything to look at besides my face. "Don't ask me to help kill you. I won't—" He swallowed hard, steadied his voice. "I *can't* do it."

If I wanted the kind of husband who would smuggle me drugs in jail, I should have married a shittier man. Pete wasn't going to do this, no matter how much I begged. Pete would protect me from anything—even myself.

Seconds ticked by while I wondered if I should apologize, and just when I didn't think I could stand the silence between us for a moment longer, a black woman in a sleeveless pink jumpsuit alighted onto the seat next to mine. "Janet Poundstone," she said and stuck her hand out. I shook it, admiring her firm grip and the smooth muscles of her arm. "I'm your criminal attorney."

Little did she know, Janet Poundstone was also my #lifegoals, because the woman was *breathtaking*. She wore her natural curls in a voluminous shoulder-length cut with a deep part on one side. Her earrings were outsized, but her makeup was understated. Her posture? Impeccable. Janet Poundstone looked like someone who woke up early enough to make coffee at home and drink it from a mug sitting down. She probably had a gym membership and a ten-year plan. Janet Poundstone definitely still kept in touch with her friends from college and had run at least one marathon in her life. She vacationed in Istanbul. She had a minimum of two thousand Instagram followers. I could totally tell.

Meanwhile, I looked (and debatably smelled) like shit. I hadn't changed my underwear since Paris. My hair was flat and stringy, my skin peaky, pale. I resembled every Pacific Northwest serial killer who never saw the sun. *Why couldn't Pete have brought me a mousier lawyer?* I thought miserably. Of course, I wouldn't make bail standing next to *her*.

"Ness," I said. And that was the end of the conversation. Janet gave a polite wave to Pete and then proceeded to get her papers out. She stood a full ten seconds before the bailiff yelled, "All rise!" Like she was psychic.

We rose for Judge Davis, a bird-like white woman in billowing black robes. She had a blunt, hawkish nose but her voice was raven-esque in both volume and timbre. "Good afternoon," she cawed crisply to no one in particular. Then she adjusted some papers; everyone was always adjusting papers in the legal system—the detectives, the lawyers. I bet the courts would go twice as fast if they gave people iPads. "We are here to hear People vs. Vanessa Brown, on the charge of murder in the first. Vanessa Brown, are you present?"

Janet nudged me with her elbow. "I am, Your Honor."

Judge Davis studied me over her glasses and confirmed that I was aware of both my constitutional rights and the severity of my charge. "And how do you plead?"

A deep breath from my diaphragm allowed me to project every annunciated syllable of: "Not guilty."

There should have been flashbulbs and gasping. I wanted people to be just as shocked as I was that I was *on trial*. But the brief silence that followed my plea suggested only deep, pre-lunch boredom. The demolition of my life was all in a day's work. "Fine," said Judge Davis. "Ms. Poundstone, your client recently left the country, is that correct?"

Janet stood swiftly in her three-inch pumps. "The victim had not passed away when my client left on an *unrelated* vacation."

"How long had she planned the vacation prior to leaving?"

It was obvious what Judge Davis was doing: she was trying to paint me as a flight risk to justify withholding bail so she and Malcolm could hoot about it later over thirty-dollar cocktails at the top of the Columbia Center. Janet replied, "The trip was impromptu, Your Honor."

Impromptu. That was good. *Impromptu* made me sound like I was spontaneous and whimsical instead of reluctant to spend my life in prison.

"And she has no family, church, or ties to the Seattle community?" asked Judge Davis.

"Along with many other thirtysomethings who move here for tech jobs."

You tell 'em! I cheered—just as Judge Davis asked, "But didn't the defendant grow up in area?"

Since when was being introverted such a crime? "She did grow up nearby, Your Honor," Janet said calmly. "If the court is concerned, we can surrender the defendant's passport—"

But Judge Davis already had her gavel in the air. "Defendant is deemed a flight risk and will be remanded until trial." The gavel swung down, and that was that—all in less than five minutes.

The court started turning over as the bailiff came toward me with his big, pinchy hands. Janet sighed, like she was annoyed to have to file more paperwork—but other than that she took this in stride. Pete had retreated, shell-shocked, to the cave of his mind, eyes fixed at the far-off horizon of a land where everything worked out like he assumed. "I don't understand," he muttered. "This never happens—"

"Listen," I hissed as the bailiff got closer. Pete's gaze drifted toward me, but I couldn't tell if he was focusing. "Malcolm said the prosecution is going to offer me a deal: rehab in California in exchange for a guilty manslaughter plea. I *know* this. If you want to know how I know this, you're going to have to *bring me what's in my closet*, OK?"

Was he even listening? "Don't worry," he said. (He was not.) I felt his hand take my left one as he patted it fretfully, his voice soft and low, the way you'd talk to a dog as the vet put it to sleep. "We'll file a motion. We'll get you out. We'll—"

Someone jerked me backward by the hand Pete wasn't holding. I only realized when I landed in his arms that it was Altan. Judge Davis went ape shit. "Sir, you are not allowed to touch the defendant!" She slammed her gavel. "I need you to *sit down*."

But Altan *dipped me* in his arms like the magnificent doofus that he was. "Smell me," he whispered.

And I said: "*What?*"

The bailiff was scrambling over the table. "Smell," Altan repeated, pressing his nose against my jaw and sniffing quick and deep, like my neck was a line of coke.

A gal's gotta breathe, so I inhaled through my nose just as Altan kissed me, open-mouthed, in *spectacular* fashion. None of this was real. I was coming unglued, dreaming with my eyes wide open. Reality was just a suggestion now, like waiting an hour to swim after eating. But no one could sleep through that gavel, yet I only heard the beating of my heart as Altan clutched me harder. Something small and smooth transferred from his mouth to mine. I almost swallowed it in surprise but managed to tuck whatever it was beneath my tongue just as someone yanked me upright and away.

It wasn't the bailiff; it was Pete.

"This trial is bullshit!" screamed Altan as he was hauled away by a different guard. "WellCorp killed Sam Stevens! Down with Big Pharma!" He twisted against the guard one last time as he was frog-marched out the door. "Vanessa Brown, I'll see you in my dreams!"

And that's when I knew for sure just exactly what the thing in my mouth was.

He'd done it. Without my even asking, that crazy sonofabitch Altan Young had figured out a way to smuggle me the Morpheum I needed to warn him that Malcolm was at Bond-villain levels of skullduggery. For the first time since I'd woken up that morning, I felt like maybe I wasn't 100 percent doomed to die in jail. I allowed myself to be tastefully elated for a full ten seconds—until I saw Pete's face.

He looked like he'd been stabbed through the heart.

FRIDAY, MAY 3

I did something stupid today. I mauled Ness in court so I could slip
her a Morpheum. Was it worth being roughed up by the bailiff and
a massive fine despite the fact I'm currently unemployed?

Hell yeah, it was.

THE BALINESE REUNION

Officer Milford was hard on the eyes, and that jail-guard uniform did *not* help. In another outfit, her middle-aged curves could have been considered graceful and Rubenesque. But between the foot-long zip fly of her polyester pants and her Batman utility belt (which held a baton, a pair of handcuffs, a radio, some pepper spray, and maybe even a cup holder), she came off as squatty, even though she was taller than me. She had resting squint face: her eyes and mouth were slits beneath a tightly curled demi-mullet of dyed auburn hair. The effect was one of permanent incredulity, like she just could *not* get over how bad you'd messed your life up now that you were stripping down at the King County Corrections intake.

"Listen up, inmate," she croaked. Her voice wasn't "husky" but deep with a phlegmy rattle. "You might be used to calling the shots in your life, but not anymore. You belong to King County now, and don't you fucking forget it."

As someone used to reading from an intake script at work, I recognized that Milford probably *had* to make this speech in order to establish her dominance over people who had a hard time giving theirs up on the first day of jail. Me, though? I was completely broken. Malcolm had proven that I was in every sense a beta, so none of this was necessary. "When I talk to you, you respond with a 'Yes, officer.'" Milford snapped. "Got that?"

"Yes, officer," I said through gritted teeth, trying to protect the pill under my tongue. I handed her my socks and jeans.

"And when I say 'lights out,' you go to bed. And when I say, breakfast, you get the hell up. Got it?"

"Yes, officer." There went my T-shirt.

"And if I say 'Jump' you say—"

Ooh! I knew this one. "How high?"

"And if I say 'Eat me out,' you say—"

I whipped around to stare at her, my elbows akimbo as I struggled with the clasp of my bra. "*What?*"

She sneered, happy to have gotten the terror she wanted from me. "How long?" she sneered. "That's what you say if I want you to eat me out. That's how much I own you now. Got it?"

This was not the most opportune moment to give up my panties, but Milford held her hand out. "Yes, officer."

I'd venture that most people entering jail were most likely to balk at the squat-and-cough portion of this intake. But for me, the panic set in when Milford told me to open my mouth. I dry swallowed the Morpheum just in time.

Once I'd been inspected, Milford ordered me to put on a set of clothes. There was a white sports bra that seemed relatively new and a pair of underwear that was decidedly *not*: it was two sizes too big, and the elastic in them was completely shot.

The whole ordeal reminded me of a factoid I'd picked up when Altan and I were at Versailles: when Marie Antoinette came to France from Austria, she had to remove all of her clothing at the border as a sign that her old life was done. She entered France wearing a French-made dress, and I entered jail wearing an oversized set of orange scrubs and undergarments that had been worn by countless women before me. And yet I'm sure we both still felt naked without the comfort of our own damn drawers.

Milford presented me with a flat, lumpy pillow and a scratchy blanket, then paraded me down a series of increasingly dismal hallways, through clanging metal doors that buzzed when opened by swipe card. The Morpheum was on its way to working. My canvas slip-ons (from King County's spring inmate collection) weighed ten boulders each.

Arriving at a row of cells so long I swear the walls tapered to a point in the distance, I was briefly reminded of the dream I showed Altan on Morpheum about the night of my assault. I had thought jail would convey to him how trapped and claustrophobic I'd felt at the time—and hey! Good news! It totally did!

This was terrifying!

Thank god I'm high, I thought dreamily, noticing that all the cell doors were solid. The jail in my dream had bars you could stick an arm through: there was air circulation and eye contact. But these six-foot-wide rooms were made of cinderblock and sealed with only one opening: the hallway-facing door made of metal with one small chicken-wire window.

I peered through them as we walked: unmade bunk beds and stainless-steel fixtures, and every now and then a woman, hunched over toilet or a novel or a hand of cards or a letter. Everyone had bad posture. Having a bed as your only piece of furniture was hard on the spine.

After approximately fifty-two hours of walking, Officer Milford opened a door, and I was so happy to see a bed that I leapt into the cell with more joy than probably any other inmate in the history of incarceration. I didn't even have time to put the pillow down: I turned into a pail of water as I fell to the mattress. By the time I splashed down, I was gone.

I woke up inside a mango.

Wait, my bad. I woke up inside a tiny room painted a *very* aggressive shade of orange, which, considering my new jail uniform, was doubly offensive. The color had been chosen by someone who had no idea how colors worked. It was guaranteed to keep you awake even in the dark.

Hot white daylight sliced though a mosquito net that cascaded from the ceiling. I moved it aside so I peer out at a small balcony near the foot of the bed, which held a wobbly café table and two matching chairs and overlooked a carpet of lush, green jungle. It was safe to assume this was Altan's dream, since I didn't recognize the setting.

Also I wasn't wearing clothes: a definite Altan hallmark.

Footsteps pounded up a flight of stairs somewhere beyond the bedroom. "Altan?" I called, wrapping the white top sheet around me like a morning-after toga and scrambling out of bed.

It had to be him. New Morpheum couldn't *possibly* be strong enough to give you permanent access to someone's dreams. Still, if either Malcolm or his Russian sidekick showed up, I was totally going to shit my sheet. *"Altan, is that you?"*

"Were you expecting someone else?" he quipped as he opened the door—and then immediately tripped over his jaw when he saw me standing there barefoot on the polished wood floor, wearing nothing but percale and relief. "Yes!" he hissed and threw his fists triumphantly in the air. "It *worked!*"

At the same time, we lunged. I jumped him like a sugar glider slapping into the trunk of a tree, and he caught me beneath the backs of my knees and turned just in time as we went down onto the bed in a heap, me on top. One taste of him and I was absolutely falling apart. Rose petals sloughed off of me every time I moved, but still I clutched my toga around me for dear life. If it came off, we'd spend the whole night gleefully drug-humping like bonobos—which would be a satisfying use of Morpheum but maybe not the most strategic, considering we had a whole conspiracy to undermine.

"What. Kind of. Conspiracy?" Altan asked between kisses.

It was shocking that he'd been able to pick up anything in my brain except the words *yes* and *more* over and over again. "I'll tell you in a second. Are we in Bali? Is this real?" I nursed a vain hope that the past 48 hours had been an especially terrible and prolonged nightmare. (Wouldn't be the first time I got my realities confused.) "Please say 'yes.'"

"Yes, this is Bali," he replied. "But no, it's a dream."

OK, but why did it have to be one or another? Couldn't a dream be manufactured in the mind but *also* the realest, truest thing you'd ever known? Our hive mind was the place I loved us most—both together and individually. There was no second-guessing in here. We were just alive.

Altan kept trying to kiss me but his grin was too wide: nothing but teeth and the kind of unbridled, cliché joy you get when you drive around on a summer day blasting your radio with your windows down. "Where did you even get the Morpheum?" I asked. "I thought you poured it all down my kitchen sink."

"I found some when I was cleaning—"

"That reminds me! I have more pills!"

"How—"

"The ones I stole from you a few weeks—"

"Right, right. I almost forgo—"

"They're in a bag in my closet," I said. "Pete thinks they're worthless. Maybe you could call and convince him—"

His teeth disappeared (oh no: come back!) as I realized nothing kills a mood like mentioning your husband to your lover. He pushed himself sulkily up onto an elbow. "So . . . Pete's not exactly a fan of mine right now," Altan said, sliding both of his eyes to the right so he looked extra shifty. "We, uh, had a fight."

Pushing the hair from his forehead to appraise where his black eye would have been if we were awake, I asked, "Is that where you got the shiner?"

"Yeah." There was a slight defensiveness to his tone. "But did you see Pete's knuckles, though?"

"Sure did. You messed them up good."

"Right? Suck it, Pete." He gripped me by the cuff of my toga and kissed me *hard*—hard enough to make Pete feel it in the Force. Poor Altan: I guess his face wasn't the only thing that my husband had bruised. But if he felt like he had something to prove, then *by all means* let's get it on—

"Wait," Altan commanded, letting go of the sheet. "What were you saying about a conspiracy?"

"I didn't say anything." *On purpose. Now kiss me.*

"You were thinking it," he insisted.

"No, I wasn't."

The air shivered Jell-O-like as it did when one of us lied on Morpheum. I winced as Altan glared at me for even trying to deceive him in here. "Start talking."

Sighing, I crawled off him and sat on the edge of the bed, adjusting my sheet. Stupid Malcolm ruined everything—even my wet dreams. "Hang on. I'll show you."

I gathered all the memories of the past two days and downloaded them into a kind of dream tablet that Altan could watch at will. "There's a lot of me waiting in a room by myself in the police station, so feel free to skip that," I said, handing the device over to him.

"Got it." He rose from the bed and moved to the table on the balcony to watch. Meanwhile, I conjured a few extra pillows and draped myself temptingly over them so that I'd be ready to seduce him when he was done getting caught up on my least excellent adventure. Probably in about five minutes. Ten at most. Once he'd scanned the video, Altan would confirm that it sucked, make love to me, tell me all the ways we would come out of this stronger, and then distract me with a classic movie-themed Morpheum adventure that would probably involve riding around in the Delorean from *Back to the Future*.

Twenty minutes went by. Neither Altan nor I had moved.

After thirty, I went over to stand next to him on the balcony. "Do you want some coffee or something?" I asked, ruffling his hair.

"Mmm? No, thanks," he said, distracted. He was watching Malcolm and the Russian terrorize me in the dream: the Sasquatch scene. "But speaking of drinking"—here he rewound the tape so that I was crying in the interrogation room with Pete—"what was in that cup?"

I looked over to see what he was talking about. "Oh, that was just some water the detective brought me. I had the hiccups."

"Are you sure it was just water?"

"I don't know how it could have been anything else."

He frowned at the screen, trying to find clues, his eyebrows knitting across his forehead. "And you couldn't wake up at all?"

"No."

"And Malcolm's friend—the Russian. You didn't recognize him?"

"I've never seen him before in my life."

"Well, look again, will you? Here. Let me zoom in."

The longer Altan studied the footage, the surer I felt the molecules of him start to change. His atoms were slowing, his synapses grinding to a halt. Altan Young, who was brave enough to travel the world and stick his hands in the Petri dishes that constituted the back-seat pockets of airplanes, was *scared*. Which was *not* how this dream was supposed to go. After all, the man was made of jokes. He wasn't supposed to take anything seriously—not even felonious charges. He wasn't *allowed* to be upset!

A thought beamed into my mind then. I couldn't tell if it was from Altan's brain or mine or the one we made when we dreamed together, but regardless, I heard a voice ask, gently, *Says who?*

It was dangerous to assign Altan and me roles. After all, I'd done that with Pete. Our marriage was designed around the unspoken presupposition that he was the strong one who only cried at funerals, and I was the sensitive, artistic one who wept through the entirety of Pixar movies. Once you wear yourself into that groove, it's hard to get out.

Altan was *very much* capable of being upset: I'd seen it in his Marrakesh dream when he and June lost a pregnancy, and in real life when we'd fought about my pill use. That I kept thinking of him as this "no worries" surfer dude who existed only to perk me up did both of us a disservice. He was entitled to feelings.

So I waited while Altan took a whole hour with the tablet, and when he was done, he placed it facedown on the table and stared out over the trees beneath the balcony for a long, quiet time. For once, I couldn't clearly read his thoughts: it was a jumble in there— a veritable gumbo of the worst possible vibes.

"So, what are you going to do about Malcolm's plea deal? Are you considering it?" he finally asked. And then, without waiting for me to answer, he added, taking my hand across the table, "You don't have to be a hero, Ness. You can take the easy way out."

"I'm not sure admitting to killing someone is 'the easy way,'" I half joked, but he didn't even half laugh. "If I take the deal, Morpheum goes to production, which means it will be out in the world. The new formula is horrifying, but even the original formula is too dangerous. People shouldn't be given access to anything that's better than real life."

"It did you some good," Altan argued. "It got you out of Seattle." *It brought us together*, he thought.

Yeah, but at what cost? I thought back.

I know people say it's better to have loved and lost than never to have loved at all, but maybe these people never had to grapple with the threat of spending their lives in prison just to make a rich man richer. "Your life will be ruined," Altan said out loud.

He'd said *your* but I could tell he meant *our* since his happiness was now bound to my freedom. If there was anything that I'd learned from his two pairs of underwear, it was that Altan preferred to travel light. He *could not*, should not stay in Seattle if I went down for Sam's death—but I feared that he would almost as much as I feared that he wouldn't.

"By the way, where are we?" I asked, trying to infuse the conversation with something—*anything*—other than how screwed we were. "I know you said Bali, but where specifically?"

"This is my old apartment." He sounded embarrassed for some reason. I mean, the paint wasn't *that* bad. "I thought you'd like to see where we could live when we're surf instructors."

Dreams always sound silly when you say them out loud, but then you end up incarcerated, and everything seems poignantly out of reach. I tried to be cheerful, playful, slightly insulting: my usual charming self. "What's with the paint?" I asked, but with my mind I begged, *Don't lose hope: I need you. Stay with me.*

"You don't like orange?" he replied. *I will. I'm trying.* "I thought it went with the tropics."

I wrinkled my nose. "It's a little—"

"Awesome?"

"—obvious."

He shot me a ghost smile, the kind designed to remind you what his real one looked like. "Well, you're the artist. We can paint whatever color you want when you get here."

Of course. *When*, as in *when* I got out of jail and we moved to Bali and Sam came back to life and Malcolm was hit by a bus and we lived happily ever after. Easy peasy.

"Altan, it's going to be OK."

"I know," he said. The air trembled. He sighed, annoyed. "Fine. I don't know. I'm scared."

"That's OK. You'll get braver."

"Isn't that my line? And aren't I supposed to be comforting you since you're the one in jail?"

I shrugged. Considering I was usually the one falling apart, it felt good not to for once. Altan would rally: he'd snap out of this fear eventually. But until then, I was happy to help him carry his worry, honored that he trusted me enough not to feel the need to put on a show. This rare and complete truthfulness was one of the things I loved most about our relationship: for us, love was never having to say *I faked it.*

He stood up and tugged me to my feet, then kissed me there on the balcony, not with the sex-crazed mania of before but softer, with pinpointed intensity. "I love you," he said.

"Shut up," I replied—not because I didn't want his love, but because I needed his strength. "What happened to 'enjoying' me?"

"I'm not sure I can enjoy anything right now."

"You will," I said, kissing him again, but Altan wouldn't surrender. Normally I could feel it when his neurons clocked out and his nerve endings took over, but he was too in his head, even as I was trying to get in his pants for his own sake: I wanted to distract him from all of us.

"I mean it, Ness." He trapped my face between his hands so I would have to look into his beautiful brown eyes. "I should have told you in Paris. I love you."

"I know," I said—because he was in no shape to play Han Solo, and one of us had to be chill.

You know how self-defense instructors tell you to punch with your whole body? That's how Altan kissed me: with *everything* he had. His mouth, his heart, his brain, his hands, his thighs, the taut drum skin of his belly all rose up at once to offer themselves to me. With the taste of Altan in Bali on my tongue, my whole body watered. But even though I was desperate for him, there was this unspoken dedication to savoring—this desire to linger over each other like a meal in which you order desserts, then cheese, then port. Then coffee. Then more port. Until the waiters are stacking the chairs and sweeping the floor and wishing you'd go home.

Every time Altan touched me, I memorized the weight of his hands, the temperature of his fingertips. Every time his mouth tasted mine, I folded it into a heavy book so I could look at it later and remember the vibrancy of the moment, how real and alive it all was, even though we were asleep. And when we came, it caught me by surprise—how deeply I felt the physicality of it in my brain, that completeness you feel as you fly apart together. Altan clutched me like the one thing you'd grab as you fled your burning house.

SATURDAY, MAY 4

Goddammit.

I thought it would be fun to take Morpheum with Ness again one last time, maybe even a little nostalgic—like, "Remember when we were addicted to this shit . . . last month?" But my stomach's not strong enough to casually whip up a little fantasy of my most perfect life that tastes just like the real thing only to wake up and realize I can't have it.

My heart's not up for it, either.

I know I can't do fancy lawyer shit like Pete can, but I can do some weird, dodgy shit to try and get to the bottom of this. So, I'm going to trail Malcolm. Figure out what he's doing. Bring Ness justice. Take her to Bali. Prove it's possible to live happily ever after. Watch her take photographs until the day I die.

Welcome to Operation Malcolm Is a Douche: Day 1.

THE ADDLED
CELLMATE

My cell had the dimensions of a cereal box, wide as the length of a single bed and twice as deep. The height of the ceiling was designed to provide a modicum of headroom to whomever got the top of the two bunks braced into the wall opposite the door. There was a stainless-steel toilet and sink—and that was it: no desk, no bookcase, no tchotchkes. No photos of past vacations or mementos of a life well lived. The walls were the color of wet sand and I was completely overcome by claustrophobia.

Even mango would have been nicer.

Who could wake up on the floor of a jail cell after spending all night in Bali and still want to live? How did I even end up down here? My body ached, probably from lying on the cold cement, but maybe also because it missed Altan. I clambered back into the lower bunk, dragged my still-folded blanket on top of me, and squeezed my eyes shut. If I worked fast enough, maybe I could go back to sleep, back to Altan, naked and disheveled beneath the mosquito netting in the sun-drenched room of his dream. *Come on, come on, come on*, I prayed.

No dice. The charcoal gravity of jail had me now; my mind was too heavy to escape. It was suddenly occurring to me in great and overwhelming detail that I was *locked in here for the foreseeable future all by myself.* Jesus, take the wheel—and drive my ass straight to the airport. How could this get any worse?

"Bitch, get your nasty ass off my bed!" a woman yelled from the door to the cell.

My forehead hit the bottom of the top bunk with a clang that made my vision go black. "Who are you?" I shrieked to the outline of the woman standing in the doorway of my cell.

"Who am I? Who the fuck are *you?*" she repeated like a meth-head version of the caterpillar from *Alice in Wonderland.* Massaging my forehead, I tried to get a better look at her. She was white and skinny in the way of unhealthy people, with thin, blonde hair that she'd fashioned into a careless bun on the top of her head. It wobbled when she careened over to the toilet, dropped her pants, and sank onto the (presumably cold) stainless steel seat without so much as a flinch. "You get top bunk, dumbass! What's your deal, taking bottom? You never been to jail before?"

Confrontation had never been my forte, so I rolled out of her bed and swung up the ladder into the top one, then backed into the farthest corner of the room—realizing too late that "cowering like a sad rabbit" was probably the opposite of what I was supposed to do on my first day in jail. Wasn't I supposed to beat someone up on my first day to prove my dominance? Would sucker-punching someone mid-piss count as an alpha move or just a dick one? Maybe it was better if I didn't anger someone who had access to where I slept—assuming this woman was actually supposed to be in here. "So are you, like, my roommate or something?" I asked.

She cackled like a car that wouldn't turn over. It went on for longer than necessary. "Oh, my god, this *is* your first time in jail! I thought you were trying to start some shit."

Funny, because I was currently waiting for her to *finish* her shit—or at least courtesy flush. "I wasn't trying to start anything: I swear," I said, barely resisting the urge to add, *Please don't kill me.*

She sighed like one does after a belly laugh. *Remember when we met and I almost kicked the shit out of you? Ah, that was fun.* "I'm not your roommate. I'm your *celly*," she said, annunciating like someone might for a non-native English speaker. Her voice was slightly slurred. "Name's Honey."

"Ness," I said, waving. Even if I wasn't shivering in a corner, waving seemed like the right thing to do when introducing yourself to someone on the john. "So, um, Honey. Is that your real name?"

"No, but I got a sweet pussy so it might as well be." She delivered this like she'd said it a few times. "Sorry. Reflex. In my line of work, I get that question a lot."

Honey seemed like a talker, which was ultimately OK with me since I tended to find silence even more awkward than talking about your vagina within ninety seconds of meeting someone. "What's your line of work?" I asked to be polite.

"Hooking."

I knew what hooking was, but still for some reason—probably sheer nerves—I said, "Is that some kind of fishing, or—?"

"Fishing!" There was that open-mouthed mirth again: I thought she would fall off the toilet. "Hysterical. Can I use that?"

"Sure. Seattl's got salmon. There's a joke in there somewhere."

Altan says that when you have to tell someone there's a joke, there is no joke, but still Honey beamed dreamily in my direction as she unspooled a fist of toilet paper from the single roll I assumed we'd have to share. She wiped and pulled up her pants as she stood, a seamless, quick motion that suggested she was used to getting dressed and undressed in haste and with minor hesitation.

"So . . . is that what you're in here for? Hooking?" I said.

"Yup. Gross misdemeanor." *Tell me about it*, I thought as she flushed. "Three-hundred-sixty-four days and I've been in here for . . . well, not that much. What about you?"

"Me? Oh. I didn't make bail."

"*Obviously*, dumbass. What's the charge?"

Usually, I like to practice when I introduce myself to people to make a good impression, but I hadn't exactly had time to nail down my delivery when I said, "I'm in for murder?" The question mark at the end made me sound *extra tough*, but lest Honey worry about being locked in with a heartless maniac, I added, "Don't worry. I didn't do it." *Reputable.*

"Yeah, no shit." She rinsed off her hands—without using soap. (*God! We lived together now!*) "You don't seem like a murderer."

"Oh," I said. "That's a good thing, right?"

She snorted as she wobbled over to her bunk, catching herself on the wall before she dropped into bed. "Not in fucking here."

Something felt off about Honey, but what did I know? Maybe she was this uncoordinated and blue with her language all the time. I poked my head over the edge of my bed so I could watch her lie there on her back. "No offense, but how old are you?"

"Twenty-three. How old are *you?*"

"Thirty-two."

"You made it to thirty-two and this is your first time in jail?" Apparently, this was the funniest thing she'd heard since *fishing.* "Man, you must've really messed up."

Assuming this was an invitation to launch into my whole saga, I opened my mouth to start. Honey cut me off. "Ugh. These *lights!*"

The fluorescent bulb that hung from the center of the ceiling was particularly awful: it gave everything the lurid yellow glow of an aquarium full of urine. Honey tossed her arm over her face, which is how I saw the puncture mark in the soft underbelly of her elbow.

I'd turned enough junkies away at WellCorp to know what it was.

"Well, I'mma take a nap," she announced—though it was, presumably, morning. (When even *I* think your sleep schedule is decadent, you know you're sleeping too much.) Honey snapped over on her side and went to sleep immediately.

So this was life now. These four gross walls, this yellow light, this orange polyester, a scratchy blanket, a shared toilet, and a cellmate who appeared to be a connoisseur of hard drugs with access to a home-brewed internal supply. What was I supposed to do with all this—make lemonade? Fuck lemonade.

My stomach roared loud enough to wake the dead, but Honey didn't move. I thought of Persephone, how she got kidnapped by Hades and dragged to the underworld, where she made the mistake of nibbling six pomegranate seeds (side note: could they not get this lady something a bit more filling?), which apparently meant she couldn't leave for six months out of the year. The ancient Greeks probably used this as a cautionary tale against women snacking, but still I was afraid the food in jail would trap me here. I was starving, but I wasn't ready to eat a meal like any of this was normal. I didn't even know where they kept the food.

Instead, I did the only thing that felt right to me: I unfolded my blanket and lay in the top bunk, listening to women's voices ringing off cinderblocks beneath the glare of that horrid overhead lamp. I squeezed my eyes shut so tight that spots blossomed behind my eyelids. I told myself they were the lights of the Eiffel Tower. I told myself I would see them again someday, and the Taj Mahal, and Angkor Wat. I'd see them all with Altan, and the long bones of his fingers, and the burn of his stubble when he kissed me. For hours, I counted the would-be stamps on my passport like sheep until my fists went slack.

Operation Malcolm Is a Douche, Day 2:

Was super stoked to get started following Malcolm yesterday—until I realized I have no idea where he lives. So, I stalked him on the Internet in an attempt to learn some things about my former boss. Fun facts:

- Malcolm grew up in Bellevue. Went to University of Washington. Majored in political science, did not graduate with distinction—despite the fact his dad made a *very* large donation that year.

- Joined a frat the same semester it made the news for grotesque hazing practices. (Had to Google what an "elephant walk" was. Do not recommend.)

- Had repulsive acne in high school. I know because there are tons of photos of him as a teenager at country club events. He must have had surgery to do something about the scars because *damn.*

- His Instagram is depressingly bland: lots of pictures of unseasoned food—grilled chicken breasts, hard-boiled eggs. He talks about protein powder like other people talk about cocaine. His gym selfies are as prolific as they are heartbreaking.

- Curiously, Instagram has no photos of travel destinations or boats—which is worth noting only because he made such a big deal about sailing the Mediterranean a few months ago. Pretty sure he spent the winter masturbating in his apartment and eating kale instead.

- Even curiouser is that he seems to have started hanging out at the lobby bar of the Fairhope Hotel. What a weird place to drink. And yet, every Wednesday, like clockwork for the past five weeks, he takes a selfie of him and some cocktail he's apparently invented that he's calling #ginception.

The captions of these selfies are deeply weird: "#ginception Wednesday." "Meet me at the Fairhope for a little #ginception." He's *really* trying to make this happen—and why? Is Malcolm so lonely he's fishing for people on Instagram to come to some rich-man's bar to sample his own line of title-pun drinks? I can't with this shit. It's too bizarre.

But the good news is: I know where he'll be on Wednesday.

Bad news: what does one wear to the Fairhope?

WEDNESDAY, MAY 8

Operation Malcolm Is a Douche, Day 5:

Hell is the Fairhope: literally, figuratively, actually, acutely. Everything about this hotel lobby is designed to give me nightmares, from the medallions in the carpet to the crystal lamps to the overly jazzy Muzak that will *Not. Stop. Playing*—even for a second. I have never been anywhere whiter than this.

In a city funded by tech money, where our multiple billionaires wear denim, who is this place for? The answer, I've decided, is New Yorkers who visit and bring shoes that aren't waterproof. Rich fat people who are most comfortable in low, wide, velvet chairs. And Malcolm, because he's a douche.

But let's focus on the positive: if you had to pick a place to spy on an oblivious dickhead with a natural blind spot for people of color, you couldn't ask for a better setting. The Fairhope has a tremendous double-decker lobby with a balcony railing running the entire length of the second level, allowing for numerous vantage points. Despite the open architecture, there are a surprising number of pockets to disappear into thanks to the phone booth-sized columns that appear to be specially designed for skulking.

The flower arrangements are behemoths, so that helps too.

The lobby bar is called The Patio (no idea why, because it's not outdoors), and it's set off to one side of the room. The bar itself is small (five seats), but patrons have their pick of *over fifty chairs* that dot the massive lobby—and that's not including sofas. It echoes like a bitch in here, so from my position on the balcony I can hear Malcolm talking nonstop to the bartender, Austin. I know Austin's name because Malcolm keeps roaring it every time Austin makes a joke.

So far, Malcolm's not doing anything unusual besides taking selfies and being loud, like he owns the place. Another middle-aged white dude in a suit came to sit at the bar, and Malcolm insisted on buying the guy a ginception.

Look, I get that buying another man a cocktail isn't inherently loaded with some kind of homosexual undertone, but the way Malcolm is touching on this dude, getting in his personal space, clapping him on the shoulder and doubling over when he makes a joke, I still can't help but feel I am witnessing a corporate version of Grindr for old white men.

Oh wait! Here's Malcolm's selfie on Insta. Caption: "Another successful #ginception reception." He's even got the dude he bought the drink for in his pict—

Wait.

Is that the Russian Ness showed me from her dream?

Operation Malcolm Is a Douche: Day 10

I am, officially, employed again: as a bike delivery guy for Snacks Now, which means I spend all day schlepping bagels and chocolate to breakfast meetings and office baby showers.

The job is menial and made even more embarrassing considering the uniform is made entirely of Spandex. I've assured my new boss I can ride a bike in jeans, but she won't hear of it. So now I'm rocking these nut huggers all over town, feeling like an asshole.

At least it doesn't rain much in the spring.

Literally, the only thing good about the job is that it requires very little thought and I can devote most of my attention to figuring out what Malcolm and his ginception friend is up to. The pay is shit, but it'll keep the lights on. I set my own hours, so I can do things like meet a journalist for coffee—a journalist like Charlie Goodman, who got my email from LinkedIn. He said he's covering Ness's case and wants to interview me, so we're meeting up on Thursday to talk about it.

God, I miss Ness. My application to visit her in jail hasn't been approved yet, and I can't tell if Malcolm is behind it or if this is just how jail works. Regardless, I hope I get in soon to see her, if only to show her my uniform. She's going to piss herself laughing.

THURSDAY, MAY 16

Operation Malcolm Is a Douche: Day 13

OK, I feel dumb. I expected Charlie Goodman to be like Peter Parker's balding, cigar-chewing boss from the *Daily Bugle* (clearly I don't hang out with enough journalists). But it turns out "Charlie" is short for "Charlotte," who is twenty-seven, and now the rampant emoji usage in her messages makes a hell of a lot more sense.

Charlie is only seven years younger than me, but it's like she's from another planet—even though she's also from California. (San Diego, to be exact.) She moved to Seattle three years ago but definitely did *not* give up Cali completely, because Charlie Goodman is a little blonde ray of sunshine. I have never, and I mean *never*, met anyone this cheerful in the Pacific Northwest.

How do I know her backstory? She gave it to me upon shaking my hand. I was like, "Hi, I'm Altan." And she was like, "Hi, I'm looking for a huge story to break so I can prove I can handle next year's election beat because my five-year goal is to be a White House correspondent. I'm an Aries, I have a cat named Whisky, and my greatest fear is his eventual death."

Part of me longed for the days before social media when you didn't feel the need to broadcast every detail about your life, but still I found her enthusiasm the tiniest bit cute. Charlie Goodman has a smile so wide she can eat an oyster sideways. I feel happier when I look at it. There are probably psychologically boosting effects of seeing so many teeth that nobody knows about. My life without Ness is that dim.

After a very long intro, Charlie got down to business: she'd been hanging around the courthouse the other day looking for a story, and she was taken by my little outburst during Ness's arraignment. As a former WellCorp employee, did I know anything about the trial that had killed Sam Stevens?

Hell yeah, I did.

I'd never talked about Morpheum to anyone else but Ness, so it felt weird confiding in Charlie. I wasn't even sure this is something I should be doing, but I clearly need help in getting to the bottom of Malcolm's weirdness. And if anyone has the energy to buy into it, it's Charlie Goodman.

Does she believe me about Morpheum? No idea. She seemed like she wanted to believe me. "This is just the story I'm looking for!" she said. It was slightly annoying that she treated my problems like her big break, but if she can help me bring down WellCorp and get Ness out of jail, I'll let it go.

When I mentioned I was mildly stalking Malcolm, I thought it would creep her out. But because "mild stalking" in journalism terms is called "investigating," she was into it. We traded numbers and agreed to meet up at the Fairhope next Wednesday, and now I have a stakeout partner who's either really cool or totally batshit. I guess time will tell.

We parted around eleven. She said she was off somewhere else. Probably to candy stripe a hospital in the middle of the night or pet orphaned hamsters at a shelter. I wouldn't put either past her.

What a weirdo.

Operation Malcolm Is a Douche: Day 17

Charlie texts a lot. I mean, *a lot*. She texts like someone who has never in her life thought, "Should I send this text?" She texts in shameful doses—amounts that suggest she doesn't have anyone to talk to out loud, but she doesn't seem to mind if I think this of her. Charlie Goodman has to break this Morpheum story so she can get on the election beat! *NOTHING ELSE MATTERS*.

I don't really mind all the texting, except when she gets pissed at me for not answering her back in less than twenty seconds. After all, I spend most of my day on a bicycle, FFS, so it's not like I have a lot of free time to be texting her GIFs.

She's starving for leads. *Who else did you work with? I need more names!* I sent her to Diana (who refused to be interviewed) and also to Dean Jacobs, who, of course, brushed her off. I gave her the names of a few of my former patients to see if they'd be willing to talk to her, but none of them were.

We met at Coffee Talk over the weekend just to touch base, and when I walked into the shop in my nut huggers, she did a literal spit take. Latte all over window. That Irish barista Ness used to like was there, and he was *pissed*.

WEDNESDAY, MAY 22

Operation Malcolm Is a Douche, Day 19

Met up with Charlie at the Fairhope tonight with what I thought was a pretty decent plan: I'd bribed a friend of mine to sit at the bar next to Malcolm and live-text everything that went on. In exchange, I'd cover his bar tab.

Charlie and I watched from a corner as Malcolm and the unconfirmed Russian from chatted up some poor woman who had the misfortune of sitting between the two of them. According to my friend/spy at the bar, she said she was in town for some convention. Malcolm was laying the "charm" on thick.

Then he buys her a ginception. (Did I mention it comes in a copper Moscow Mule mug? It's, like, ninety percent ice.) My buddy pipes up, "Hey, I'll have one of those," but the bartender says he just ran out of syrup or some shit. Obvious lie, because he ended up making one for Unconfirmed Russian (officially named now, according to Charlie) a few minutes later.

When the lady finished her drink and got up to leave, I was terrified that Malcolm would try to slip into her elevator or something extra horrifying, but eventually he left. Unconfirmed Russian was the last to go.

My friend's bar tab was $85 for three cocktails. Charlie felt bad and offered to split it with me. I absolutely hate the Fairhope.

THE "CAMERA"

It was Wednesday, and Janet Poundstone would be coming to visit for her regularly scheduled consultation like she'd done every Wednesday for the past three weeks. I waited for her in my bunk, peering through my "camera"—a cardboard tube I'd snagged one day when Honey finished all the toilet paper.

Before you go thinking I'd lost my mind again, trust me: I *knew* this wasn't a real camera. But it functioned like one when I put it to my eye in that it allowed me to block out the chaotic ugliness of jail. "The camera" gave me a sense of managing, made me feel like I was in control of *something*, even if it was just one vignette at a time. If I tried hard enough, sometimes I'd manage to find a composition that was pleasing. I'd pretend I was in Paris, or London, or Tokyo—and Altan was with me, just out of frame.

Now and then, Honey would come in from lunch and catch me lying on the floor, peering up at her water cup poised on the corner of the stainless steel sink. "How's the angle?" she'd say.

Bless her for indulging me. "Not quite right. A little more to the left? Much better," I'd lie when she nudged it, because there had to be beauty somewhere in this hideous cinderblock compound. I just had to pretend I could see it.

I did a lot of pretending in jail, but that's because Honey spent a lot of time strung out in her bunk. Not that I was jealous or anything: *I* certainly didn't need a chemically sponsored vacation from this shithole with no privacy or autonomy. But it would have been nice to break up the boredom with a bourbon. Or at least some Morpheum.

Man, I really missed Morpheum.

As far as cellmates went, Honey was a good one in that she tidied up after herself and didn't stab me in the night. I'm kidding about that last part—there didn't seem to be a ton of inmates who knew their way around a shiv. Most seemed like regular women who had been felled by any combination of childhood trauma and shitty relationships and a lack of financial opportunity—a tale as old as time.

Honey and I weren't exactly close, so I hadn't yet gotten the entirety of her backstory. But she was full of intriguing little mysteries. She pointed her shoes in opposite directions next to her bed "to confuse ghosts." She origami-folded her bath towels into elephants and teddy bears that she left on her bunk like we lived on a cruise ship. She sang when she was bored, high, off-key, and shamelessly. I appreciated that about her. Sometimes it felt like shame was all I had.

"What's on the agenda for today?" Honey drawled up from her bunk. Without chairs, she and I didn't speak face-to-face as much as we did face-to-ceiling. At this rate, I'd get bedsores by June.

I said, "I got a meeting with my lawyer today. You?"

Honey yawned. "Feelin' cute. Might go down on Milford later. I don't know."

Fun fact about Honey: she had an opioid habit. Though she'd settle for whatever passed for intravenous drugs in a pinch, she preferred the oxy that she got from Officer Milford in exchange for cunnilingus. Officer Milford was the one who had processed me after my arraignment, and her haircut and her piggy face did nothing for my nether regions. That they conducted what Honey called "quid pro ho" in the janitor's closet made the activity even more unappealing. I imagined the nasty stench of bleach and mop water; the dampness of the floor. All of it seemed unpleasant, and I hadn't even gotten to the power dynamic yet.

"Do not judge me, bitch!" Honey had said the night she told me where she got her drugs.

"Honestly, I wasn't," I'd replied, which was only half true. On one hand, I totally understood what it was like to be willing to degrade yourself for a pill. On the other . . . *mop water.* "I just wish you had someplace nicer to, um, conduct your business."

"Awww," Honey cooed. "That's actually really sweet."

When Honey was high, for lack of anything better to do I stayed in my bunk as a kind of lookout in case she needed to be woken up. This was completely unnecessary, but it felt nice to give myself a job. My "camera" to my face, I'd try not to think of all the *real* pictures I wasn't taking outside these walls—or wonder what Altan was doing. I hadn't seen or talked to him since our Bali dream. For some reason, he hadn't been "approved" to the visitor's list or the roster of people I was allowed to contact from the bank of grubby public phones outside the cafeteria. Curiously, I wasn't able to get anyone approved besides Janet (as my lawyer, she got the thumbs-up by default), and every time I asked the warden or the guards why this was, I was told I couldn't know for "confidential reasons."

One of the worst parts about being embroiled in a conspiracy with unimaginably deep pockets in a world where most people would do almost anything for money is that you can't tell the difference between what's real and what's orchestrated. Your life looks like a dream, an alternate reality pasted over what looks like the real world. Or at least that's what I thought when I recently saw the warden with a new shiny watch. Had it come from Malcolm?

Was the warden in on the scheme? I stayed up late wondering, looking through the toilet paper tube I'd squashed in the half inch of space beneath the locked door of our cell so I could watch the guard's boots parade past in the well-lit hall.

In short, I was *thriving*.

Just because I couldn't talk to Altan didn't mean I hadn't heard from him at all: he'd written me a letter. Well, it was a note, really (considering all the stuff he scribbles in that journal of his, I expected it to be longer), and it was folded around a thick stack of bookmark-size hardware-store paint swatches. The note read: "I still like mango, but you do you." This was Altan for: *Go ahead and plan that life we're going to have together, because this is all going to work out.*

In my mind, I painted that crazy bedroom of his a hundred different colors. When Honey was high, I'd spend whole afternoons treating myself to these grand fantasies of life abroad, eating guavas, photographing the lush orchids of our Balinese garden. I'd imagine the light in the afternoons when Altan would come home from surf instructing. I'd kiss the salt from his skin and we'd have sex beneath the mosquito netting of our bed before cooking lobster for dinner.

Before he passed away, Sam Stevens had similarly gotten wrapped up in dreams of his dead wife. I'd felt sorry for him at the time for thinking he didn't have anything worth staying awake for—not even his daughter. But now I understood that sometimes you can live in a jail even if you're not locked in. Grief is its own kind of prison.

So I'd think of Altan. I'd think of Sam. And then I'd think of Pete for good measure—because he hadn't visited me either. After my arraignment, he'd disappeared without so much as a goodbye. The look in his eyes when Altan kissed me in court was shock mingled with an embarrassment for being so aghast, as if he was disappointed in himself for not adequately imagining what "my wife ran off to Paris with her coworker" looked like. Then there was hurt in there, too, the kind of pain you'd gnaw a limb off to escape from.

I hadn't gotten to tell him I was sorry/grateful/worried about him. I never got to say that I wished I hadn't let the baby thing eat me alive from the inside out, that I'd been honest from the get-go with him and myself—that I'd gotten help sooner to straighten out my thoughts so I could have real conversations about our future instead of skulking around with my pills.

When I slept, sometimes I dreamed about Pete—mundane, unremarkable scenes. We'd go for a drive. We'd have coffee in the neighborhood. We'd hike through Discovery Park, me squinting because I forgot my sunglasses, Pete giving me his because he was a gentleman. Every time I woke up, it felt like someone had died, the sadness heavy on my chest, Pete's shadow nearby and just out of reach.

Honey's voice would float up from her bunk below. "Dude, you awake?"

I'd sniff and swipe at my eyes with my fists. "Mmmhmm."

"Just wondering," she'd say, because really, what was there even to talk about?

When Officer Milford opened the door to our cell, she was already barking, "Brown, stop looking through that toilet paper tube"—I was developing something of a reputation for being a trash lady—"You look creepy as hell. Lawyer's here. Let's go."

I stowed the cardboard tube in my chest pocket (never leave home without it!) and clambered down my ladder. Before I hit the floor, Honey was moving faster than I even thought possible. She beat me to Milford's side, cooing, "Hey, baby, what you doing later?

My jaw still hurts from the last time but I think I can make it work—"

Milford shoved her so hard she fell back into her bunk. "Get out of my face, inmate!" she said. I didn't know for sure, but I think this was part of their arrangement: Honey would do something flagrantly disrespectful to Milford, and then Milford would take her away to "have a word" with her in the janitor's closet. "Do you need a talkin' to, you stupid slut?"

"Oh, yes, please!" said Honey, her eyes shining. Honey never looked more alive than when she was about to get drugs.

Milford narrowed her eyes. "Let me deliver Brown to her lawyer, then I'll deal with you, you skinny sack of shit."

(I mean, with charm like that, who *wouldn't* want to go down on Officer Milford in a mop closet?)

Milford marched me to one of the small, featureless rooms on the other side of the block that inmates used to meet their lawyers. She screamed the entire way—"Hey, Gonzales! Wipe that smirk off your face." "Daniels, if I see you throw away your breakfast again, I'll feed it to you through a goddamn tube"—but nobody seemed to notice. *That's* how much noise there was in here: half the time you couldn't even tell someone was insulting you. There were just too many abuses to keep track of.

This was why I looked forward to my visits with Janet: of all the people in my current social circle, she was the least likely to call me a cunt. She wasn't exactly as chatty as I would have liked in a lifeline to the outside world, but it was enough to see her every week if only so I could marvel at her outfits.

Janet had a lot of wacky ideas for my defense, but the only option that was *not* viable (according to her) was the truth that Malcolm had orchestrated Sam's death from the beginning. Since there was no proof, it didn't matter if my version of what happened was real or not. With this in mind, she kept trying to come up with some new Twinkie defense to explain why I'd told a room of wealthy white dudes that I'd killed a man while high.

"Have you ever been diagnosed with SAD?" she asked me the first week she came.

"Seasonal affective disorder?" I clarified, in case SAD was a new kind of depression (that I probably also had). Pretty much everyone in the Pacific Northwest was at risk for SAD in the winter, when statistics like "Seattle had cloud cover for 93% of January" start clogging up the news. "I've never been formally diagnosed," I told her. "Is SAD a good thing to have, defense-wise?"

"Probably not," Janet said and made a note. "What about vitamin D deficiency?"

"No, but can that cause you to kill someone?"

"No precedents"—Janet squinted as if studying something written on a chalkboard in her mind—"yet. I'll have to research."

Maybe it was the vitamin D recollection, but that night I dreamed about that one February Saturday that Pete and I drove east in search of the sun. We finally found it in Walla Walla after four hours on the road, and we were so excited we pulled over at a Dairy Queen and ate Blizzards in the car with the moon roof open.

Last week when Janet came to visit, I realized I had no idea how she was being paid. "Pete's covering my fees," she told me when I asked, adjusting one of her bracelets (she had seven on each wrist: fabulous). "He said you two will sort it out in the settlement."

"Ah." I tried not to wince at Pete's name. Considering I'd lived with him for more than a decade and now found myself cohabitating with a far less endearing roommate, I couldn't help but wonder how he was doing.

"Do you see him much?" I asked Janet.

She replied, without looking up from my case file, "We have coffee every morning."

It was touching that Pete wanted daily updates on my case—assuming that's what they were meeting about. Of course it was. Why else would Pete want to regularly see a woman as bright and accomplished and put-together as Janet Poundstone? Suddenly, she looked up from her notes with uncharacteristic nosiness. "What happened to you two anyway?"

"Pete didn't tell you?"

"Honestly?" she said, leaning back in her chair and crossing her arms across her chest in a way that was just the *slightest* bit accusatory. "I'm not sure he knows."

And this was when I'd realized I'd never gotten the chance to tell him anything that had happened: not really. I'd tried in Canada when we went away for the weekend but had failed spectacularly when my memories caused me to hyperventilate in a restaurant on date night. Pete was totally in the dark as to what had happened with Malcolm and Altan and Morpheum—only now, I was even more sure he wouldn't believe me if I tried to tell him.

"I can explain. Can you ask him to come see me?"

Janet drifted forward again, resumed flipping through her files, and said with that professional cool that refused to sugarcoat facts simply because we both had ovaries: "I'm not sure he'd like that."

I stared down at my hands, ashamed. A tongue of anger flared toward her for refusing to deliver my request, but a deeper part of my heart that was glad. As much as I wanted to feel like I was entitled to even *more* opportunities to justify my actions, I know Pete deserved someone that would protect his peace of mind. I was just sorry that that woman turned out to be Janet instead of me.

Milford and I finally arrived at a short hallway lined with the interview rooms (two on each side). The windowless doors were closed to the hallway like a doctor's office, and for similar reasons. Even on the inside, there were no microphones or recording devices in the lawyer rooms. They were the only truly private spaces in the whole jail—except maybe the janitor's closet.

"They're in four," Milford said. I was halfway to room four before my heart seized on the wrong word.

I spun and asked, just to be sure: "Did you say *they*?"

THE SWEETENER

Walking into that conference room, it was almost too easy to pretend I'd just gotten home from work to find Pete reading in the living room. His usual armchair had been swapped for one of those molded plastic nightmares you sit in at the DMV, but he was making the best of the industrial furniture by reclining, his long legs crossed in front of him. His tie had been removed, presumably stowed in a pocket somewhere, leaving his collar undone. He was overdue for a trip to the barber: his hair looked shaggy and boyish as he ruffled it absentmindedly while poring over some papers. In the split second before he looked up, I was seized by an urge to smooth it for him. It's what I would have done back when we still loved each other. It hadn't been so long ago.

Janet was also here, looking stunning (as usual) in a cream sheath dress—sleeveless (also usual) to maximize the view of her arms. I'd bet her raincoat was also sleeveless. If I had arms like hers, I'd show them off, too.

She stood and gestured to the chair next to her. "Come on in. We have a lot to discuss."

Tell me about it.

Seated at the table, I flicked a glance at Pete, who stared back, unsmiling. "We finally got some good news," said Janet in her no-nonsense alto. "The prosecution offered you a deal: plead guilty to involuntary manslaughter in exchange for rehab in California."

Just like Malcolm had promised. My relief was an Altan-style fist pump in the back of my mind. I was *so* tired—of public bathrooms, of moping around all day, of having no purpose. If Malcolm's plan was to wear me down, it had worked. Let him sell his little pills. Maybe they'd be used against ISIS or al-Qaeda and not against innocent civilians: who was to say? And why was it my problem? Why did it all have to hinge on me?

"Is that a good deal?" I said as Janet slid the papers toward me so I could see. I looked at them like I spoke lawyer.

"*Really* good. Honestly, I've never seen a deal this lenient for a crime this severe. WellCorp has offered to fund your rehab, three years' probation, zero jail time."

I expected Pete to be as relieved as I was. After all, his duty to me was done: my life was saved, we could get divorced, and he'd live out his days content with having done the right thing. But for some reason, Pete pulled the stack of documents away from my reach. "Ness, I want you to think about this. Involuntary manslaughter is still a felony."

"So?" I said. I was already imagining the mud baths, the massages, all that sweet, sweet mental healthcare.

"So, your life might be different after the rehab. You'll have to disclose the fact you're a convicted felon on your job applications."

"Not worried," I replied. After all, I'd probably be working under the table in Bali and beyond.

"You'll have to put it on your *visa applications*," Pete pressed.

"Like for credit cards?"

"Like for immigration."

Oh.

"So, what you're saying is that I wouldn't go to prison, but I also would have a hard time leaving the States, which would mean I'd still be in jail, just an America-sized jail?"

Pete's head bobbed up and down a fraction, a movement that was trying to be too small to see. Janet saw it.

Having previously thought I was all out of raw material with which to hate Malcolm, I was pleased to find a fresh new vein. "No deal," I pronounced. Maybe before Morpheum, back when my idea of traveling was all just a silly pipe dream, I could have traded my stupid notions of seeing the world for a practical life where I could wear colors other than orange. But I didn't want that now, and Altan would never go for it. I needed a future where I could come and go freely, otherwise what was the point?

Janet adopted a tone that sounded like she was trying to negotiate nap time with a three-year-old. "Ness, I know it's not ideal, but this is how the system works. Ninety percent of cases don't make it to trial. The court calendar is backed up for months. You could be waiting for a date for a year—"

"It doesn't matter," I said, cutting her off. "I won't do anything that doesn't let me leave."

She drummed the fingers of her left hand on the table once in frustration: her nails were painted coral. "Vanessa, as your *official* criminal attorney, I strongly advise you to *take this deal.*"

Oof. The edge in her voice could have shaved Altan's beard. It was almost enough to scare me into compliance, but Pete intervened before I could agree to anything. "Hey, Janet," he said. "Mind if I talk to Ness alone?"

She shot him a look of annoyance that was multiple fathoms deep: it landed somewhere between "Don't screw up your job" and "Don't screw up *my* job" and "Don't screw up your heart, because we *talked* about this, Pete: we talked about this *numerous times.*" But after a moment, Janet got to her heels and smoothed her skirt as if it had a direct link to her nerves.

"Ness, give the deal some thought. Call me if you have any questions. I'll see you next week."

Pete, gallant as he was, stood and beat her to the door so he could pull it open and close it as she left. He took a moment to steady himself, allowing me a view of his back—the same view I would have had from my bed at home when he was getting ready for work in the bathroom. When he turned to face me, he reached for his throat to adjust the tie that wasn't there. Upon realizing this, his hands flopped to his sides, then landed in his pockets in an attempt to be casual. "Hey," he said.

I beamed at his awkwardness, at the fact that—despite the profound weirdness of having him visit me in jail—Pete was *here* and we could talk. But where did I even begin? All the words crowded my mouth, trying to get out at once.

"Um, so, Janet's right," he started. "You should take the deal, but I wanted you to know what it meant."

"It was cool of you to tell me. You didn't have to. You know I wouldn't read the fine print."

"I thought about that," he said brightly. "I was like, 'Wouldn't it be funny if I didn't tell Ness about the immigration thing and then I saw her getting deported on *Border Patrol*?'"

I snorted. "Now *that's* a cold dish."

Hands still in his pockets, he gave a little shrug. "Well, I'm not good at revenge. I guess that's why I'm still here."

There was something sad about the way he said it, like he regretted having a soft heart. Who could blame him? I bet it hurt like hell every time he came to my rescue.

Suddenly, he strode back to the table, jerked a chair out and sat down, his palms flat in front of him, all business. "At your arraignment, you told me Malcolm talked to you about this deal, about California—but he *couldn't* have. I checked the visitor's logs at the police station: he didn't come back to see you after I kicked him out, and you didn't mention the deal then—presumably because you didn't know about it. So I wondered how you knew. And then I wondered about what you had in your closet . . ."

It took seventy-five years for Pete to figure out what to say next. Had he found the Morpheum? Had he taken it? Could he have figured out what it was on his own? More importantly, after everything I'd done, was he saying he was willing to trust me one more time?

He finally went with: "I hear the coffee sucks in jail."

I mean, he wasn't wrong—the coffee totally sucked in jail. It was *powdered.* From a *canister.* Add some lukewarm water from the spigot in the canteen (not hot enough to scald a baby, much less one of the guards), and you could make a gritty, tan sludge in the bottom of a paper cup. It was completely pointless: too cold to warm you, too weak to wake you, too flavorless to distract your palate from the queasy taste of eggs made in bulk. "It straight-up blows," I replied, but what did coffee have to do with Morpheum?

Pete's mouth quirked up like he knew I'd say that, and he reached into his pants pocket and placed something on the table, sliding it toward me beneath the palm of his hand. It was a lavender packet of Opal, that zero-calorie sweetener being touted on TV as "The one that *won't* give you cancer!" (Of course, that meant it would, eventually.) "What's this for?" I asked.

"To improve the coffee."

"Doesn't work." I tossed the packet back to him. "I already tried the Opal they have in the cafeteria. Coffee still sucks."

Pete crossed his arms, refusing to take the packet. "Maybe you should switch to tea then. Before bedtime."

"I don't drink this in my tea, either. I don't even *drink* tea."

He sighed, exasperated. "*Maybe you should start,*" he said, leaning on every word. "Before bedtime. Right before you go to sleep." He poked me with his eyes like I should be inferring something, but I had no idea what.

To appease him, I picked up the packet, which was a little more crumpled at one end than the other. Having tumbled from a pocket, I'm sure the battered state of the paper was completely justified—but then I remembered whose pocket it came from.

Pete was methodical, intellectual, detail-oriented, clever—enough to break open one of the Morpheum capsules he found in my closet. Meticulous enough to pry open the seam of the Opal packet, funnel the powdered guts of the pill into the opening, reseal it with a tiny bit of glue, and iron the whole thing under a dry towel to diminish the wrinkles and make it look like no one had tampered with it in the first place.

I whispered, "Is this Mor—?"

"No," Pete said, cutting me off. "It is absolutely *not* that."

"Oh," I said, somewhat disappointed. "OK."

A beat passed before he went on. "But if it were—"

He shrugged, trying to assemble a disaffected expression, one you would wear if you didn't really care about the topic at hand. "If it were, how would you show me that side effect you mentioned in court?"

"Hypothetically speaking?"

His face was even. "Purely."

I stood and pulled him to standing, reached my arms around his waist, and turned my head so that my cheek was flush with his heart. "It would work like this," I said.

He flinched against this inappropriate tenderness before he settled and buried his nose in my gross jail hair. I closed my eyes and inhaled the smell of our life—Indian takeout and lavender laundry detergent and the overpriced conditioner I kept in the shower that Pete didn't think I knew he used. For a moment, I ached to go back there, to when we were happy, and I was clean, and the future was bright—and all we had to do was decide where to go for the weekend, what to have for dinner, whether or not to have kids.

"Well, then," Pete said. "Enjoy your tea tonight."

"Sure," I said. And then I let go.

Operation Malcolm Is a Douche, Day 26

I was on my way to meet Charlie at the Fairhope lobby for another Malcolm stakeout when I got a text from her: *Call me when you get to your usual spot and don't hang up.*

So, that's what I did. She picked up on the first ring, and I was like, "Where are you?" And she was all, "Oh, hey, I'm at the Patio Bar at the Fairhope. Did you get my text?"

I looked around trying to find her and that's when I saw her sitting at the *actual bar*, dressed up AF in heels and a skirt: total Malcolm trap. Sure enough, he was on the stool next to her, chewing on a cocktail straw and staring unabashedly at her (admittedly nice) legs. He was alone: no Russian. Charlie repeated, "I *said*, did you get my text?"

Don't hang up. "Yeah, I got it," I said, and before I could tell her just what a bad idea it was to be within arm's reach of Malcolm, she screeched, "What do you mean, you can't make it? It's my birthday!" She dropped her voice and hissed loud enough for Malcolm to hear, "I got waxed for you. *Brazilian.*"

I swore I heard Malcolm's boner make a diving board sound in the background: *sproing.* "Yeah, well, screw you, too," Charlie said, then slammed the phone facedown on the bar without hanging up so I could hear Malcolm swoop in.

He was all, *Hey, baby, did some asshole stand you up on your birthday?* ("I'm so done with Tinder," Charlie groaned.) *So what's your name?*

(Amanda.") *What do you do?* ("Marketing at Amazon.") *Poor you*, he chuckled, like having a job is the same as having cancer.

He offered to buy her a birthday drink. "Sure thing," said "Amanda" and tried to order a glass of wine, but Malcolm wouldn't let her.

"You've got to try one of Austin's cocktails," he said, and then he ordered on her behalf (ugh) a ginception (bingo!)—"which isn't even on the menu," he bragged. "Austin makes it just for me."

I had to watch her drink it while Malcolm slimed all over her— touching her hair, her knee, leaning in to whisper in her ear. I don't know how she could stand it, but she flirted with him like he was Chris Evans. When his drink was done, he simply paid the tab and stood to leave. "You should get home," he told her. "It's late. Can I call you an Uber?"

"No," she said. "I'll be fine."

"Please. I insist."

"No," she insisted back—presumably because she wanted to dish with me after he went. After a bit more back and forth about the Uber (he's such a control freak!), Malcolm finally left. I got down to the bar just as Charlie was asking Austin for another ginception, but he said he was out of syrup.

Again.

Charlie settled on a glass of wine, and I got a beer, and we moved away from the bar so Austin couldn't overhear our conversation. Charlie was "totes bummed" that she didn't get more info other than learning ginceptions taste like ass. I complimented her ability to both lie smoothly and tolerate Malcolm's gross hands on her. She shrugged like it was no big deal and said, "I have a lot of practice with shitty men." And I was like, "Because you're a reporter?" And she went, "Also that."

I could tell she was rattled. I would be too if my job description entailed having to pretend to be *not* sexually repulsed by someone like Malcolm.

How did Ness manage to do it for so long?

Charlie was yawning like crazy when she finished her wine, said she was on a deadline, and told me to go get a cup of coffee from Austin so could finish her work. By the time I brought it back to her, she was curled up like a kitten in one of those big velvet chairs, fast asleep. And I mean *fast*, because I tried to shake her awake and she barely moved.

Lightweight.

Fortunately, I'm used to hauling semi-conscious women out of bars. The *last* time I had to do it—at the Signature with Ness—the bartender gave me ten kinds of hell about my intentions. But Austin didn't even look twice when I threw Charlie's arm around my neck.

What a prince.

So now we're at my place because I don't know where she lives to get her home. Charlie is asleep on my floor because I never bothered moving the mattress back up to the loft. And even though there's room for both of us, I'm sleeping in this goddamn IKEA armchair (*again*) to prove I'm not a total piece of shit.

I should just buy a sofa and open up an impromptu Airbnb for people who can't handle their booze, but the acquisition of furniture is a dumb idea since Ness and I will be leaving for Bali.

Any day now.

THE WAR
WE NEEDED

It was one thing to accidentally start mild-melding with a coworker and then go along with it for intellectual (followed by emotional) kicks. It was completely another to voluntarily open up your brain to the person who was supposed to know (and love) you better than anyone else in the world only so he could hear every nasty thing you'd whispered to yourself about him behind his back. I thought of this as I lay in my bunk chewing my nails, waiting for lights-out so I could take my meds with Pete.

With Altan in my head, there was no context; my brain to him was an attic full of someone else's junk. But considering that Pete and I had lived together for ten years, he was going to recognize all that junk: the grievances I'd held onto, the histories I'd revised, the lectures I'd only pretended to listen to—all the little sins I'd committed against him and lies I'd told in the name of kindness, or harmony, or in an attempt to make myself more lovable. On Morpheum, Pete would see me more naked than I'd ever been with him before—so naked it was like I wasn't even wearing skin.

Why was I even afraid? Weren't you *supposed* to be completely honest with your life partner? Wait: no. Of course not. No one deserved anyone at cask strength. Even with Altan, I watered myself down for his own comfort. Historically, I'd used more water when it came to Pete, but maybe now that we were older, he deserved a higher proof.

Honey stumbled into our cell. "What are you doing in my bed, bitch?"

Oh good! Her rendezvous with Milford had been successful. She'd sleep like a log tonight. "Honey, you have the bottom bunk, remember?"

"Oh. Yeah. Right. I was just messing with you."

She wasn't, but that was fine because she collapsed into bed with her shoes on and was snoring instantly, leaving me to freak out freely about the emotional and ethical issues that arose from dream-cheating on Altan with Pete using the drug I'd used to dream-cheat on Pete with Altan in the first place, even though—and I cannot stress this enough—none of us were having actual fluid-exchanging sex then or at the moment.

As dodgy as it was, I *had* to dream with Pete. My freedom—my *future*—depended on whether or not I could convince my almost-ex-husband of a ridiculous medical conspiracy, layered on top of the debatably more difficult job of persuading him I was sane to boot. Altan would understand why I did this, assuming he ever found out. Which he wouldn't, because I wouldn't tell him.

With that conundrum shelved (for now), all I had to do was take my medicine. Rip the packet, swallow the powder. Don't think about Pete, or what it'll be like to have him in your head, or how much it will hurt to see what you've done to his heart. Don't question if you still love him, or how much, or if it'll be hard to walk away from him after this. Tear the paper now in three, two, one.

"Lights out, bitches!" came Milford's distant voice in the hall. The room went dark.

I tilted my head and dumped the dust in my mouth like a Pixy Stix. The grit of the powder coated my tongue, and nothing happened. Uh-oh. Was Pete's sugar-packet innuendo a product of my not-so-reliable mind? Had Pete even visited? Was I sitting here mainlining sweetener like the truly insane? *Was I even in jail?* But then I felt it, the *whoosh* of the drugs as they grabbed my ankles. I barely had time to clutch my blanket as I went down.

The party was in full swing when I arrived in the dream, so presumably Pete was hosting at his place. He had conjured an impressively appointed ballroom candlelit by a pair of tremendous brass chandeliers that loomed from the ceiling, casting the soft, flattering glow of a PBS period piece. Combined with the man-sized fireplace at the end of the room, there was enough light to compensate for a time before electricity.

Satin-upholstered walls reflected the sheen of the candles, and huge darkened windows at the wall opposite the fireplace did their best to make the room feel airy, but the effort was negated by the empire-waist dress I was wearing. It was a cage for my ribcage.

Where are my jeans? I grumbled, dodging a violinist's bow. Edging along the chair rail in true wallflower style, I was determined to avoid the dance floor, where women spun in cap-sleeve gowns on the arms of men in waistcoats. I'm not sure how I realized I was at the Netherfield Ball from *Pride and Prejudice*, but when I did, I was torn between rolling my eyes and chuckling into my long white gloves. *Of course*, Pete was dreaming about books; the man never left a chair without one. As nerdy as it was to fantasize about literature, there was something cozy and tender about my husband's innermost mind. Sweet Pete was such a literal Romantic.

Hold up. Who was *that*?

In knee-high boots, dark trousers, tailed coat, and ivory cravat, Pete swept into the party from some unimportant drawing room, looking like Mr. Darcy come to life. Those sideburns! That scowl!

The man put the *Oof* in *aloof* as he moved through the crowd with intimidating grace. Which was *definitely* weird, because Pete in real life was an amicable guy—that time he punched Altan notwithstanding. More often than not, he was quick to smile and prone to stammering when he got anxious, a gentleman who thanked waitresses for refilling the water and told strangers to bless themselves when they sneezed.

Here, though, he looked dangerous, and when his eyes locked with mine across the room, I felt like prey, tasty and screwed. He came toward me, his boots drumming in time with my heart. Even when he reached for my hand so he could raise it to his lips, he didn't drop his eyes from mine for a second.

"Good evening," he murmured over my knuckles.

"Um, hi," I said, and *oh my god*, when the air left my lungs, I had a hard time getting more. It would have been easy to blame my cramped diaphragm on this stupid dress, but since this was a dream, I knew the truth: Pete left me breathless in a way I'd *never* felt for him. Even on our wedding day, when I saw him in his navy suit, freshly shaven, blonde hair the closest it had ever been to neat, I had been overwhelmed with something more like relief than lust, like I'd seen a lifeboat on the horizon and knew I'd been saved.

But in here, Pete belonged to no one but himself, and he did *not* give a shit if I drowned. I felt the draw of his proximity, that magnetism of people who only want to repel. The corner of Pete's mouth twitched up a little to show me he knew this.

"Soooo, yeah!" I said too brightly. "It's me, Ness."

"I know," he replied. Subconscious Pete had a serious, quiet voice—a murmur that was both somber and sultry, like a boudoir Batman. Who *was* this guy? Where was my husband? *Who cared?*

The violins struck up a new song, and Pete pulled me onto the dance floor. I tried to protest—"No, really, I can't, I don't know how"—but he just stationed his hand civilly in the small of my back and said (not rudely, but still as a demand), "Shut up."

So I did. We waltzed an entire song in a silence that for once I didn't feel the need to break—even though subconscious Pete was *really* into prolonged eye contact. Even with these unobstructed windows into his soul, I could barely read him. Altan's feelings came through clear as cable, but Pete's whole head was shadowy, rabbit ear antennae during a hailstorm. I came at his brain from seven different angles and was blocked at the door every time. "What are you doing?" Pete finally asked.

"Trying to read your mind."

"You could just ask."

Yeah, but I could also do that when I was awake, so what were the drugs even for? "Fine. Farthing for your thoughts?"

There was that lip quirk again, enough to acknowledge the fact that I'd made a joke without giving it the respect it didn't deserve. "I was wondering if love was real," he said.

Sure. Casual. Same thing I think about in my sleep. Unlike Conscious Pete, Subconscious Pete cut right to the chase. "What made you think of that?"

"You in that dress, for starters"—

To which I thought: *Gulp.*

—"But also, as a philosophical exercise," he said in an unpracticed way that suggested he might *actually talk like this* to himself. "After some debate, I've concluded that I think love is real, but our perception of it is false. Love is far more utilitarian than the poets make of it, don't you think?"

"Um, OK," I agreed weakly. Did I mention that I *liked* Pete's boudoir Batman voice? It was soothing and elegant, similar to his usual one but with the humor and insecurity dialed all the way down so that there was nothing but the confident purr of his mind. For the record, Pete wasn't pontificating like he'd thought about all of this before and then just felt like bringing it up to sound impressive. I could feel him chewing on this question in a way I never had—even though I'd claimed to have loved two men for much of the current year.

"I think the main problem with society's perception of love is that we treat it as being *so* precious," Pete went on, glancing occasionally above my head to make sure he wasn't going to steer us into the punch. "We've spent centuries painting pictures and writing songs and coming up with ways to convey and celebrate this 'magic.' But love *isn't* magic."

"OK, so what is it?"

"It's water: common, abundant, flavorless, boring—absolutely critical to survival. If we thought of love as something you *had* to consume on a daily basis and then probably piss out at some point, I think our expectations would be a lot more reasonable."

I mildly choked on a cough because I was unprepared for the idea of "pissing out love." Still, he had a point: anyone who's ever been single on Valentine's Day could tell you love had a tendency toward being totally overhyped.

"In conclusion," Pete said, "I think humans are capable of caring deeply for one another, but I also think we've historically overestimated our ability to do this. Thoughts?"

Flashback again to our wedding day, to that moment I'd stood in front of Pete and promised him *everything*—things I didn't even have at that point. How was I supposed to know that fate or my own crappy concept of self-discipline would throw me a pill that would end up reshaping the way I thought of the world?

If our vows had been along the lines of, "I promise to love you with 85 percent of myself and will strongly think about babies I don't want to have," would I have ever taken Morpheum in the first place? Maybe not. But the pressure of being someone's ideal got to me, and I understood again why Altan left June: it's impossible to hold someone's whole happiness in your butterfingers.

Pete twirled me beneath his arm: somehow, my feet knew the steps. "I think love is one thing, and true love is another," I told him. True love to me had always implied you were supposed to honor that love before yourself. And maybe in some cases, you do. Not having sex with another person? OK, fine. Not thinking about another person? Not fantasizing about another person? Not befriending another person? Not befriending yourself, or your fantasies, or the private desires of your own heart? I felt like I could be true to Pete from the nose down. But my eyes and my brain and my loyalties still had to be mine.

"I suppose the next logical question is: do you believe in true love?" Pete asked.

Unfair, considering he was dressed as every regency romance hero come to life. It was enough to make even the most hardened cynic want to say *yes*. "There's no such thing as true love," I said. How else could you justify loving two people at the same time?

"Ah," sighed Pete in deep satisfaction, like after a Thanksgiving meal. "That explains *everything*."

Did it?

OK, enough of this. Speaking of explaining, it was time to come clean. "Pete, do you know where you are?"

"Netherfield," he replied, twirling me under his arm again.

"Well, sort of. You're asleep. You took a pill from the closet tonight. Remember?"

His brow creased. It worked with the rest of his broody-Darcy look. "Yes," he said slowly, like he was remembering a dream, only the dream was his real life. "The pill was pink, and you're in jail."

His reaction wasn't the pants-shitting, mind-shattering panic that Altan and I had shared. Curiously, Pete seemed suspiciously cool with all of this. He didn't even stumble as he whirled me past the buffet. "So how are we in a dream together?"

"That's the Morpheum side effect I was telling you about in court. You can dream with people. Anything you like."

"Anything," he repeated, dropping the end so that I wasn't sure if it was a question or a confirmation. "Interesting."

With that, all the other partygoers disappeared. The music still played, but the musicians were gone, and I hadn't done any of it. "I see what you mean," Pete said, as he made a bottle of champagne hover across the room. He caught it by the neck, sucked a liberal amount of it down, and then tossed it behind him, where it vanished into thin air before it could smash on the floor.

Whoa. It had taken Altan and me a while to adjust not only to the *concept* of dream weaving, but also the actual execution of it. Pete was, freakishly, a natural.

It felt like someone had just thrown me the keys to the idling Ferrari that was Pete's brain on drugs. Driving him would be so much fun. Was it too late to opt for that? Telling my husband about that time I got addicted to drugs and mind-sexed another man suddenly seemed like a waste of perfectly good Morpheum—but he needed the truth. It would be easiest to tell him in a dream so he could absorb both the info and my intention. Maybe here he would realize how much I had never meant to hurt him.

On the dance floor, I stopped short and dropped his hand. The violins continued. What an elegant soundtrack for a slaughter. "So, now that you know what Morpheum can do, I need to show you what I did when I was on it."

Giving him the footage of all those weeks with Altan would take too long for him to absorb, so I gathered photographs of my memories: the nightmares, the baby fear, the shame, the pills . . . and Altan. And the dreams, and the time we accidentally had sex in Paris, which was awkward and terrifying and exciting in a way I'd never felt. There was the wild glee of our adventures, and the depth of our intimacy—how the pills made us *feel* things, could transmit emotions, memories, regrets: the magic and the mundane and the misunderstood. I packaged all of this into a black box, and then I solemnly handed it to Pete so he could unpack it all like the world's most devastating Christmas present.

He opened the lid, and in a flash had pinned the photos to one of the ballroom's damask walls, turning it into a corkboard cluttered with a murder detective's theories, threads around thumbtacks tethering to Post-It notes, all of it leading to one large photo of Altan and me, in Paris—the real Paris, not the one we'd dreamed about. I looked at it and shuddered and how heartless it all seemed.

But if I were heartless, then my heart wouldn't be breaking as I watched Pete regard the big picture and understand for the first time that what I'd given Altan was more valuable than my body. I'd given him my mind, my past, my secrets—things Pete never even knew I'd squirreled away. I'd let Altan penetrate me in a way Pete never had, and the pain of that knowledge was so sharp I caught my breath, having almost forgotten that when I cut someone on Morpheum, we both bled.

"So, Altan was taking the pills, too?" Pete said as he studied the wall, his hands clasped behind his back, like my misdeeds were just paintings at the Louvre.

"Yes," I replied, hoping frankness *now* would win me points for all the deceit I'd racked up before.

"And you told him about your assault?" There was a dark academia to Pete's voice, like Oppenheimer describing what he could do with atoms.

"I showed him. In a dream."

He still wasn't looking at me. "Before you told me?"

The order of these events was important to him for some reason. "Yes."

"Ah."

He drifted toward the fireplace, where he braced a hand against the mantel and looked into the flames. The candles in the chandelier blew out, leaving just the fire and the long shadow Pete cast on the wall. "And you fucked him in these dreams?"

"Only twice. And one of them was a mistake."

"But the other?"

The air crackled with electricity—proof that it had always been there, even before Edison had figured out how to put it in a bulb. "I'm so sorry," I whispered. "I didn't mean for any of it to happen. It just . . . did."

He felt that—yes?—the sheer freakishness of this whole situation? Falling in love on Morpheum was like getting hit by a comet or run over by a submarine: these things didn't *happen* except to people who were truly unlucky. And that's how this all started, bad luck. It had nothing to do with Pete, or the kind of man he was, or the husband he'd been to me. "You know that, right?" I said out loud, but only the fire crackled in reply. "Say something," I begged.

Pete's voice was lifeless. "I can't."

If Pete fought back, I'd know this was a war and not a massacre. For us to move forward, Pete had to scream at me, give me what I deserved: we needed catharsis to get closer to square. Otherwise he might believe that I'd destroyed him, and he needed to be whole—for his sake. And for reasons of my legal representation, but mostly for him. I wanted him to get the victory he deserved. "Tell me how you feel, Pete, *please*. This is what Morpheum is for."

I thought he'd insist on sparing me again—after all, he'd spent years watering himself down for me, too—but then he said in that smooth subconscious growl, "You want to know how I feel?"

Yes, I thought. *Here it comes.* The war we needed.

Into the fire, he whispered so softly I had to strain to hear over the crackle of the flames, "I'm so angry at you I am consumed by it. Every part of my body, inside and out, *burns* when I think of what you did, how carelessly you treated the life we built together—how little you trusted me to understand."

Boosh: there went my infantry. He wasn't done: "Every thought I have of you gives me hives. When I see your shit in our apartment, I feel like I have food poisoning. I want to vomit to get you out of my body. *That's* how angry I am. I am allergic to your memory."

Pew, pew, pew: the cavalry was being mowed down. I was all for catharsis, but this was a little much. Yet I knew Pete couldn't help it. He was reacting to the drugs in that weird, blunt way of the uninitiated, tapping into a part of him that he didn't indulge in the real world. And unfortunately, that part of him was really, *really*, totally understandably (but still kind of awkwardly) pissed at me.

Pete rounded on me. With the fire behind him he was red and gold and menacing. "I don't care how many times you and Altan had sex, in real life or in whatever the hell this is," he spat. "You *wanted* him so bad you almost killed yourself with those pills. You would have rather died with him in a dream than lived a real life with me."

Kapow: left flank, right flank, up in smoke.

"And it's unforgivable, how *stupid* you were," he roared. "Especially, and this is the most insulting part, when you consider what a grade-A piece of shit Altan is. Did he even tell you how his marriage ended?"

My mouth was dry from the heat of the fire. Instinctively, I took a step back, maybe to avoid whatever Pete was insinuating. "He told me he and his wife were trying to have a baby for years, and he couldn't handle the stress."

Pete twisted his face in a sneer. "Oh, he was stressed alright. But did he tell you what he did to relax?"

The tentative fingers of my mind reached toward Pete's to try and snatch the answer, but he felt me, and his skull clamped shut. "Of course he didn't. You should ask him—if only so you know the kind of man you threw me away for, because you don't. You think you do—that these fucking pills of yours make you two special—but you don't know *shit*."

Boom: that was it, command post obliterated. Pete had won. My back hit the wall, and he plastered his body to mine, one hand holding both of mine captive above my head, the other wrapping my throat in a caress that was either murderous or sexual. Either way, it was the tiniest bit exciting in the way of haunted houses and scary movies and other things that only *felt* like they would kill you.

All he had to do was deliver the *coup de grace*—literally, the stroke of mercy—our marriage needed to die. I'd only broken us up: it was Pete who deserved to destroy what was left.

"But you know what pisses me off the most?" he whispered, his thumb tracing along my jaw. "In spite of everything, I can't hate you. Even though you deserve it, even though it's good for me, I can't stop wishing you were still here."

Suddenly, I was afraid. I was terrified he *wouldn't* kill me when he *had* to. One of us had to put a stop to us, and I didn't have the power. Pete knew that. He'd always been the strong one.

Says who?

"I know how you felt when you were addicted to those pills," he said hungrily, "how willingly you poisoned yourself. I know,

121

because I do it all the time. I think of you, and then I die a little, and then I do it all again."

His lips hovered against mine. I felt our muscles tense against each other's like we were bracing for collision. He was in so much pain. I wanted to suck it from his blood like venom, carve out the dead tissue, kiss his wounds, good as new. I closed my eyes and surrendered, lifted my mouth to his—

"What the shit?" I heard someone say.

When I opened my eyes, Officer Milford's face was looming over mine. Honey was next to her, and both appeared to be standing on the bottom bunk, trying to shake me awake. "Brown, you lazy taint stain: get up already!" Milford barked. "You got a visitor!"

"Oh, OK," I said with a yawn, trying to look normal, like I hadn't just attempted to seduce my husband in our sleep.

THURSDAY, MAY 30

Operation Malcolm Is a Douche, Day 27

This morning, Charlie woke up in the bed on my floor screaming bloody murder. I have never seen anyone this messed-up by a nightmare before. She was twisted in the sheets, trying to kick her way out, shrieking "LET ME GO, YOU BASTARD!" at the pillow. I jumped on her to try and calm her down (WTF was I thinking?). That only freaked her out more. She was all, "I WILL KILL YOU, MOTHERFUCKERS!"—and then she got an arm free and punched me right in the face.

Two black eyes in as many months: excellent.

It was the smack of her knuckles hitting me in the eye socket that snapped her out of whatever trance she was in, but she didn't look sorry as I rolled on the floor groaning about my face. When she realized she was awake, she promptly exploded into tears.

Now, any instance of a woman waking up crying in your apartment is a tragedy in itself, but watching spunky future White House correspondent Charlie Goodman sob her heart out on your pillow is like watching a puppy die. What's the etiquette here? Do I comfort her or just pretend it's not happening? I knelt down on the floor and asked stupidly, "So, um, can I help?"

I thought Charlie would punch me in the face again, but she grabbed me by the shirt and hauled me into her so she could shriek into my chest. For the record, I am seriously not making fun of her here: I've never seen anyone this upset about *anything*.

When Charlie had finally chilled into the sniffling/hiccupping phase of crying, I made her a cup of coffee that she drank at my counter, a blanket wrapped around her shoulders. Halfway through, she said, "How did I get here?"

Not a good sign. I told her she fell asleep at the Fairhope, and I brought her here to crash because I didn't know where she lived.

"So weird," she sniffed, unable to recall any of it. She remembered the dream she had, though. It was a super strange sex dream involving Malcolm and the Unconfirmed Russian, who wasn't even at the Fairhope last night. "And at the end," she said, shuddering over her coffee, "they killed my cat in front of me. They hung her from a butcher's hook and gutted her over my bed. But the wildest thing is, I feel great. Despite the dream, I feel super well-rested." Her laugh was nervous. "Like you said you'd feel when you woke up after taking Morpheum. But that's crazy, because I didn't take any Morpheum. Right?"

I didn't know how to tell her what I thought was in a ginception, but "fortunately" she didn't make me. She just put her head down on my counter and cried and cried and cried—which gave me at least ten minutes to wonder how Malcolm did it, considering he never touched her drink at all.

After Charlie left, I got a call from King County saying my application to visit Ness had finally been approved. Few things have been going my way lately, but this is absolutely perfect timing.

THE
CONFESSIONAL

I rolled out of bed and followed Milford as quickly as I could, shaking off the Morpheum residue as I went. I hadn't even had time to brush my teeth or even wonder who the hell was here to see me. It couldn't have been Pete: we'd been sleeping together not ten seconds ago. (Ten more seconds and we might have been sleeping together in a different way, but that wasn't the point.) Maybe Janet had come to bully me into taking the deal?

Oh, god. Please don't let it be Malcolm!

Where Milford was supposed to turn left to take me to the legal conference rooms, we instead went right through a door that was new to me. The hallway beyond it was designed like a shooting range gallery in that it was demarcated on one side with partitions that gave the illusion of privacy, kind of like confessionals. In each stall was a backless stool, a black-handled phone receiver, and a shallow countertop that dead-ended into a Plexiglas wall.

When birds stun themselves accidentally flying into patio doors: that was me, seeing Altan for the first time in weeks.

"Control yourself, Brown, or you'll go back to your cell!" shouted Milford, yanking at the tail of my shirt. I hadn't even realized I'd managed to get a knee onto the countertop like I was planning to throw myself over. Stupidly, I smashed my palms on the glass (they always do that in movies), and Altan matched on his side so that we looked like shmucks in an intro to miming class.

His expression? Bittersweet wasn't the right way to describe it: it was too polite for emotions this massive. The feeling was more like torture-joy, grief-stacy. I knew, because I felt it too. *Sit down*, he mouthed, and so I did, brushing my eyes with the back of my hand as I picked up the greasy phone that hung to my left and said, "Hi."

"Hey," he replied. That was all we could manage. What else could you say in a situation like this? Does humanity even have the words to express a longing this violent? And even if it did, could you utter them into the receiver of a tapped phone line in a jail, or would they just evaporate in protest?

Altan looked even thinner, as if that were possible, but also tighter somehow, like his muscle mass had increased by stress-clenching for weeks. In Paris, he'd gotten his hair cut in a messy pompadour, but now it was growing out. Long, straight locks fell into his eyes, but he was too busy watching me to brush them away.

We studied each other like we had at the office during our first few days on Morpheum, when we kept trying to read the other's mind, trying to figure out if the drug worked when we were awake. It didn't: I knew that. But still I reached toward Altan's brain with my own, trying to brush his thoughts. After a moment, he shook his head sadly as if to say, *No, I can't hear you either.*

He had another black eye. At least, I thought it was new. "You been hanging out with Pete again?" I pointed to his face.

"Oh that? No. Just an accident," he said. "How are you?"

I wanted to crack another joke, but apparently I had used up my humor allotment on the shiner reference. "Miserable."

He nodded. "Me too."

A huge bouquet of yellow tulips wrapped in white paper lay before him on his side of the counter. "I went to Pike Place," he said. "I thought you could use a snack for your insatiable eyes."

This wasn't the first time Altan had attributed my photography habit to a gluttonous sense of vision. The way he tells it, my eyes are a gout-ridden Henry VIII with a turkey leg in each hand. I love the comparison so much. "That's really sweet." I swallowed hard. "I haven't had much to look at."

"What *have* you been looking at?"

"No." My hands fluttered in front of me like two little birds. "Um— I can't— Just— Tell me what you've been up to. Don't leave anything out."

"Ness . . ."

"*Please*, just talk. I'll be OK in a minute. Just talk."

So he did. He told me about his new delivery job, and how much he hated people who ordered La Croix by the rack—but not as much as he hated people who ordered six packs of La Croix in ten different flavors. He jabbered through half a dozen stories in as many minutes, just so I could calm down, lose myself in the rhythm of his voice, the predictability of his punchlines. It was Paris all over again: coffee and croissants, chitchatting about nothing special, telling stories with our words instead of our memories.

"In every office, there's a Malcolm," Altan was saying. "A smarmy asshole who thinks he's better than everyone else. At one office, there's two, and the only reason I care is that they take turns tipping me. One of them will be like, 'What did Cummings give you last time?' and I'll say, 'Twenty bucks,' so I'll get twenty-five. And then the next day, Cummings will be like, 'What did Sweeney give you?' and he'll make it thirty. I'm wondering if they're going to ceiling out at some point, or if I can get them high enough to pay my cellphone bill."

I laughed weakly, startled by the sound of it. "You should get a pool going at work. I'd put money on fifty."

He looked relieved to see me not teetering on the verge of tears. "Yeah, well, I don't have a lot of friends at work. It's kind of a solitary job. Besides, you can't really grab a beer after your shift because of the Spandex. It's just too weird."

I sniffed another laugh—my second in as many minutes! A new jailhouse best for me. "Personally, I wouldn't mind seeing you in Spandex," I teased.

"Why? Do you need even more nightmares?" The words were already out of his mouth before he realized what he'd said. "Sorry," he winced. "That was insensitive."

"It's OK," I said, trying to recover. "I haven't been having nightmares, actually." *Unless you count getting ripped a new one by my suddenly sexy husband.* I hadn't had time to figure out if that had been a good dream or a bad one.

"Um, speaking of nightmares . . ." Altan scanned the room to see if any guards were obviously watching us. When none of them were, he said, "Take a better look at these flowers," and thrust the bouquet toward the glass. Hidden among the greenery and tucked into the plastic fork that usually holds the card was a photo of Malcolm and . . . hang on a second. Was that Dorian Meh, the Russian of my dreams? (Wait: the Russian that was *in* my dreams. You know what I meant.) The two of them were mugging for the camera, holding up copper Moscow Mule cups in what looked like—a funeral parlor? The Lincoln Bedroom?

"Where did you get this?" I breathed into the phone.

"Instagram."

"And you printed it out?"

"I didn't know if I could bring my phone. Besides," he added, shifting in his seat, "the guards are listening."

Ugh. Jail was the *worst*. How was anyone supposed to discuss shady illegal business over tapped lines?

It was probably too late to institute some kind of secret code, but it didn't hurt to try. "Those flowers remind me of a dream I had once," I said carefully. "It was right before my arraignment, and there were these two guys who kept chasing me all night."

Altan caught my drift and pointed at his bouquet. "The flowers in your dream were the exact same as these?"

Considering Dorian Meh had a pretty forgettable face, the memory of him was crystal clear. "The exact same."

This meant something to Altan, though I couldn't tell what. "What a coincidence," he said. "Thanks for letting me know."

And that was the end of the conversation: no room for follow-up questions, like *How the hell did you find a man I met in my mind? Why is Malcolm hanging out with this dude for real? What are you doing that makes you afraid of being overheard by law enforcement types? Just how screwed am I?*

Nope: time for more small talk, which was fine—I'd listen to Altan read the phone book if it meant I could be within ten feet of him (albeit separated by glass). "So," said Altan. "Your turn. What have you been up to?"

Oh, golly. Let's see. *Staring through a toilet paper tube. Napping with my junkie cellmate. Almost having sex with my ex-husband in a dream . . .*

My eyes glazed over for a moment as I recalled the most exciting thing that had happened to me in weeks. It was good that Officer Milford woke me when she did, because who knows how far I would have gone with Pete—or how good it would have felt? His big hands flashed in my memory, one gripping both my wrists above my head, the other firm (but not tight) around my neck— funny how I hadn't been afraid. Despite the clear and present danger, I trusted him completely. Talk about a mind-fuck.

"Ness?" said Altan. "Is everything OK?"

What a dumb question for someone in jail—but what else was he supposed to say as I sat there, staring into space? There had to have been a reason I was thinking about Pete, other than how utterly, fantastically confusing he was in a dream . . . Oh, right! Now I remember. "I've been meaning to ask you something," I said.

Altan leaned back in his chair so he could hoist one leg across the other. "Go for it."

"Why *exactly* did you and June get divorced?"

Silence. Prickly, static-filled silence hissed out of my phone receiver like a gas. Then he swallowed audibly. "I told you already. She lost the baby in Marrakesh, and the stress of trying to get pregnant again took its toll on us."

My fingers tightened around the receiver. "And that was it?"

"Did Pete tell you what happened? Because he's not supposed to break attorney-client privilege—"

"Pete didn't tell me anything except to ask you," I said calmly. "So I'm asking you. What happened?"

Sometime early in our relationship, while Pete was still dropping his vast amount of literary knowledge on me during dates, he told me Hemingway was once challenged with writing a story in only six words. Hemingway came up with: "For sale: baby shoes. Never worn."

Boom. Mic drop. I thought only Hemingway could tell you everything and break your heart with just a handful of English, but it turned out Altan could, too. His mouth moved up and down as he tried to think of something to say, and when there was nothing, he swallowed hard again. "One day, June came home early from a business trip."

That was it. That was all I needed to know, because no one comes home early from a business trip and lives happily ever after. The scene played in my mind as easily as if we were on Morpheum:

the distant slamming of the front door, the footsteps on the stairs, his name on her lips—*Altan, are you home?* The soft squeak of the bedroom door hinges—Altan, glorious and sweaty, snapping his head toward the *thud* of a handbag hitting the hardwood floor. The gasp of the woman beneath him as she scrambled for the sheets.

The only thing I couldn't picture was June, because Altan had never introduced her to me—not in real life, not in dreams. I'd never questioned it before: I was too enamored with him to wonder about his ex-wife's memories, her mannerisms—the face she made when she found her husband giving it to someone else in their bed.

"I'd been thinking about divorce for a while," Altan said into the phone. "All the baby stuff stressing us out? That was true. I wanted to see how I felt with someone else—*if* I could have feelings for someone else. When I realized I could, I knew it was over. I was going to tell June when she got back from the trip." His knuckles whitened on the phone. "I didn't know she was pregnant."

Oh, shit. "She was pregnant?" I asked, adding a little extra judgment in my voice. No, I'd never met June, but the unspoken code of women stated that I should feel angry on her behalf.

"That's why she came home early," Altan said desperately. "She wanted to surprise me with the news."

My heart was pounding, slow and steady in my ears. "What happened to the baby?"

To his credit, he didn't look away. "Another miscarriage."

A bolt of electricity fired from his heart and landed smoldering in mine. I remembered his grief in Marrakesh when they lost the first pregnancy: to lose the second (especially given the *extremely shitty circumstances*) must have killed twice as hard. Part of me completely identified with the weight of guilt that big. But then part of me remembered that he *hadn't told me any of this*, and the door to my sympathy slammed shut.

"The doctors didn't know why," he went on, staring at the flowers on the counter. "Said it could have been stress. Or shock. Or bad luck. She had a history, so maybe it was—"

"How many times did you cheat on her?" I asked.

He sighed. "Does it matter?"

In the same way manslaughter is different from first-degree murder, yes, it mattered. When I refused to give him an out, he finally admitted, "It was more than once."

"*Jesus*, Altan. How could you?"

I hadn't even heard Officer Milford sidle up behind me. "Brown, your time's up," she said, but I ignored her in favor of watching Altan's mouth move up and down like a nutcracker. He was trying to form an argument. It usually didn't take this long. "I was lonely," he said. "I was so damn lonely—"

"No, I meant *how could you lie to me?* I asked you on the plane if you'd ever cheated on June, and you said no."

"Why didn't I tell you the one thing I'm most ashamed of in my life? Because I didn't want you to know what an asshole I am!"

"Brown, that's *enough*," said Milford, her hand on my elbow. She was dragging me backward, but I held on to the receiver.

"I *need* to know what an asshole you are: I've made large life decisions based on the fact that I assumed you weren't an asshole!"

"Yeah, well, you're an asshole, too," Altan retorted with all the panache of a grade-school bully. "Look what you did to Pete!"

"That has nothing to do with this," I spat as Milford finally wrestled the receiver out of my grasp. I hoped Altan could still hear me when I shouted, "And fuck you for bringing it up!"

He jumped to his feet and splayed his hands against the glass like Dustin Hoffman at the end of *The Graduate*. "Did you ever think that's why we belong together?" His voice was muffled, as if underwater. "We're too messy for clean people."

Who are you calling messy? I thought, as Officer Milford forced me down the hallway of the jail I was in for killing someone because I refused to stop stealing pills from my workplace since I needed them to cheat on my husband when I was high.

Fine. Maybe I was a *little* messy. Granted, no one's perfect, but some people's errors are small enough to be forgivable. Others go for broke in the fuck-up department—and that's where Altan and I lived: among rusted refrigerators and eyeless dolls in trash heaps where nothing worked right. Which was bad only if you didn't know you were there in the first place.

Officer Milford berated me all the way to my cell. "Brown, you overgrown cum stain: when I say you're done with the phone, you are done with the *phone*. Understand?"

"Yes, officer," I said, staring at my shoes.

"I'm revoking your visiting privileges for a month. Prove that you can *listen*, then you get your shit-for-brains boyfriend back."

I opened my mouth to argue, but remembered 1) I was a beta now, and 2) Altan did, in fact, have shit for brains. "Sorry, officer."

She shoved me through the door to my cell without even bothering to antagonize Honey (who had apparently gone back to sleep curled against the wall) and left me standing there in the small space between the sink and the bunk beds. In lieu of anything satisfying to kick—a chair, a trash can—I whiffed my foot through the air like a doofus. Mother. Fucking. Altan. Young.

Multiple times, in dreams and in person, he'd lied to me— which was unacceptable because our whole relationship had been founded on psychic radical honesty the likes of which had been unprecedented in the history of human trust. Altan and me: I thought we were pioneers. But it turned out we'd been the same as all the other couples who don't make it because one of us was trusting and optimistic and the other shady and full of shit.

The worst part was what this knowledge had cost me. I'd wrecked my life (and Pete's, *and* Sam's) to be with Altan. And yes, I chose all of that—just like I'd technically given Sam all those pills—but still, I couldn't help but feel like I'd been duped. In redacting this seminal moment (pun *totally* intended) from his past, Altan had played me as surely as Malcolm had. And in that moment, he was almost as despicable.

"So, who's Pete?" Honey said to the wall. She didn't even bother rolling over so I hadn't even known she was awake.

"Pete?" I said.

"Yeah, Pete, as in"—here she made her voice Marilyn Monroe breathy—"*Oh, Pete! Yes, Pete!* You moaned his name all night."

Honey pulled up to one elbow and half turned from the wall. She looked as smug and serene as the woman in the "Grande Odalisque" painting I'd seen in the Louvre with what's-his-face.

Pretty sure I turned the color of my top. "*What?*"

"You don't usually talk in your sleep," she drawled. "So come on: who is he?"

Good question. The sweet guy I had slept next to for a decade was not the imposing man I met in a dream last night—just like Altan wasn't the down-on-his-luck divorcée he'd sold himself to be, so now I didn't know if I knew anyone. The problem with Morpheum is that it allows you to see people better but at the same time spotlights all the things you still don't understand. It gives you a boat to sail in and a horizon that never gets closer.

So who *was* Pete?

I shrugged my shoulders and sprang up into my bunk. "No clue."

THURSDAY, MAY 30 (CONT'D)

Operation ~~Malcolm Is a Douche~~, Day ~~27~~ FUCK YOU
PETE ^

Remind me to buy Pete a drink to thank him for *totally ratting me out to Ness about the reason June dumped me.* I mean, SHIT! (!!!!!) This was *not* the way I wanted to hang with Ness in jail, because she got *pissed* when she found out I'd been selective with my info, especially as it pertained to my ability to support loved ones in crisis while also keeping my dick dry. Which is fair: she's allowed to be pissed. I should have told her (especially when she asked). But also—and maybe this is an unpopular opinion—but I feel like she overreacted the tiniest bit.

It's not like I cheated on *her.*

Anyway, Ness got dragged out by the guard before we could resolve this thing, so now I have to wait until visiting hours on Monday to make sure we're cool—assuming she keeps me on her list of approved visitors.

Four days to stew is a long time.

The situation with Ness is starting to feel like it did with June when we were trying to get pregnant. Ness is in jail going through all this wrenching physical and emotional stuff that I can't help with. I'm over here eating Doritos and being worthless. Maybe that's why I'm so hell-bent on trailing Malcolm even though it's borderline stupid: it keeps me connected to her so I don't drift away. Again.

The good news is that before Ness cast a hex on me, she was able to confirm that Malcolm's sometime Fairhope date is the same Russian-speaking dude from her (and Charlie's) dreams. So now I have a more solid lead as to who might be behind this, even though I don't know his name.

I thought Charlie would be excited about this development when I met her for dinner, but she didn't have the heart to get stoked. Was pretty lackluster in general. I guess having your cat murdered repeatedly in a sex nightmare will do that to you.

She spent the whole day trying to find Malcolm's Russian friend, poring through old newspapers, but she came up empty.

To cheer her up, I gave her the tulips I bought for Ness. (Obviously, I took the picture out of them first.) I mean, what else was I going to do with them?

I hope they work.

THE BOY SCOUT

The thing about jail is that you can't escape it. Yeah, I know that sounds obvious since containing alleged bad people is the whole point, but what I'm trying to say is that you can't escape *anything*—not the building, not the people, not yourself or your personal feelings of rage or sadness or despair. There's no friend you can call or walk you can go on or Netflix to binge. It's just you and a world of hurt that overtakes every moment your eyes are open. And as fun as it is to do jigsaw puzzles in the common room, they don't really take the edge off *all the injustice being visited upon you.*

Besides, half the pieces are missing. Not good for morale.

All of this to say that even though I was primarily pissed at Altan, I went ahead and got pissed at Pete for good measure because I had nothing else to do for the entire day after our dream together. Honestly, it was offensive that he hadn't come to visit. Didn't a near-death blow-up on a magical drug trip with his wife warrant Pete's full attention? What's a gal gotta do to get prioritized around here?

Feeling like you've been relegated to a back burner sucks.

Two days after my dream with Pete, Officer Milford appeared in the doorway of our cell. "Hey, belle of the balls. Lawyer's here to see you."

I sat up in my bunk, where I'd been contemplating paint samples for the past two hours. "Does that mean me? Or . . ."

"Yeah, it's you." Milford shot Honey a glance that clearly said, *What a dumbass.*

Honey sniggered. "Which lawyer is it?" she asked Milford. "The hot one?"

"No. The guy." Before I could wrap my mind around the fact that these two had possibly discussed the sexual attractiveness of my lawyers behind my back, she added, "And, Brown, if I get word that you're throwing tantrums again, I'm going to shove your boot so far up your ass I'll be wearing you like a bedroom slipper."

"Good one," Honey cackled.

"Shut up, ass wipe—or you'll be keeping my other foot warm!"

Honey's reply was more like a purr than an acknowledgment. "Yes, *ma'am.*"

I leapt out of my bunk and into my shoes (spent two days perfecting that move). As anxious as I was to see Pete, I was equally anxious to not have to watch Milford and Honey's mating ritual.

In our usual interview room, Pete was sitting at the table looking like he always did: a little skittish, slightly bent from all the reading, his hair a mess—like nothing at all had changed. "Oh, hey, Ness," he said as he stood. Milford shut the door behind me. The broody aristocrat of the dream was gone. "How are you?"

Yet another stupid question to be asking people in jail. They should make a whole subset of greetings for people going through hard times, like *How's your crisis going?* Or *Tragedy treating you alright today?* "Oh, you know!" I said brightly, feeling that back burner beneath me flare up a notch. "Just sitting here, twiddling my thumbs, wondering when you were going to feel like paying me a visit."

"I know," said Pete with a guilty flinch. We were both still standing. I was squaring up for a fight, but Pete crossed his arms over his chest and hunched his tall frame in deference. "I should have come yesterday."

"Ya think?" I swept my arm to the side dramatically. "Look, I get that I'm not the poster child for people who are good at confrontation, but you can't just have a fight like we had the other night and then *not* come talk to me about it—"

"What?" he said.

Ugh. Pete was too smart to play dumb, so his trying it really set me off. "You know *exactly* what I'm talking about!" I said. "The *Pride and Prejudice* dream we had on Morpheum where you ripped me a new one about how awful I am and then Milford woke me up before we got to maybe rage fuck. Ringing any bells?"

His eyes went as wide as saucers—big flying ones, not down-sized salad plates. "Wait, wait," he said helplessly. "Rage fuck?"

"Yeah, that hot, angry, emotional sex you have in the middle of an argument."

"It's real?" he whispered.

"Rage fucking is *definitely* real."

"Jesus Christ, Ness!" He reached for me and put his hands on my shoulders, more in panic than in anger. "*Was the dream real?* Were you in it, too?"

If anyone can sympathize with the balls-out wackiness of realizing Morpheum lets you make cameos in other people's brains, it's me. But I wasn't in the mood to be charitable since I already explained all this and he had a history of not listening to me. "Of course, it's real! I *told* you Morpheum had a side effect!"

"You also told me you were pregnant, like, six weeks ago!" His voice was strangled. "So, sorry if I was *skeptical.*"

Touché.

Pete let go of me and melted down into his chair, head in his hands. News of possible pharmaceutical mind-melding would be confusing enough to throw most people into a mild existential crisis, but he would take this harder than most. There wasn't a lot of room for gray area in Pete's gray matter; he liked things black and white.

"Pete?" I said to the back of his head. He didn't answer. He was off somewhere wrestling with this knowledge. Now that I'd seen the elegance of his mind, I could imagine the scene in his brain: there were likely five Petes in a mahogany-paneled library, quaffing scotch and throwing out phrases like "I daresay," and "Hear, hear!" and "But what does this mean for England?" In short, I imagined my husband's thought process looked like that movie *Inside Out* except every emotion was Winston Churchill.

He startled when I brushed his shoulder. "Pete? Talk to me."

When he finally lifted his head, his face was as rosy and wrinkled as a baby bird's. He burst immediately into tears.

In the decade of our relationship, I'd only ever seen Pete really cry once—when his grandfather died, and even that wasn't at the gravesite but later in the evening, in the privacy of his childhood room. He'd cried facedown into my lap while I rubbed his back and felt that awful, heartbreaking impotence of bystanders. The next morning, he'd apologized for the outburst, like he'd actually inconvenienced me with the fact he had feelings.

So Pete crying was kind of a big deal.

I dropped to my knees next to his chair trying to get him in my arms, but he squirmed away to hide the flush of his face, the crumple of his mouth, the way he dragged his hands across his eyes in the pathetic way of an overtired child. "Stop fighting," I said—a fitting motto for our marriage. It seemed like one of us was always trying to come off as more put-together than we were.

Finally he gave up and joined me on the floor, where he crushed me against his chest and the familiar smell of dry cleaning. His surrender felt . . . honest. And it was weird that it took me a moment to define it, but that's how rare it felt to glimpse him undone.

"I thought you'd lost it," he sputtered into my hair. "I thought the drugs had wrecked your head."

"That's fair," I said softly. "For a while there, I wasn't doing so good."

"If you had poisoned Sam on purpose, I would've stood by you—"

"I know, Pete—"

"Even after everything that's happened—"

"Pete, I know."

"And then in the dream, I said those things—about how angry I was, how much I wanted to hate you." He pulled back so he could look at me, his blue eyes watery and shot through with pink. "I was hoping it wasn't real, that it was all in my head and you didn't see, but you did, didn't you?"

I nodded. It was hard to speak with this kickball in my esophagus, but still I tried. "Dude, you are *so* pissed at me." It came out in a laugh-sob as I smoothed his hair. (His face cracked briefly into a smile, if only to ease the tension.) "It's OK. Be as mad as you want: I don't blame you." Kneeling on the ground, I took his hands in mine. "Just know it was an accident. Pete, I *swear* I wasn't looking to hurt you—"

"I know," he said. "Ness? I know. I felt it in the dream."

I sighed in *deep* satisfaction, the kind you can't usually get in jail. Half of my angst instantly dissipated, because now Pete *knew everything* he needed for both repairing his heart and sorting out my case. That the truth was out and in the hands of the smartest man I knew—and he *believed* me—felt like skipping away from a plane crash.

"The crazy thing is," Pete said, pushing himself to standing. "I feel better after the dream—not *great*, because I still think you were an idiot. But better."

I wasn't even offended, first because he was probably right, and second because I was so pleased that we were being honest with each other. He reached a hand down to help me up. "Maybe I just needed to scream at you."

"You don't need a pill to do that. You can scream at me all you want sober—but you have to come see me to do this."

"Point taken." He snatched a tissue from the box on the table and handed it to me. "We never were good at hard topics."

"That's what's great about Morpheum: it forces you to have conversations you wouldn't have awake." *Unless one of you was crafty enough to avoid certain subjects altogether,* but whatever.

"I can't tell if that's a good thing or a bad thing," he said, arranging the scattered chairs back into their spots around the table. (Pete couldn't help but promote order even in times of emotional crisis.) "That drug it's—it's like meth for your id. Ness, I wanted to *kill* you. I felt like I could have *done* it. And it was . . . terrible. But at the same time . . . *amazing*. Do you know what I mean? You feel that free."

It was hard to imagine Pete being addicted to anything besides his books, but for the first time since I'd known him, there was a viable candidate for a new obsession. "Now you know why I liked it so much. In your subconscious, it's like you feel completely entitled to your feelings in a way that you overthink when you're awake."

"But the dream is also *your* subconscious, and so you're entitled to *your* feelings, so where do you draw the line?"

The memory of our dancefloor discourse on love came back to me. "Hasn't that been the question all along?"

The room finally put back together, Pete sat at the table with me. He rubbed his temples and stared at the laminate of the tabletop. "Jesus, I need a drink."

My voice was the tiniest bit bitter when I said, "Have one for me, too."

Suddenly, Pete froze, as if he'd just been hit by a meteor consisting of a *lot* of key plot points—like how I couldn't drink because I was in jail for maybe murdering one of my patients at Malcolm's behest. (When I'd handed Pete my memory box in the dream, I'd thrown in some extra details so he'd be up to speed on most of WellCorp's ne'er-do-welling.) His hands slapped as they fell to the table. "The plea bargain."

"Think I should still take it?"

"No!" he said, horrified. "If this pill fell into the wrong hands, I don't even know what would happen. Could someone hijack your memories or your identity? Would you even know it happened, or would you think it was just all a dream?"

Hadn't I been saying this to Altan all along? Now that I'd travelled with him, his idiotic enthusiasm (or enthusiastic idiocy) when it came to Morpheum made total sense. *Take the pills*, he'd said. *It'll be fun. We'll figure it out the details later. What's the worst that could happen?*

This, Altan. The answer you were looking for was *this*.

I said to Pete, "I don't know the full extent of what Morpheum can do, but Malcolm is definitely exploring torture possibilities. In the dream before my arraignment where he told me about the plea deal, he . . . did some things."

"What kind?"

Those particular details were not included in Pete's briefing as a courtesy to him. "Bad things."

Something passed between us then. I didn't know what it was—not forgiveness or absolution but maybe a kind of truce that fell somewhere between "till death do us part" and "the enemy of my enemy is my friend." So many questions revolved around the past and the drug, but one thing was clear: we needed to stop Malcolm for reasons that went beyond my personal future.

"I'll call Janet and tell her we're not taking the deal," Pete said. He muttered as an afterthought: "She's gonna be pissed."

Poor Pete was always so worried about pleasing the women in his life. "Does Janet even get pissed?" I said. "I can't imagine her getting herself wrinkled."

"Right? I bet she sleeps on an iron." He smiled, imagining it.

"Or in a panini press," I offered, trying to prolong the joke— just like old times. Being married to Pete wasn't *all* arguments: sometimes it was fun.

It had been a lot of fun. He looked at me like he remembered that, too, and before nostalgia overtook us completely, he got to his feet. "Well, I guess I better go. I've got dragons to slay, marriages to dissolve. Full schedule."

"Right," I said, standing as well. "Me, too."

Was this it? This couldn't be *it*: not when the cracked femur of our love was just starting to fuse, not when Pete had laughed at my panini press joke! We hadn't felt this easy and normal in ages. *Think, Ness!* I commanded, following Pete to the door. *Figure something out. Make him stay.*

"So, um, thanks for the dream"—I heard myself say—"sailor."

Face? Meet palm. *Sailor?* What was I trying to do? And why did I sound like Katharine Hepburn all of a sudden? Oh, right: so I could claim I was *totally* kidding when I added in that same saucy black-and-white movie voice, "We should-ah do it again sometime."

Pete could have laughed this off or ignored it as he waved goodbye, and it would have been over: just another one of my stupid antics—that time I asked my husband to continue abusing his position as a lawyer to smuggle drugs to me in jail and keep me company while I slept. Classic Ness. I thought he'd shake his head fondly and chuck me under my chin before he left. (Here's looking at you, kid.) But improbably he froze with his hand on the door handle. "Seriously?"

I was awkwardly close when I said, "Yes?"—my gaze trained to the stretch of throat above Pete's collar so I wouldn't have to look him in the eyes. He'd missed a spot shaving.

I'd only noticed because of my insatiable eyes. Maybe Pete and I had been doomed all along: the man's greatest wish was to gaze at the same face for the rest of his life, and while this was a lovely, tender thing, I didn't know it wasn't *my* thing until I took a pill and fell in love with a man who also preferred landscapes to portraits.

Assuming my love for Altan was real and not a drug-induced side effect we hadn't thought to document. Assuming Morpheum *wasn't* just a nocturnal version of ecstasy that makes you rub up against any decent human that you found yourself in a dream with. Assuming I had made the right decision. Without a second experiment to confirm these hypotheses, I would never be sure that Pete and I were supposed to end up this way.

"What about Altan?" Pete said.

"We're on a break," I replied, which was technically true. With my visiting privileges suspended for a month and no way to resolve our argument, Altan was out of the picture for the next 30 days. So what was I supposed to do—mope around with high Honey? Assume he and I still worked after I found out our whole relationship had been built on a lie? *Not* take the opportunity to get to know my husband the same way I knew my lover for no other reason than making an informed and scientific decision before proceeding with my divorce? Was love not like water in that you *needed it to not die?*

"What happened?" Pete said.

I was still concentrating on his neck. "I took your advice and asked him why he and June really broke up."

"Ouch." In my periphery, Pete winced in sympathy, which was generous. "I'm sorry. Are you OK?"

"I don't know." When I finally reached his eyes with mine, I saw concern there. But was it enough? "I don't know anything about Altan right now except that he isn't here," I said. "But you are. I'm lonely and I'm scared and I want someone to stay with me. And while I recognize that I've been awful and that you are completely within your rights to tell me to go fuck myself, I'm really hoping that you don't."

"Why? Because you want me to do it for you?" came his immediate reply. He'd delivered this with a wink—a real one!

My eyebrows flew up past my hairline, burst through the ceiling of the jail, and then broke the sound barrier on their way to orbit Jupiter. "*What?*"

Pete swallowed the grin that threatened his cool. "You heard me."

And with that, Pete pulled three more Opal packets out of his suit jacket and dropped them in the chest pocket of my orange top next to my cardboard tube. It was the smoothest thing he'd ever done—in the waking world, at least. My knees went on strike.

"You brought more? I thought you said you didn't know the dream was real."

"I didn't, but I made more packets in case I was wrong. It's been known to happen every now and then. I like to be prepared."

Pete admitting he was wrong was on par with crying in terms of rare events. The man had gone from weeping to seduction to quoting the Boy Scouts. My libido had whiplash. It was the most (enjoyably) exciting thing that had happened to me awake since Paris.

"So, I'll see you tonight?" he said as he opened the door.

"Um, yeah," I said, my heart going crazy. "It's a date."

FRIDAY, MAY 31

Operation Malcolm Is a Douche, Day 28

I met up with Charlie for coffee today, just to see how she's doing. She looks better than yesterday but seems to have lost a bit of her perkiness. Her hair wasn't as meticulous as it usually is, and she had bags under her eyes. I mention it only because it's out of character for her—not inherently *bad*. She told me she didn't sleep at all. I told her I didn't blame her.

Anyway, she was a bit keener to plot against Malcolm for the good of her journalism career (and maybe personal revenge), so we decided to try and come up with a plan to . . . prevent Malcolm and some Russian dude from torturing women in their dreams? In order to . . .

??????

Like, seriously: what the hell?

It's all so weird I can't even begin to figure out how it all adds up, but if Malcolm can roofie people without their knowing and then bring a third party into the dream, couldn't we reverse-roofie Malcolm, jailbreak *his* mind together, and figure out what he's up to?

We sketch a plan:

1) Continue trailing Malcolm and his #ginception movements. Take notes. Take pictures. Who's he meeting? Who is he drugging?

2) Get Morpheum. Take Morpheum.

3) Charlie figures out a way to smell Malcolm again. When she does, I smell *her* and *also* take Morpheum, and then we'll all be connected in the dream. (Right?)

4) Charlie and I go in—undercover—and figure out what the hell is going on between WellCorp and the Russians.

5) Gather evidence? Tell Ness's lawyer, Janet?

6) ?????

7) Ness gets out of jail

8) Profit!

OK. This plan is ridiculous, but we have nothing else going on so it's worth a shot. The trickiest part will be getting the Morpheum to get into Malcolm's head in the first place. Even *if* Austin would make us a ginception, I'm not super excited about the idea of being locked in a dream with no escape. Which means, we need Original Morpheum in order to do this safely, and the last time I checked, the only known available supply was in a shoe in the bottom of Ness's closet.

So now I'm going to call Pete and see if he'll give me some of the drug that encouraged his wife to leave him for me.

The good news is that this won't be awkward at all!

THE
TROJAN HORSE

All afternoon, I lay in my bunk thinking about Pete as Mr. Darcy in those tall black boots. For the first time since arriving in jail, I was horny—which felt like a good thing, a much-needed human thing. Until now, I'd been like Altan in our Bali dream, all in my head. I'd been like I was during my first few days in jail when I barely ate. But now, I was back in my body, and my body was starving for a man I'd had access to for the past decade, but of whom I'd never fantasized like *this*.

There was something thrilling, almost illicit, at how forbidden Pete had become, both because we were (allegedly) getting divorced and because I saw in his mind how much anger and vanity he'd hidden in that skull. Why hadn't he shown me this in our marriage? What else was he hiding? I wanted all of him, like a mainline to his heart. I wanted that moment when you look at someone's psyche for the first time and really *see* them, like witnessing a whole new spectrum of light, all those colors we cannot fathom are suddenly turned on, and the rush of it, that breathless *whoosh*: it's delicious. I wanted to feel that again, but more than that, I wanted to feel it from Pete.

"Honey, you awake?" I whispered five minutes after they turned out the lights.

"Duh, bitch. What you want?"

"Nothing," I whispered back. "Just checking."

Smooth.

Logistics were always the enemy. How the hell was I going to indulge a clandestine pill habit with a cellmate? I held an Opal in my hand in the dark, wondering if she'd hear me tear it. Then, because I couldn't stand the thought of getting caught, I ate the whole packet, paper and all.

The things I do for drugs.

The dream was pitch black and smelled like Poseidon's boxers: crab stench and mildewed wood and a saltiness that was either ocean or body odor—or both. "Pete?" I whispered, half-panicked. My fingers collided with a body as I groped the darkness.

A gruff voice (not Pete's) hissed, "Watch it!"

"Pete!" I said louder as twenty people panic-shushed me all at once. This was . . . not what I had in mind. Just as I was about to Nightcrawl out of there in search of someplace less freaky, someone snaked a pair of arms around my waist from behind. Pete had employed that move thousands of times when I washed dishes at the sink; I'd know it anywhere. With his mouth to my ear, he said so softly that I wasn't sure he was actually talking: "Be quiet."

"Where are we?" I mouthed back.

"Inside the Trojan Horse."

Well, that explains the stink. I dialed the repurposed-boat funk down a notch, hoping Pete wouldn't notice. His mouth was on my ear again, the fog of his breath sending chills down my spine and into more intimate places. "We've already gotten dragged into the city. Now we're waiting for everyone to fall asleep before we attack."

"Oh, OK. Cool."

As far as I could tell in the dark, I was pressed face first against one of the wooden walls of the horse, cramped somewhere between Ajax and Odysseus, Pete on my back like a cape. At first, he held me around my waist to keep me from getting jostled too much, but eventually he commandeered enough elbow room to move his hands up to my shoulders.

Instantly, I was transported to any Saturday morning in our neighborhood, the two of us waiting for our turn to order donuts and coffee. In the real world, Pete took any opportunity to juice the stress from my shoulders as a way to pass time in lines. It was just this thing he did, back when I was entitled to such displays of affection, before we'd get our order to go, rush back to our apartment, and let the coffees get cold on the counter while we had sex with the curtains open for the sheer novelty of making love by daylight. Whatever weak sun there was would stream through the window and glint off the dust we never bothered to clean. The air shimmered like magic.

I felt myself lean back into the memory as Pete's fingertips grazed my collarbone; it was odd that I could feel them. "What am I wearing?" I asked the dark.

He took his right hand from my shoulder and splayed it on my belly, ran his palm up the front of what felt like a leather bodice covered by an armored breastplate, until I felt his fingertips return to my neck. "You seem to be dressed like Wonder Woman. The new one: not the one in Spandex."

"Then what are you wearing?"

"Same thing." Against my cheek, the corner of his mouth quirked up a smidge.

I choked on a laugh and got *shhhh*ed again as I thought how nice it was to joke again. I wasn't sure we'd ever get there.

"Hey, remember when we used to go get donuts at Top Pot on the weekends—"

"No talking," Pete ordered. "You'll get us in trouble."

Well, fine. I was just as happy to be massaged in silence. Pete moved his ministrations from my collarbone to my shoulders before trailing down my arms to massage each of my hands, in turn. There was no hurry or explanation in his movements. After all, we were stuck in the Trojan Horse without our phones: what did people do before Instagram to pass the time?

At first, it was easy to tell myself this wasn't sexual at all: Pete was just . . . helping a friend with muscle pain! But then his hands slipped deeper down the bodice of my armor to massage my sternum—and beyond. "What are you doing?" I whispered.

He helped himself to more of me, like my body was an unattended bowl of grapes. "Whatever I want."

Who *was* he right now? This was dangerous—by design. This wasn't some in-the-moment flip from bloodlust to actual lust that I could later blame on a slip of the mind. Pete's seduction was altogether slower, more psychological, like he wanted me to think about sex with him, and then overthink it, and then think about Altan and choose him anyway. That was the speed of his fingers as he moved them to the insides of my thighs, up and down—never high enough to give me what I wanted but knew I shouldn't. "Tell me what to do," he said darkly.

The answer, I knew, was *stop*. Just because I was lonely in jail and mad at Altan didn't mean I had to jump Pete within the opening minutes of our first cognizant dream together. He could keep me company with his pants on: I knew that. But there was just something about the dark, and the time travel, and the quiet, and the room full of other people, and the freshly verboten feeling of being touched by my husband who wasn't supposed to be touching me anymore: it was different enough so that what Pete was doing felt somehow . . . not like sex. So not like sex that I barely felt guilty when I said, "Higher."

He pressed home, and when I gasped, thirty unseen Greek dudes went *shhhh*. "Like this?" Pete asked.

I nodded along his shoulder so he could feel it, but still he felt the need to confirm. "You want it like this?"

"Yes," I hissed, spinning in his arms so I could face him, kiss him, ignore all the shit both between us and waiting in the wings. After what had felt like years of war, I wanted to feel if only for a moment that we'd never fought, that we'd stayed together, peaceful and prosperous, and that I'd never wandered. "Keep going."

"Keep going?"

Was he deaf or something? "Yes. Yes. Please."

A fist banged against the wood somewhere, and Pete's hands withdrew from my body quick as fish. "What?" I cried, confused. "What was that?"

"That's the signal." It was too dark to see his face, but I was able to use the smirk in his voice to imagine it. "Time to go."

He poured out the trap door with everyone else, presumably to ransack Troy, while I writhed alone in the horse.

Pete: 1. Ness: 0. I hadn't even known we were playing.

The sand-colored city was crackling with chaotic orange flames when I hauled myself out the door. The huge front gates behind the horse had been flung open, and streaming through on leather sandals was the Greek army, bellowing as it smashed into handfuls of groggy Trojans, who'd come out to see what the noise was.

Pete was sprinting at the front of the Greeks, sword drawn and already smeared with blood. It would have been comical to see my mild-mannered lawyer husband running around like an overzealous LARPer if he didn't look *so damn good* doing it. Who needed 300 Spartans? I only needed one Peter Brown in a leather miniskirt.

He clasped my hand as he flew past and led me up a side street, the night air cooling as we moved away from the fire. Turning a corner, we found a Trojan squad barreling toward us, their curved scimitars slicing the night sky. Pete tossed me a sword (where had he gotten the spare?) and told me, "You know what to do."

I did know. We killed *everything*.

For hours, he and I were nothing but murder. We worked as a team, moving from palace to palace, slicing bad guys in half without thought. There was no shortage of assailants: they streamed out of the night in Pete's perfectly measured doses—never so many that we got overwhelmed, but never so few that the fight felt easy. I could feel him pulling the strings at my side, devising new traps and plot twists, weaving the story tighter as we went. Altan and I had never been so controlling: usually, we'd put the dream on like a record and just go with it. But Pete was remixing, adjusting every detail, a control freak in paradise.

It shouldn't have been so delightful to skewer faceless soldiers the way we did, but actually it was kind of relaxing not to have to talk or think. Only reflexes were necessary, and those were automatic. That we weren't on the losing team was nice, too: it felt good to win for once.

On the huge marble terrace of a palazzo high in the hills overlooking the city—that's where we ran into the closest thing to trouble Pete would allow. He and I were back to back, disposing of a ring of Trojans as they came at us one by one. "How you holding up?" he asked, running his sword through some dude's gut.

"Not bad," I said, truthfully, sidestepping a Trojan as he charged me. War was easy when you had cheat codes. "Are we going to do this all night?"

An arrow sliced the air: Pete caught it and then used it to stab a guy in the shoulder. "Did you want to do something else?"

I took a running leap at an oncoming soldier, wrapped my thighs around his neck, then dove backward in a handspring to cast him over the balcony edge. "No," I lied. "This is fine."

Even Pete's guffaw sounded bloodstained: that's how hearty it was. My lack of chill for him had been clear since the war started: I'd spent every free second perving on his body and his mind. That he could direct the dream and act in it at the same time was impressive. The man was such a virtuoso, I couldn't help but wonder what else he'd be good at.

"Maybe we'll take a break soon," he said. "Are you thirsty?"

"For water?" I kicked some Trojan nobody in the face. "No."

Look at us, flirting! Who knew killing imaginary people could bring us closer together? In all seriousness, it felt good to fight *with* Pete instead of against him, and I wondered if he had designed the dream this way to force us back to a state where we had each other's backs like we'd promised all those years ago.

"Behind you!" shouted Pete.

I turned in time to watch the dagger he'd flung slide neatly into an eye socket. It was the guy I'd thrown over the balcony; somehow he'd climbed back up.

Troy was an inferno below us, her streets ringing with the clamor of steel and bronze, thick, acrid smoke belching up in hot, black clouds. Firelight glinted off the sweat of Pete's body. He was filthy and gorgeous and devoted to protecting me—but only (and this was the best, most respectable part) as a failsafe for when I couldn't do it myself. "Thank you," I said.

Ash rained down on him as Pete nodded to acknowledge I was talking about more than the dead guy. "Any time."

He threw his sword onto the marble floor of the balcony, which (I guess) meant we were done with the war for now. "What else do you do in these dreams of yours? I'm open to suggestions."

Oh. I had a suggestion, but even in a dream controlled by my subconscious, it felt a little forward to say, *Make me come hard enough to forget I'm in jail*—at least not right off the bat.

I shrugged and racked my brain, trying to remember all the dreams Altan and I had shared. Most of them had been as adventurous as this, but I remembered the boring parts best. Even on the night we blew up the Death Star, there had been a long stretch of the two of lying on top of the Millennium Falcon, looking up at the stars and discussing our favorite movies in high school. "I usually do normal stuff," I told Pete, omitting the damning use of *we*. "Walk, talk, drink coffee. But, like, in space."

"Normal stuff," Pete repeated with exaggerated casualness, mocking my crappy attempt to play it cool. He sauntered toward me, his leather skirt leaving very little to the imagination. Maybe we were in the Bronze Age, but he was as hard as stone. "Like sex, but in ancient times?"

"Um, sure." I felt myself blushing as my top teeth bit into my bottom lip. "Something like that."

He backed me up onto the edge of the balcony overlooking Troy and hoisted me onto the railing, which was designed at the perfect height to align my hips with his. "Something like this?"

I wrapped my arms around his neck so I wouldn't go over the edge and kissed him with an urgency that bordered on violence. He sank into me like sheathing a sword, but it was the sound of him sighing into my mouth that damn near made me come on the spot. I wanted this, the sex, but also to feel like I was his again, and he was mine, and I was if not forgiven, then at least allowed to come home. I wanted to unburn the house where I'd left the stove on, resuscitate the dog I'd locked in a hot parked car. I wanted Pete and me to live again. Pete wanted it, too. It was obvious.

In real life, marital sex—like our relationship—had always been sweet and respectful. But Pete in here was rougher, his demeanor cooler, his voice deadly calm when he gripped my hair and yanked it backward so I'd look him in the eyes, crazed with lust and something darker. "I want you to be honest with me," he said. "Promise?"

"Yes." *Sure. Fine. Whatever you want.*

"Did Altan fuck you like this?"

Wait. "*What?*"

He repeated like I was simple: "Did Altan? Fuck you? Like this?"

"No," I gasped, truthfully. Dream sex with Altan was whimsical, leisurely. *This*—whatever this was—had just become personal and thrillingly dirty. Pete pulled out and draped me belly down over the balcony so I could watch Troy burn beneath me. "Did he fuck you like *this?*" he asked, taking me from behind. "Tell me how he did it. Was he gentle?"

"Sometimes." It was both mortifying and freeing to be pried open like this, my secrets shucked like oysters, exposing all that shame I'd tried so hard to hide. Why had I even been afraid? Pete was so strong. He was strong enough to know the truth.

"He made you come," Pete surmised, and when he felt my body clench at the memory, he said, "He made you come like *this.*"

Without warning, an orgasm ripped through me like a *zap* from a car battery. I was shocked at how familiar it was, how close it had been to an Altan dream. "Did you say his name?" Pete asked. "I want to hear you say it."

My whole body was twitching in spasms, so it was impossible to isolate the muscles needed to shake my head. He pulled another wave within me like a tide; it crested for a long moment, like a threat. He snapped, "Say it!"

"Altan!" I shrieked as I lost my footing and nearly knocked myself out on the marble railing. This was magic sex; the physics of it were nonsensical. How? I mean, *how*? How had Pete hijacked my body so thoroughly?

I was halfway to the floor when Pete pulled me back up and resettled me precariously on the balcony ledge, wrapping my legs around his waist. The center of my body twisted, drawing everything in toward the core of an exploding star—the biggest bang. There on the verge of flying apart at the seams: that was when I realized none of this was about my pleasure. This was Pete's need to prove his dominance. Anything Altan could do, Pete could do better. Beneath the machismo of this display was a vein so human and tender. Even though Pete was trying his best to distract me, still I saw the truth.

He dragged his teeth up my throat to murmur in my ear, "What I'm about to do to you is unprecedented, and it will never be repeated. You are about to come so thoroughly, so completely that all orgasms from this moment on will pale in comparison. Altan will never make you come like this. He will spend his life trying, and every time he fails, you'll think of me. *This* is the coldest dish I can think of."

All of it was terrifying, and exhilarating, and still I trusted him even as he threatened me with sexual annihilation, and I was so high—higher and higher. And higher, my heart beating, my muscles burning, until I reached the full face of the sun, that glorious heat of zero gravity. There was nothing but light and stillness and Pete's breath in my ear as he said, "Now."

I fell through the clouds like Icarus, wingless and sticky. The descent was brutal, and I crashed, grasping Pete like he could save me, screaming until I heard my own voice, mindless, answer when he growled, "Tell me you're sorry."

"I'm sorry!"

"Tell me you love me."

"I love you!"

"Say my fucking name."

"Pete! Pete! Jesus Christ, Pete!"

MONDAY, JUNE 3

I spent the weekend planning this elaborate display of apology to Ness at visiting hours today. I was going to sacrifice a Coffee Talk Americano to the trash can and then try to win her over with a copy of *National Geographic* pressed against the glass. But at the jail they told me Ness couldn't have any visitors for a month. I can't call her, because she doesn't have a phone—and she can't call me (even if she wasn't pissed as hell) because she's not allowed to dial anyone except her lawyer for some reason. So . . . how are we supposed to make this right?

I asked the guard, "Can I leave a message?" And she just laughed and laughed.

So now Ness has thirty days to think about what a jerk I am. When I see her again, she will have either forgiven me entirely or stockpiled a month's worth of rage. I better go buy more magazines.

Meanwhile, Charlie *still* can't find any connections between Malcolm and Russia, and Pete won't return my calls to give me any Morpheum.

This is going to be a long June.

There's probably a joke in there somewhere about my dick and my ex-wife, but I'm too sad to make it.

FRIDAY, JUNE 7

Operation Malcolm Is a MEGA Douche, Day 29

Was delivering La Croix around Pioneer Square today and guess who literally almost killed me when he cut into the bike lane in order to park his BMW illegally in a loading zone?

Malcolm Jacobs, that's who!

Did he recognize me in my helmet and sunglasses? No.

So, did I lose my shit and call him a grade-A wanker afflicted with a micropenis? YOU BET I DID!

He flipped me off as he was walking into the Pioneer Building—the one off the square where you can find the Underground Tours of Seattle. It's pretty touristy (duh), so it's odd that he was hanging out there. After I made my delivery, I checked the directory in the lobby of the Pioneer Building. Not much of interest—except a sign in Cyrillic. Google Translate tells me it's the Ukrainian Consulate of Seattle.

So that's why Malcolm doesn't have Russian connections.

I texted Charlie this news. We'd been looking at the wrong country all along! She was able to pull up some footage of events taken at the Ukrainian consulate over the winter, and guess who we found shaking hands with the Ukrainian president's attaché? An extremely unremarkable-looking millionaire named Ivan Boyko who nonetheless appears very familiar.

What I'm about to write is so ludicrous that I'm afraid to commit it to paper for fear of looking like an idiot later, even if it's only to myself. But:

Is Malcolm shopping Morpheum to the Ukrainian government?

Like, I know Malcolm is a complete asshole, but is he capable of something close to actual, literal treason?

Wait a second. Of course, he is.

Operation Malcolm Is a Douche, Day 40

I've been trying to get ahold of Pete for like two weeks to score some Morpheum for Charlie's and my mind heist. He won't get back to me, which is super mature. I emailed. I texted. I left him seven voicemails, all, "Hey, can we meet up? I need a favor. It's to help Ness." *You know, that woman we both care about? The greater good in this stupid romantic rivalry you insist on maintaining?* But all I get is the cold shoulder. I'm half tempted to show up on his front stoop again, but I don't think my face can handle a third shiner.

So there's nothing to do but deliver snacks and check on Charlie and wait for pills. Operation Malcolm Is a Douche doesn't require any more stakeouts at the moment, but still I make excuses to meet Charlie for drinks at bars we can afford so I can maintain some kind of social life and hear about all her grand schemes.

Now that I've told her about what Morpheum does, she can't wait to get her hands on more—says this is a "career-making story" and she will "definitely win a Pulitzer" for her firsthand reporting *inside the mind* of a traitor. That's what she's going to call her article, by the way. She thinks she should pitch it to *The New York Times* instead of local. She is so full of energy and optimism that sometimes I just concentrate on the faces she makes, the sparkle in her eyes. Do all twenty-somethings have this much hope? Did I ever used to? Or was I always bracing for this level of calamity?

I honestly can't remember.

FRIDAY, JUNE 14

Operation Malcolm Is a Douche, Day 42

Charlie texted to tell me she hasn't had a good night's sleep since the Malcolm dream: says she's too freaked out to be in her apartment alone. I asked, "Don't you have a boyfriend to keep you company?" But apparently, future White House correspondent Charlie Goodman doesn't have time for relationships.

I knew where this was going. "Want me to sleep on your sofa tonight?"

She didn't even bother with the whole "Are you sure? Is that OK?" dance. She just said, "Be here at nine," then texted me her address.

Charlie's apartment is way nicer than mine—one of those newly renovated joints in Belltown that's small but made exclusively out of right angles, so it feels bigger than it is. Charlie had stuff on every surface: candles and knickknacks, pictures of San Diego she'd taken to remind her of home. Her photos weren't nearly as good as Ness's but they were taken in the hope that they might be: the angles were meant to be interesting, the light was trying to be poetic. She doesn't have Ness's eye, but still Charlie framed her photos, and it's cute how young she is, how much she believes in herself.

On the sofa was a throw blanket and an extra pillow—two things I do not have at my apartment (a sofa makes three). Charlie even had an extra toothbrush—a whole bathroom drawer full of them, with accompanying single-serve toothpaste tubes, like this was a hotel.

I'm ashamed to say I fixed my hair in the bathroom. I don't know why; maybe it was all the estrogen.

When I came out, she was waiting for me in the hall in leggings and an oversized T-shirt from someone's bachelorette party. Her hair was done up in an endearingly sloppy ponytail, and she'd just washed her face.

Help yourself to anything in the fridge. The light switch is over here. Thanks so much for doing this. It'll be good to have someone around besides the cat, she said, and when there were no more instructions to impart, she stood on her tiptoes and kissed me on the cheek. "Goodnight."

A casually meaningless kiss on the cheek is about as on-brand for Charlie as her pictures. I'm sure she meant nothing by it, but when she went into her bedroom and closed the door, I stood in the hall like a creep for longer than I should have.

And then I went to sleep on the couch, like a good boy.

SUNDAY, JUNE 23

Operation I Miss Ness, Day 52

I slept on Charlie's sofa again and dreamed I got a phone call from Ness. "Hey, baby," she said (even though she never calls me that IRL). "What have you been up to?"

In the dream, I was so excited to talk to her, but we ran out of things to say after five minutes once we'd both established that we were bored and miserable and wanting to move to Bali already.

So, we sat there in silence, and it felt so high school—like when you'd call a girl and talk for hours, and even when you'd exhausted all topics of conversation, you still didn't want to get off the phone. And she'd be like, "You hang up," and you were so weird and smitten that you'd be like, "No, *you* hang up," "No, you"—and this would go on for a whole ten minutes.

It was like that, but depressing. "I hate this," Ness said in the dream, and then I said, "No, *I* hate this." And we went back and forth, trying to convince the other of our individual misery.

She told me, "Altan, I don't know what to do." And all I wanted to do was say, *No, Ness, I don't know what to do*, but instead I told her, "Just hang on. We're almost there."

Even though we're nowhere close.

What a shitty dream. Even so, it was really nice to see her.

THE TEA PARTY

I was ready to go at 9 a.m. every morning: teeth brushed, face washed, bra on. That was the extent of my beauty routine in jail, but I made sure it was all done by the time I heard Officer Milford release the lock on my door. "Guess who's here," she'd started deadpanning.

Pete delivered Morpheum every morning before he went to work, having replaced Janet as my primary legal contact, much to Milford's annoyance. "You need to get that lady lawyer back," she told me once during my escort. "She's better on the eyes."

Debatable, because every time I saw Pete waiting for me in that interview room, my eyes were pretty thrilled. "Hey, gorgeous," he'd say, kissing me on the cheek. He didn't used to call me that, but maybe he was dialing up the compliments a notch to be kind. Considering I didn't have access to moisturizer, I didn't exactly mind.

"How'd you sleep?" I'd ask.

"Not bad," he'd say—the joke being that I knew the answer already since I'd been with him in his head. Having just spent eight hours together, we didn't have much to catch up on. But still, these encounters had to look like actual legal meetings to keep the guards from getting suspicious, so Pete couldn't just hand me my Opal and leave. Since he was busy with his regular case load on top of helping Janet with mine and also being my personal drug mule, Pete used this time to sift through his emails while I read magazines he stashed for me in his bag.

This was the best part of my day, like how Sunday mornings at home used to feel: the two of us putzing around the apartment in our own little worlds, colliding every so often with some tidbit from the news or a reminder that the car needed its registration renewed. I missed that comfort level that came from prolonged contact. Pete and I could trade in the trivial. "They closed the Coffee Talk by your office for renovations," he told me one morning out of nowhere without looking up from his laptop.

"Oh, no," I said automatically, not at all that upset.

"Diana told me when I bumped into her on the street. She says hi, by the way."

Diana was my former coworker at WellCorp, who was as brilliant as she was ballsy. While we weren't ever close (she seemed to prefer the company of her plants to that of Altan and me), I respected the hell out of her knowledge of pharmaceutical chemistry and her love of squabbling with Malcolm. "How is she? Still at WellCorp?"

"Unfortunately."

I clucked. "Too bad."

It was all small talk. Married talk. The kind of talk so boring you reserve it for your spouse because he or she is legally obligated to endure it. "You know what sucks the most in here?" I'd say out of nowhere. "Single-ply toilet paper. It's the *worst*."

"I bet," Pete would answer, fussing with a spreadsheet.

Being married was so boring at times. I missed it so much.

When Pete would leave left for his office, he'd slip me an Opal packet as he sniffed me, and he'd say, "Smell you later"—which was now his favorite way to say goodbye. (What a dork.) I'd spend the rest of the day in a flurry of activity: making my bed, doing puzzles in the common room, a few half-hearted sit-ups in our cell—anything to trick Honey into thinking I was a bright and functioning person, so clean I squeaked when I farted. Nothing to see here! No signs of dysfunction or substance use for *miles*.

Then at night, Pete and I would share dreams so intense and perverted I wasn't even sure they were legal in some states.

It began with the Trojan War and Pete's determination to ruin all subsequent orgasms of my life to spite me for cheating on him. (Spoiler alert: my orgasms were still fine.) From there, it escalated into increasingly inspired book-themed acts of sexual revenge that honestly did not feel like punishments at all, and yet we both pretended they were because this was the game. Even in dreams, Pete had a hard time saying *I'm still mad that you broke my heart*. So he said it in other dark and nasty ways—controlling, sometimes insulting ways that I really, *really* liked.

At the beginning of my Morpheum sobriety (you know, like, two months ago), I purposely tried not to think about Morpheum sex, because *damn* the sex with Altan was good. I'm talking physically, spiritually, psychologically, emotionally, astral-ly (is that a thing?), completely: I came on all levels. When Altan was inside my body while I was inside his mind while he was also inside *my* mind was like opening a series of nesting dolls only to find the biggest one at the center. It's an infinite loop, having sex in a dream, a wormhole within a wormhole. You became so tangled with someone it altered your DNA.

That was Morpheum sex with Altan.

Morpheum sex with Pete was . . .

Better.

Have you ever had a dream where the role someone you know is played by someone you don't? That was Morpheum sex with Pete, familiar and foreign at the same time—less nostalgia, more déjà vu, the sensation of having experienced this before even though I hadn't. It was Pete, but it also wasn't Pete, and I couldn't tell who was the actor and who was the role. Was Subconscious Pete his real self and Waking Pete just the way he watered it down? Or was he projecting in his own mind the image of what he thought I wanted? Was his anger toward me really this profound or did he like the game as much as I did?

I didn't know. The only certainty was that I'd never been so physically and mentally fucked by anything in my life, and that Pete was capable of it shocked me every time. Apparently, my husband was a funny, sweet, mild-mannered lawyer in the streets—and a sadistic sex wizard in the sheets. Which. Was. *Wild.* Because I'd watched this man floss every night for over a decade, and it turned out that beneath his obsession with dental hygiene beat the heart of an animal: unyielding, maniacally devoted to my pleasure and the power it gave him to give it to me.

And for the first few nights, I didn't mind *one bit.*

Take the time Pete took me to one of Jay Gatsby's lawn parties— which he did just to score points in an argument we'd been having since the night we met. "You know I hate this book," I grumbled as we made our way across the lawn to a spectacular tent. As usual, I was dressed impeccably for the occasion, courtesy of Pete's mental atelier: a beaded shift dress that sizzled every time I moved.

"My brain, my rules," he shrugged in his tuxedo, his hair completely compliant for the first time in his life, slicked back smoothly along his head so that he looked period-appropriate in his spats. "Besides, I guarantee you're going to like Gatsby after this."

"Doubtful," I groused.

Bypassing the party completely, we headed inside the sprawling mansion with staircases for days and stumbled into the master bedroom, complete with the gilded hairbrushes on a marble-topped dressing table. The walls were upholstered in red velvet. There was a ghastly amount of fringe.

"Do you think this is what Gatsby meant when he said he was an Oxford man?" I joked, hauling open the doors to the walk-in closet. "I mean, who the hell needs *this* many—"

Shirts. The floor-to-ceiling shelves were full of shirts: folded, not on hangers, not in plastic. Just how Pete liked them. The smell of starch was overwhelming. It made my eyes water for totally non-emotional reasons.

I closed the door and composed myself for Pete's sake. (It wasn't my party: I shouldn't be crying.) "So what comes next, Old Sport," I said, hoisting myself on the high canopy bed. "Are you going to make me have sex with you as Jay Gatsby?"

"Almost," Pete said as *another Pete* (Twin Petes!) in a pink suit appeared in the doorway. "I want you to have sex with *him* as Jay Gatsby."

In my wildest Morpheum dreams, it had never occurred to me to make a *golem of myself*, much less use it for this. "Why can't I just have sex with you?"

"Because then I can't watch," said original Pete sensibly as he pulled a chair to the foot of the bed and sat down with his cocktail. "Don't worry," he said lightly, as Gatsby Pete came toward me, removing his tie. "Now lie back and do as you're told."

I did. Three times. (And yes, Pete was right: after getting to rough Gatsby up in bed, I like the book a little more now.) It was the most indulgent, ridiculous sex in my life—until the time Pete and I went camping in a dream and he asked me as we snuggled by the fire, "Have you ever read *Bear* by Marian Engel?"

I hadn't, but Pete gave me Cliff's Notes in real time.

The next morning, he came to visit me in jail with his laptop and his shy smile, like he was part embarrassed and part proud of what we were doing at night but not brave enough to mention it. "Are you drinking tea?" I asked, noticing his cup.

"Remember that storefront three blocks from our building? They opened a Steepologie," he replied with a shrug. "Thought I'd give a try."

"Ah," I said. *Remember when you turned into a grizzly and went down on me until I lost my voice from screaming?* "That's nice."

"Morning, sunshine," Honey chirped when I woke up after a particularly inspired take on *Moby-Dick*. I peeked over the edge of my bed to find her looking up at me sweetly, her head resting in the crook of her elbow.

"Um, hey," I said, unnerved by her cheerfulness. Honey wasn't exactly a morning person. Or a night person. In fact, she wasn't really an anytime person unless she got her pills. "What's up?"

"There was a fight next door last night. Jacinda got the shit beaten out of her."

Rumor was that Jacinda had been using her celly's toothbrush to clean the toilet because they'd had a fight about Scrabble rules in the common room. I guess she got caught. "She OK?"

"Dunno. They came to take her to the infirmary around 3 a.m." Honey didn't seem to be in a particular hurry to impart these details, like the woman's life wasn't the point of her story. "All hell broke loose: lights came on, guards were running around shouting. It was funny, though: you didn't wake up, even when I shook you in case they needed us to do a count."

I should have known this was coming: Honey was a bloodhound when it came to mind-altering substances, and yesterday was Milford's day off, so her nose had been in high gear. "That's so weird!" I said with exaggerated brightness.

"Sure is. Got me wondering though."

She looked at me so I'd be forced to ask, "About what?"

"How you get your drugs in here."

"*Drugs?*" I snorted and climbed down my ladder. If I moved fast enough, the panic on my face would blur and maybe she wouldn't see. "You're crazy. I don't do *drugs*."

"Yeah, I thought that, too, but then I remembered your first night here—the one where you passed out in my bunk. When I dumped you on the floor you didn't even flinch. No one sleeps that long or that well sober. So, what do you take—Vikes? Fenty?"

"I don't take anything!" My hands were shaking as I applied toothpaste to my toothbrush, hoping Honey hadn't been taking cellmate advice from Jacinda. "I'm just a heavy sleeper."

She glared at me so I'd know she thought I was full of shit. "Sharing is caring, OK?" The edge in her voice glinted off the fluorescent lights. "That's all I'm saying."

Funny, because she'd never offered me any of *her* drugs.

That afternoon, when I caught her rummaging around my bunk "looking for a hair tie," I decided it would be too risky to take Morpheum that night. Which, apparently, scared the crap out of Pete because he practically snapped my spine the next morning when I arrived for our meeting. "Where were you last night? I thought something bad happened."

He was in a full-blown panic, nothing like the collected persona of his dreams. I was sorry to have made him worry, but also relieved to see that he still did sometimes. Subconscious Pete could be eerily calm. "Everything's OK," I explained. *Classic* jailhouse blunder: celly thought I was high because I didn't wake up when Jacinda got a beatdown, and then she accused me of bogarting drugs, and now it's "a thing" that will *totally* get resolved the second Honey gets more pills when she goes down Officer Milford.

"Oh," said Pete lightly, trying to absorb this, but I could tell he was concerned. "Maybe we should stop."

"No!" I said, because I *loved* our dreams for the surprises and the sex, but more than that I loved them for that giddy, grinning feeling I had all day when I was awake. Jail was ten times more enjoyable when you had a deep pool of sex fantasies to replay in your mind. Lying in bed for most of the day, I'd wonder what Pete was planning next, what we were doing, what it meant.

The dreams gave me hope and purpose and things to chew on. The pills were a time machine, because now I found myself fascinated by Pete the way I was back in the era of our library date, before I knew everything about him. I'd become obsessed with all the things I didn't yet know about that can of bookworms he called a brain. I had to pry it open, and *soon*, because admittedly, my whole "recreate the Morpheum experiment to know Pete better and make the right decision about our divorce" scheme hadn't gone *quite* as planned. He and I didn't talk much in dreams. There was too much other stuff to do.

After all, a Pete dream was a work of art that demanded your full attention. The worlds he built were impossibly rich: the costumes were complex, the fabrics sumptuous, the music clear and lively, and the perfumes? A Pete dream contained all the world's best fragrances: tobacco, fresh bread, lavender, coffee, old paper. It had been so long since I'd smelled anything besides bleach and steam and the fug of people living in close quarters. I got lost in the details, could spend hours just sniffing things in silence. A Pete dream didn't leave time for chatting, not when there was so much beauty to appreciate. And sex to have.

Together, we reenacted all the great romances of literature. Pete was King Arthur, Odysseus, Orpheus, Marc Antony *and* Julius Caesar once in the same night. The scale was so grand, the scenes so epic that it took me almost two weeks before I finally realized that the only man I hadn't dreamed yet about was Pete, himself. Surely, an oversight. Didn't my husband know that I was fascinated by him just the way he was?

"Let's do something," I said one afternoon at the Mad Hatter's tea party. My outfit was that of a college-era Halloween-party Alice: crinoline, pinafore, no panties. The dormouse kept knocking plates off the table. Pete, who was channeling the Tom Petty version of the Mad Hatter with the sunglasses and smirks, kept tasking me with cleaning up.

"I am doing something," he said silkily as the dormouse pushed a spoon onto the lawn.

I rolled my eyes and crouched down to fetch it so the Mad Hatter wouldn't get the satisfaction of seeing my ass. "Want to go for a walk?"

He frowned, confused. "Like in *The Lord of the Rings*?"

"No, like . . . a regular walk." Not everything had to be a sexual epic. "We could go to Cap Hill, get donuts at Top Pot like we used to. You know, hang out. Make fun of joggers. Usual stuff."

"Sounds boring," Pete scoffed, pouring another cup of tea.

"To you maybe, but I haven't had a decent cup of coffee in *months*."

When I thought of my favorite Altan dreams, I remembered Marrakesh, and the night he had shown me all the footage of his travels, and the time he gave me the keys to his memory so I could thumb through high school beach bonfires and his childhood dog and scenes of him folding dumplings with his grandmother. It was in these dreams when I felt closest to him, and I wanted Pete the same way, open and vulnerable—and *relaxed.* In Pete dreams, his mind was always humming, adjusting the scenery, calculating the next step. What did he look like when no one was watching?

My skirt primly pulled over my lap, I sat cross-legged on the lawn next to Pete's chair. "Take me to your childhood," I demanded, catching a pop-fly scone courtesy of the dormouse. "I want to see your favorite Christmas."

He chuckled to himself, since he'd historically been the one who told me what to do in dreams. "I don't have one."

"OK . . . Oh! Show me Janet when you knew her in college. Did she always dress so well?"

He shook his head, eyes unreadable behind his sunglasses.

Was I going to have to have sex with him for this information? Settling myself on his placemat, I planted a Mary Jane on each of his armrests. "What do I have to do to see your senior prom?"

"My past is not on the menu," he said smoothly.

I pouted. "Why not?"

"Because." He stuck a finger into the pot of clotted cream and held it out to me so I could lick it off. "I don't want you poking around in my memories."

I got that Subconscious Pete was into power moves, but this seemed excessive. After all, I'd shown him my secrets. It was only fair that I got to see his. "Come *on.*" I knocked his hat off and tugged a little on his hair, like I could open his skull like the lid of a pot. "One little peek?"

He roared in a panic and flung his arms around his head like he was trying to protect himself in an earthquake, "Dammit, Ness, I said *no!*"

His sunglasses fell off in the struggle, and I saw the raw, uncut fear in his eyes. For that one unguarded moment, the wall around his mind slipped, and I read him as easily as I could Altan—not enough to know what he was afraid of, but to know that he was, in fact, afraid—more afraid of my seeing one particular memory than he was of anything else on Earth.

That was all I got before he powered his force field back on. "Hey!" he said, scrambling for his glasses, groping for some tea cakes, trying to restore the good-time feel of a madcap party before I ruined it with my desire to see him more deeply. "Know what's more fun than my memories?"

He ducked his head beneath my pinafore, and when I felt his mouth on me, my stupid, traitorous body obeyed and tipped back into the cups and saucers, where I lay twitching in the tea as it flooded the table, warm and wet. His was a good effort, but not good enough to totally distract me from what I'd seen in his brain:

Pete was hiding something. Something *big*.

WEDNESDAY, JUNE 26

Operation Malcolm Is a Douche, Day 42

I know we don't *need* to go to the Fairhope anymore, but I dragged Charlie there anyway to see if we could figure out how the bartender dopes the drinks. If we could just figure out the secret ingredient, maybe we could steal it instead of waiting on Pete to cough up some pills from Ness's stash?

Malcolm was at the bar without Ivan Boyko. He ordered ginceptions for himself and a woman reading a book in the lobby who was in town for her friend's wedding. (The bartender used the same ice, the same gin, the same shaker as he uses for all other drinks.) It was hard watching her drink the cocktail, knowing what he was probably going to do to her tonight. Charlie and I flirted with the idea of trying to knock it out of her hand, but then Malcolm would recognize me and our stupid sting operation would be over.

Maybe the woman won't realize what's going on. Maybe tomorrow morning, she'll just think she's had a nightmare and will move on with her life. I hope so. I don't want anyone else to go the way of Charlie Goodman: Future White House correspondent, current insomniac.

Charlie asked me to stay over on her couch again, so here I am, scribbling in my little diary while she watches Netflix on her laptop in her room. Even though there's a closed door between us, I admit it's nice to be in an apartment with someone else.

THE ROSE

Pete's mind on the night of our wedding anniversary was a summer in a century fond of corsets. The one he'd dressed me in was the ivory hue of old piano keys and featured a lace-trimmed scoop neck that really decked out my décolletage. A set of mutton chop sleeves laced to the bodice, which was then lashed to a full, floor-length skirt embroidered with gold threads. The rustle it made when I moved suggested there were at least three—no, wait: *four*—sets of petticoats beneath.

This is going to take forever to pry off, I thought, which reminded me of an (other) argument Pete and I had been having for years. Ever since our library date, he'd been trying to persuade me that poems were born from humanity's earnest desire to celebrate love—but I was convinced they'd been penned only to fill dead air in the time it took to peel a lady out of her clothes. (How do I love thee? Let me count your stays.)

"You're so unromantic," he'd accused back then.

Well, look at us ten years later: I was so romantic that I loved *two* men, and Pete didn't even trust me with his darkest secret. So, who was the cynic now?

In the nights since the Mad Hatter dream, I'd come no closer to cracking the Pandora's Box Pete called his past. The exercise was reminiscent of earlier in the year when Pete was all, "Why don't you want to talk about having babies?" And I was like, "OMG, shut up," only this time, Pete was the one doing the dodging. Because we had a history of this game (and because I knew what calamity to expect if the secret keeper refused to cough up the truth), I felt entitled to keep prying. After all, he'd eaten all my oysters. I felt like I deserved some of his.

But I wasn't just curious: I was worried about him. Granted, Morpheum had messed up my life pretty bad, but aside from the jail time, that drug had also helped me address a lot of skeletons in closets I otherwise wouldn't have gotten around to cleaning. If Pete had demons, I was more than happy to exorcise with him. The power of love compelled me.

"Did you kill someone?" I'd asked a few nights ago. Pete was building a little house on the prairie while I sat in the shade of the only tree for miles as I watched him chop wood shirtless. By that I mean he was shirtless. I wasn't. But with the sun gleaming off of him like that it was only a matter of time before we both were—which had probably been Pete's plan the whole time. The sex we'd been having was maybe supposed to be more of a distraction than actual revenge. Now that I suspected this, I couldn't unsee it.

"I didn't kill anyone," Pete grumbled, raising his axe ominously. "Stop asking. You don't want to know."

I very much wanted to know. "Did you cheat on me?"

The axe came down and lodged in the tree stump he was using as a splitting block. "No."

"The last man who kept secrets from me cheated on his wife." I never mentioned Altan's actual name in a Pete dream—you know, unless Pete wanted me to.

"I haven't cheated on you." He picked the axe back up. "Yet."

"Can you cheat on me if we aren't married anymore?"

"Believe me, we are very much legally still married."

Tell me about it. Only married people bickered this much. "If we're still married, that means whatever you tell me won't hold up in court. So come on: who did you kill?"

"And why don't you trust me?" I shouted from the front row of Plaza de Toros de Pamplona last night. Pete was playing matador. (Was this *The Sun Also Rises*? Probably. That he was dabbling in Hemingway probably hinted at a deep-seated need for *even more machismo*.)

"I do trust you," he called, sidestepping a bull with a swirl of red satin.

"So tell me the thing."

"I can't." He drew a long, thin sword as the bull rounded on him. (Pete's dreams had also turned more weapons-focused than usual. Obviously a defense mechanism.) "It's not like that."

"So what's it like?"

I'd been peppering him with questions for the entirety of the dream, thinking I could at least annoy him into letting something slip. But Pete refused to give up even an ounce of his past in the fear that if he let one thing go, I'd somehow pull the rest out of him. Secretly, I dialed the bull up to eleven. From the far end of the stadium, it hoofed at the dirt. "Who was your first crush?" I shouted.

"Nope!" sang Pete as he draped the cape to his side.

"The best concert you ever went to?"

The bull bellowed.

"Ness, cut it out!"

"What about the thing you most regret?" I tried.

Pete snapped his head in my direction, and for the briefest moment, I saw the pale fear in his face right before the bull gored him in the stomach. *Oops.*

Because I knew he wasn't actually going to die, I took my time in crawling down onto the sand so I could check on him. "Why are you so obsessed with my memories?" Pete grunted when I arrived at his side. Blood bloomed along the front of his white shirt as he clutched his hands over the wound.

"Because they made you who you are." *And you told me I wasn't allowed to look at them.* "And I want to get to know you better."

"You *are*," he insisted.

But I wasn't. At no time, awake or asleep, were Pete and I spending time together without an agenda or an entourage. The talk we made in the mornings was too small to matter, and then at night, the plots were predetermined by Pete, who refused to go off script. In the weeks we'd spent high, we'd yet to have a full conversation about anything meaningful going on in our lives—our real lives. Not this. "What am I learning about you now: that you can't take a horn to the pancreas?" I snarked. "What do you think Morpheum is for, anyway?"

"Fucking your coworkers?" he spat.

Fighting, like fucking, was just another distraction. I wouldn't take the bait. "You seem to be confusing oral sex with verbal sex. News flash, genius: you can still be intimate *without your penis.* Don't you roll your eyes at me!"

Oh, wait. The eye-rolling was probably because he was bleeding out. His face was as pale as garlic. "Peter Brown," I scolded, "don't you dare die on me just to get out of this—"

He disappeared from the scene.

"—conversation!"

If the point of Pete's withholding was to drive me insane, then it was working. Maybe the idea of keeping a secret from me was another trick in his emotional BDSM toolkit, or maybe he really didn't trust me after all these years together. The point was that after weeks of dreaming, I still didn't know him well enough to tell the difference. He was even more mysterious than before I'd gone in.

I wandered around the garden Pete had concocted in the dream, enjoying the splash of the fountains and the labyrinthine hedges carved expertly into scrolls like I'd seen at Versailles. It was nighttime, and the color of the flowers had been washed in indigo, but somehow the lack of visuals made the perfume of the roses more pronounced. Pete had picked a conspicuous place to ignore our anniversary.

"Night has come," said an unseen voice. "In the dusk, my words grope their way to find your ear."

Well, maybe we *weren't* ignoring the date after all. "Come on out, Romeo," I said to the night.

"Not Romeo. *Cyrano de Bergerac.*"

Was that that movie where Steve Martin had an even bigger nose than usual, forcing him to real-life catfish his crush using a hotter guy but his own linguistic skills? *Roxane.* That was it. I wasn't looking forward to having sex with Toucan Pete, but he would figure out a way to make it enjoyable. My pleasure had become both perfunctory and predictable: always guaranteed. I sighed. "Well, whoever you are, put your hands where I can see them."

Pete's voice was as soft as the night itself. "It is easier to speak my heart in darkness."

There was a rustle to my left as the silhouette of a man stepped out from behind a hedge. He wore a musketeer's cloak and a plumed cavalier hat with the wide brim dipped over his face. "I love you," he said. "That is all. Just three words, and yet, they don't do justice to the immensity of the feeling. Every ounce of my soul, every breath of my body sings only for you, Vanessa."

Vanessa. Not Roxane. Not Eurydice. Not Helen or Juliet or Penelope, or even Ness, but my actual name, Vanessa. Of the two of us, Pete was clearly the poet, because all I could think to say was *Whaaaaaaaaaaaaaaaaaaaaaat?*

What was this? Had the bull knocked something in Pete's soul loose? He said, "I just wanted you to know, tonight of all nights, that the world beyond these dreams without you is too cold—life, too sad. Since you left, there is no color or music or flavor or fragrance. Every joy I've ever felt is locked away with you."

My hand trembled as I took a juicy red rose from his outstretched glove. OK, this wasn't the secret I was expecting, but still it felt like a *pretty big reveal.* In dreams, we'd pretended to be countless other couples (most of them doomed), and now, here we were: having an honest conversation about our feelings, which meant I could say that I missed him too. I missed the Pete I slept next to for all those years, the chatty one with his trivia tidbits and groan-worthy jokes. Sexy as he was, Subconscious Pete only reminded me of the sweet, everyday version of the man who loved me and made me feel safe.

Cyrano swept the hat off his face with a deep and gallant bow. I barely had time to register that the hair color was wrong before he stood back up. When he showed me his face, I tried not to scream.

It was Altan.

Except it wasn't Altan. It couldn't have been, and besides, the eyes were wrong: they had none of the real Altan's mischief. But still, for a moment shorter than the beat of a hummingbird's wing, I believed it was him, and my heart was cleaved open before being cauterized just as fast, leaving a wound that burned like hell to realize he was still out of reach.

But beneath the searing of that pain was another, like a saltier, underwater lake: Pete had declared his love with another man's mouth. This anniversary "confession" was just another one of his literary schemes to get under my panniers. We were nowhere closer to a truth or trust between us—and maybe that was the answer I was looking for but refused to accept: *Pete wasn't interested in cultivating these things with me.*

I looked at him and said as sweetly as I could, "Pete, honey, do we have a safe word?"

"No," replied "Altan."

"Well, can we make one?" My breath came out shaking. "Because it's official: this is *too* much."

Pete ran his hand through Altan's long hair, and in the moment his face was obscured, it switched back to the one he usually wore. "Sorry," he said glumly, embarrassed that his "gift" hadn't gone over well. "I thought you'd like it."

Ladies and gentleman, the brilliant Peter Brown, whose mind was powerful enough to do anything *except read the room*. "Pete, it's our *wedding anniversary!*"

"I know! But . . ." It was rare to see him speechless in dreams. He was usually letter perfect in his confidence. Maybe he was just as exhausted by this charade as I was. "I— I didn't know what would be appropriate. Because you're in jail. And we're maybe getting divorced—"

I noted his use of maybe before I went ahead and put him out of his linguistic misery: "Well, it's not *dressing up like the man I accidentally left you for.* I need something else. Something real."

"We're in a chemically manufactured dream," he said, taking me into his arms. I let him, even though I was mad: I was also that shaken. "Our options are kind of limited."

Into the velvet of his cloak, I said, "You know what I mean. I need the real you." For all the crazy sex we'd had and wars we'd fought and whales we'd hunted, for the first time in a dream with him, I was afraid. First, I was afraid that if he knew how devastated I was, he'd just use it against me in a different dream as part of his game.

The second and more serious reason was: I was terrified this was all he was capable of. What if there was no basement floor to Pete like there had been to Altan? What if all he had in this skull was imagination without tenderness? Sure, meaningless sex was fun, but . . . there had to be more to him and me. Right?

Pete ran his fingers comfortingly up and down my back. I could hear him thinking, even though I couldn't hear the actual thoughts. When he'd decided what to do, he pulled the ribbon that laced my corset and the whole dress fell off me at once, like a cicada husk. Beneath it was a pair of worn-in leggings and my favorite sweatshirt—the one from a college trip to the photography exhibits of the J. Paul Getty Museum in California. It was the exact outfit I would put on if I was home.

When Pete melted off his own layers of linen, he was wearing jeans and a T-shirt I bought him on our honeymoon in the San Juan Islands. "Is this better?" he asked.

I wanted to cry. I wanted to cry so hard. "It's perfect."

The night sky of Roxane's backyard poured in over our heads, surrounding us in an even deeper, mica-flecked black. The stone path of the garden arched backward and morphed into an asteroid about the size of a single-family home: you could walk on it, but not terribly far without tracing your steps. The terrain was barren and rocky, punctuated by three small volcanoes. Beyond the unimpressive horizon, the vast void of space stretched farther than I could imagine, pinpointed by private galaxies invented by Pete.

"What is this?" I said into the purest quiet there ever was: no ambient noise—no cars whooshing over wet roads, no buzzing of light bulbs or humming of HVACs. Not even the music of the spheres jingled in the distance.

"It's *The Little Prince*." Pete said.

"Another book?" I tried not to sound disappointed.

"Don't worry: there's no sex in this one," he said, like he was reading my mind. "It was my favorite book when I was a kid, but I still read it now. You appreciate it differently as you get older. Or at least I do, anyway."

Pete's voice sounded more like his old self, less formal, more conversational, with an undercurrent of excitement I recognized when he talked about books in real life. Suddenly I could imagine him in our apartment, feverishly fussing over the built-ins in our living room, trying to find his copy so he could show me a favorite part. I'd been looking at him for weeks, but this was the first time I saw him in what felt like forever. "Is *this* your crazy secret?"

He sighed, more in defeat than annoyance. "Can we just not talk about that for, like, five minutes?"

"Fine. OK," I said. After all, he'd taken me to his special book. I didn't want him to shut it so soon.

"So, the story is about a man who crashes his plane in the Sahara," Pete explained as we walked the surface of the small planet. The dust beneath my bare feet felt so fine, like powdered sugar. "And as he's trying to fix it, this little kid walks out of the desert and introduces himself as the Little Prince. He's an alien, and he lives on this asteroid." Pete gestured around to the empty space. "As you can see, it's pretty luxurious."

"I wonder what the HOA fees are," I said, playing along. Pete rewarded me with a half-smile when he held out his hand for the rose he'd given me in the garden.

He stuck it into the ground so that it was growing straight out of the dirt. "No HOA fees, but the property comes with a girlfriend."

I looked down to where he was pointing. "The kid's dating a flower?"

"Told you there was no sex." Pete laughed his real laugh: not whatever sinister chuckle or disaffected snort passed for humor in his dreams. "Even when I was a child, I was like, *How the fuck do you date a rose?*"

It was a fact that Pete was far too wholesome to have ever used the F-word before thirteen, but I liked that he imagined himself a badass, reading his French literature in his childhood room. "I learned later that the rose is a stand-in for the author's wife. Apparently, Mr. and Mrs. Saint-Exupéry fought like hell, so he gave the rose a bit of an attitude in the book."

"That's something only married people would do," I said.

Pete agreed, sitting down on the surface of the asteroid next to the rose, like it was a campfire. "Only married people are that passive-aggressive."

He and I would know.

I sat next to him, crisscross applesauce, enjoying both his good mood and the interactive book report. There was something in him that suddenly reminded me of Altan: maybe it was the honesty, or the wistfulness, or the angle of his jaw as he looked up at the stars. Maybe it was the realness of Pete that I was seeing for the first time, that tense reluctance as you bare your underbelly, that mild hope as it triumphs over a fear that was misplaced.

"Anyway, the Little Prince decides to leave his planet because he's so sick of his bitchy rose. But before he goes, he tries to put this glass dome over the flower to keep her safe. She refuses it to be difficult, like 'No, no. Don't worry about *me*. I've got four thorns to protect me. I'll be fine.'"

"Ugh," I said. "These two were the *most* married."

"Seriously." Pete reached behind him and pulled up a tiny tree that had taken root in the dirt, a subconscious gesture that I found profoundly sweet. He was weeding a planet that wasn't even his. "*Now* it's obvious, but when I was a kid, I didn't get it at all. I thought the prince was a jerk for leaving her alone without her bell jar or whatever, but it was what she wanted, so what could he do?"

When Pete flicked his gaze to mine, I felt a rare bubble of his memory: a video clip of me flung across our apartment door, begging him not to leave—comical considering he thought I was pregnant with another man's child at the time, so the concept of one of us stepping out had more or less already been established. Still, as he gripped the doorknob to the soundtrack of my keening, I felt him tear between giving me the protection he knew I needed and the out he assumed I wanted. Beneath that swam the shadow of that monstrous secret, a memento amore to remind him that his devotion to me *had* to be larger than life. *All of this is my fault*, he thought—but for Pete's sake, *why*?

He shifted his eyes back to the ground, where he tore up another small tree that had grown in the time we'd been sitting there. It was funny how reluctant he was to look at me now that he'd fallen back to his usual Pete persona. "Anyway, the Prince travels all over space trying to be happy, but eventually he starts missing the rose right around the time he figures out he's too heavy to escape Earth's gravity. Convenient timing," he mused. "People are always figuring out they want someone the moment the door to it slams closed."

"So, how does it end? Does the Little Prince go home?"

"Well, he lets a snake bite him so he can ditch his body and be light enough to travel back."

Jesus, where were *The Hardy Boys* when you needed them? "You mean he *dies*?"

Pete snickered as if my outrage on behalf of a fictional character was comically misplaced. "You don't know if he dies for sure. It's supposed to be ambiguous. As a kid, I totally believed the Little Prince got home, but when I read it now, I can't help but think that *of course*, he dies, and the rose is dead too because no one took care of her, and the whole thing is so sad and French."

I was surprised at his pessimism as he hopped up to his feet to pry up an even bigger tree. (Was he growing them on purpose to give him something to do?) "So before he dies, there's this part where the Little Prince is talking to the pilot about leaving his rose, and he kind of blames himself for it. He says, 'I was too young to know how I should love her.'" The tree was putting up a fight: Pete pulled harder. "Maybe we're always too young to know how to love right. Maybe love is a curse in that we're always destined to get it wrong."

Was he always this melancholy? Was that why he put on these dream shows for me in his brain? "You don't believe that," I pronounced.

"I know I don't. Which is why I feel stupid."

"You're not stupid!" How could this guy talk about my husband like that? "Being a divorce lawyer while also being a hopeless romantic is the ultimate intellectual exercise. Not many people can pull that off."

He shook his head, straining against the roots of the tree. "I'm not sure I do."

Didn't Pete know how brilliant he was? How amazing? How wonderfully he loved me? What was *wrong* with him? I got up to help him uproot the tree, and together we were able to yank it out of the ground. "Why *did* you become a divorce lawyer anyway? Wait: I take it back. Don't tell me," I said when I saw panic touch his eyes again. *Don't slam shut.* "Instead, tell me why you brought me here for our anniversary."

He shrugged, slipped his hands in his pockets, kicked dirt into the hole where the tree had been. I knew Pete wasn't keen on showing me his memories, but his mannerisms were so defensively boyish it was like seeing him when he was seven. "You asked for something real, and this was the first thing I thought of. I guess it's how I feel about you. Or something." He heaved a teenager's sigh and turned his eyes upward to the wide infinity of space. "When I was young, I believed in the happy ending. And then I grew old, and I don't. It's like the magic, it's . . . gone."

"Look!" I insisted, sweeping my arm toward all the galaxies he'd invented at the drop of a hat. "We are here: together, in your favorite book, *in your brain*. How is this not magic?"

When he looked at me, his eyes were soft and sad. "Ness, this isn't the magic I want."

Oh.

Oh, Pete.

I knew that I had hurt him. I knew that he was angry, and disappointed, and that he felt betrayed. I knew these things but I never bothered to experience them. I hadn't stopped to feel how much it hurt Pete to keep me company in here, to have me so close to his wounded heart and to a nerve he would rather die than have exposed. The books he recreated, the sex he spun up—yes, they were distractions, but more than that they were ballast. Pete needed me at an arm's length even in his own brain. After all, he had no interest in any of this: experiments or dream trips or inexplicable mind-melding engineered by sleeping pills. The only thing Pete had ever wanted the simple, enduring magic of living happily ever after.

It was the one dream he couldn't have on Morpheum.

"Anyway," he said, trying to salvage the moment, like he always did. He turned toward me as we stood there next to his rose as it stuck out of the planet's pitted surface like a headstone. Carefully, he dipped his head to brush my mouth with his, as if he were afraid to feel the memory of the years we loved each other, all that sharp, bloody shrapnel I'd left in his heart. "Happy anniversary from someone who never figured out how to love you right."

It was tempting to debate him, but why did I always have to have the last word? "Back 'atcha," I said. "This year I'll try harder. Assuming we're still married."

He smiled sadly at the preposterousness of it all. "We are still married," he said. "And that sounds like a plan."

THURSDAY, JUNE 27

Operation Malcolm Is a Douche, Day 43

Speaking of being a shitty sleeper, I was up all night worrying about that lady at the Fairhope, so I ditched Charlie's couch at 5 a.m. and went back to the lobby with a cup of coffee hoping to catch her coming down from her room so I could see if she looked like she had permanent psychic damage. (I hate Malcolm even more for making me spend any more time here than is strictly necessary.)

Good news: I spotted her at the checkout desk. She seems OK. Like, I don't know what "not OK" would look like if you were terrorized in your dreams, but she's not crying uncontrollably, so I guess it's fine?

Charlie texts me: "Where'd you go?"

Me: "Back to the Fairhope to check on that lady."

Her: "Stop by Top Pot on your way back. I feel like a donut."

Presumptuous.

Part of me knows I shouldn't be playing boyfriend with her, but the other part of me really likes donuts. And Charlie. So I text her back: "What kind?"

THE
DINNER DATE

I was ready to go at eight instead of nine the next morning, desperate to see Pete after our dream inside his favorite book. Had I really not checked on him at all while all this was going on? I must have, right? At some point, surely I said, "Hey, how are you?" But I'm not certain I'd ever banged on the door of his own grief and shouted: "No, really. I see you trying to put on a brave face, but this is an official welfare check so give me proof of life."

I'd never said, "So is it actually cool that we're dreaming together, or are you just doing this to be nice?"

Or: "You can let Janet take care of all this if it's hard for you to see me. I completely understand."

In my defense (not that I deserved one), I wasn't sure I knew *how* to check on Pete. After all, in the entirety of our marriage, Pete had never let on that he needed anything more than his books and his armchair—so maybe that's why I was so blindsided by the baby conversation in the first place. When he wanted to talk about wanting a family, it had never occurred to me that he was even capable of wanting things besides coffee or tacos.

But *why*? What was up with the stoicism and the outsized sense of duty he felt toward me? I needed to know if only so I could help him break it; he didn't think straight while under my influence, and he needed to be clear headed. Today I would force this topic out loud in the real world. I would stage an intervention for our morning meeting. As soon as the guard came to get me to take me to Pete.

Any second now.

Honey wandered in from breakfast, looking worse for wear. But I didn't have time to worry about her: I was too busy worrying about Pete. "What time did the clock in the cafeteria say?" I asked.

"Ten-thirty," she moaned, dropping lifelessly into her bunk. She didn't leave for lunch and neither did I, afraid that if I stepped out the guard wouldn't know where to find me. It was best to stay put and wait.

By three, I was really freaking out—not because I wouldn't get my drugs for the night (after all, I had extra packets from when Honey was too up in my business for me to safely take them). But who could even sleep at a time like this? Was Pete OK? Not once in the past month had he missed our morning meeting. Maybe Malcolm had gotten to him. Maybe he'd been hit by a Lyft. Maybe he'd eaten the sushi from that takeout place I refused to eat at because it got a C grade once and now he was dying in our bed.

An hour before lights out, I went to the bank of payphones to call Janet, still the only person I was approved to contact. Maybe I was being paranoid, but then again, I was also embroiled in a conspiracy involving my disgusting boss who was capable of unspeakable cruelty, so maybe I wasn't overreacting after all.

"Ness?" Janet said on the first ring. Even though we hadn't talked since Pete had started bringing me Morpheum, I could picture her veneers flashing. (Kidding: she had her real teeth.) "Is everything OK?"

Wherever she was, it was noisy: people talking, the roar of the pans in the open kitchen—a restaurant. I heard the pop of wine being uncorked. It had been forever since I had wine. "Sorry to bother you. I was wondering if you'd talked to Pete today."

"Pete?" She sounded confused.

"He missed our meeting this morning, which isn't like him. I was worried something happened—"

"No, he's fine," she said. *Pause.* "He's right here. We're having dinner. Would you like to talk to him?"

My palms broke into an immediate sweat. "Um, no, that's OK," I said quickly, trying not to do this math. Pete plus Janet, minus me, multiplied by wine equals . . . a very lovely evening enjoyed by two professional colleagues and nothing more. "I was just worried. I gotta go. It's almost lights out."

"Well, wait a second, let me put him on—"

But the phone had already been slammed into its cradle and I was already running back to my cell, praying Honey would be miraculously gone when I got there because I was *really* in the mood to be alone. Pete had stood me up in favor of his nice-smelling colleague who had the freedom to go to restaurants.

Which was fine. He was entitled to that. After all, I had Altan, and his visiting privileges would be reinstated soon, and we'd make up from the fight we'd started a month ago, and all would be well. My waking, rational brain knew that even though we were married, *Pete and I were not together.* But still, I'd wanted . . . what? Closure? The respect of being officially dumped? The piece of Pete's heart he still hadn't given me in all these years? What would I even do with it?

When I finally pounded up the hallway into my cell, I found Honey on her hands and knees, puking into the stainless-steel toilet. "Oh, shit!" I said. (There's nothing like the smell of vomit to snap you out of an emotional tailspin.) I jumped for her hair, which had escaped her elastic and was close to falling into the toilet. "Honey, what's wrong?"

"Need oxy," she said, then retched into the toilet. "Milford's been. Out sick."

"When was the last time you had any pills?"

"Three. Days."

I was not intimately acquainted with the ins and outs of opioid withdrawal. "Is that a lot to go between pills?"

"For me? It's forever." Honey collapsed onto the floor. I wasn't *quite* sure her aim had been good enough to safely lie down that close to the toilet. Everything was a slippery mess.

"Should I call a guard? Get you to the infirmary?"

"*No*. They can't know. Milford will get fired."

"Yeah, and then where will you get your drugs?" I scolded— probably a little too harshly. After all, not everyone was married to a lawyer who delivered fresh supplies daily.

"Her son. In college," Honey panted. "She needs money. Tuition."

Oh. Well. It was so easy to paint people in two-dimensions. That's probably why kids were prone to doing it.

What else did Honey and Milford talk about in the mop closet? Maybe their relationship more than quid pro ho.

"I just want to sleep," she moaned from the floor. "If I could stop shaking, I could sleep. Then maybe it wouldn't hurt so bad."

Now that I'd tapped into the pain of the people around me, I couldn't ignore how unfair it was that anyone had to hurt at all— especially when we had the science to solve for this kind of thing. Honey was the one who had said it best: *Sharing is caring.*

"Come on," I said, pulling her up under her armpits. She was so light I barely had trouble. "I know what will help."

I tucked her into bed and went to the sink. "Fuck water," she protested when I poured her a cup, hoping her voice was loud enough to mask the tearing of the Opal packet from my pocket.

"Water always helps," I reasoned with my back to her. As I found myself drugging my cellmate without her knowledge or consent, I tried to channel the cheerful practicality of Mary Poppins instead of Malcolm's creepy meddling. *Just a spoonful of Morpheum makes the DTs go down.* Or something like that.

The powder dissolved with a quick swirl of the cup, and I wedged myself into Honey's bunk so she could lay her head on my lap. "That's it," I urged, tipping the cup toward her mouth. "Get all of it. You need to stay hydrated."

After she drank, she collapsed on my thigh, shivering. "I don't want to do this," she sobbed. "It hurts so bad. I can't."

Would the Morpheum get her through this? I had no idea. Since I probably wasn't going to sleep much anyway, I figured I'd stay up and make sure she didn't accidentally aspirate, because the *last* thing I needed was to accidentally kill someone else. "Shhh." I petted the top of her head. "It's going to be OK. I'll take care of you."

Honey had already started twitching as she neared the edge of sleep. To seal the deal, I stroked her hair some more and started humming that old chestnut, "Hush, Little Baby," even though the song had never sat well with me. How gross is it to give a live bird to a newborn?

"I used to sing that song to my daughter," Honey said.

Her tone was neutral, factual, with that famous Morpheum forthrightness. Maybe all the oxy in her system was interfering with the sedative? Maybe the pill was working on her while she was awake? "You have a daughter?"

Honey nodded against my thigh. "She'll be eight next month. I'll still be here."

This was math I could do quite easily: Twenty-three-year-old mother minus a middle schooler, carry nine months, equals Honey probably got pregnant at fourteen years old. "Where is your daughter now?" I asked.

"With my uncle."

That's nice, I thought. It was good that Honey's family had been able to help her out. "Do you know where the father is?"

"I told you. He's my uncle."

Oh. Oh god! *That's fucking terrible*, I thought, readjusting the equation. Divide by sexual abuse and family drama, multiply by stress and poverty, subtract a high school diploma and mental health care, and here was the answer to Honey's everything: her career, her attitude, her nighttime fear of monsters, the stuffed animals she made out of bath towels, her drug use. "Is your daughter safe with him?"

Honey sniffed. "For a few more years."

"Would you like to see her?"

"Very much."

"Think of her. Picture her in your mind. Hang on to that, OK?" I smoothed her hair some more, trying to coax her into the bliss of a Morpheum sleep. "Good night, Honey. Sweet dreams."

When I finally felt her relax, I wiggled out from under her and cleaned up the floor with toilet paper so I could flush all the evidence that she'd been sick. The cell smelled dank and sweet but that would dissipate eventually, and I could do a better clean tomorrow—as well as get her some fresh bedding. The guards called for lights out, and when they finally killed the fluorescents, I breathed a sigh of relief. We hadn't gotten caught. Honey would sleep off her sickness. Maybe she'd wake up well enough to swear off pills.

With Honey within sniffing distance, it was probably a bit too intrusive to take Morpheum tonight. While peeking in on her dreams was a tempting way to take my mind off the fact that Pete was out on a date while I was stuck in here mopping up barf, even I recognized that was going a little too far.

Besides, what was the point of taking a break from jail when it was always there waiting for you when you woke up? If Pete needed space to grieve (even if it is with his brilliant lawyer friend), then so did I, because there was no more pretending or hiding or dreaming of other, better things: this was my life now.

There, at the foot of Honey's bunk with her feet in my lap, I finally cried my heart out for so many reasons. It was the kind of visceral, open-mouthed bawling you can only do when you're by yourself because it's just too embarrassing otherwise. But as Honey was unconscious, there was no one to impress. I was finally, terribly, alone.

TUESDAY, JULY 2

When I told Charlie I usually go to Din Tai Fung on the Fourth of July to remind myself of my Taiwanese roots, she let slip that she's never been before. (*Seriously?*) So I insisted we go for dinner tonight. At the restaurant, she let me do the ordering and didn't balk at any dish that came out. Gustatory bravery is a quality I really value in people.

We didn't talk about our mind heist. We didn't talk plans. We just talked about normal shit: movies, the news, the weather (I've never been so happy to talk about weather). I even said this to her, like, "Isn't it nice to talk about stuff not related to the government conspiracy involving my former employer?" And she laughed her big Julia Roberts laugh, and I looked up at her, and I pictured it in a flash: my reaching across the table and putting my hand to her face and kissing her, the way couples do when they've been together for a while.

It shocked me, that vision—that I could be thinking of anyone besides Ness. But goddammit I'm so lonely. It feels like June all over again, and I don't want it to—and I won't let it. And yet, sometimes I like to pretend that I might slip if only to make myself less sad for an evening.

So yeah, I flirted with Charlie. Not my best game, but enough game to keep her entertained all night. We had too many beers. We stumbled up to Cap Hill with our arms around each other to stay upright and found a karaoke bar where things got *really* shameful. And then I put her in an Uber and sent her home to her cluttered apartment with her subpar photos and her extra toothbrushes.

And even though she wanted me to stay over, and *I* wanted to stay over, and she said I could sleep in the bed, (I believe her exact words were: "I could sleep in wherever I wanted"), I went back to my shitty little studio. I've been up all night: too drunk, too hungry, too horny, too lonely to sleep. My snack delivery shift starts in four hours, so it doesn't pay to sleep now anyway.

I wonder if Charlie's up. I should text her.

No. Bad idea.

Speaking of texts, look who's blowing me up at 5 a.m.? My old pal, Peter Brown! He says:

> *Call me.*
> *Call me now.*
> *I need you to do something for Ness.*
> *Goddammit, Altan. I can see you reading these. Call me.*

I've spent the past ten minutes typing something in reply just to make those three dots appear on his phone, and then I delete it. I picture him going ballistic on the other end. I mean, of course I'm going to call him back: I need those pills. But it's fun to toy with him a bit considering I've been trying to get him on the phone for a month.

Here's another text! What will this one say?

Oh, shit.

THE TESTIMONY

I woke up in Honey's bunk leaning against the wall. She was out cold on her back, snoring with her mouth wide open. I must have dozed off during my vigil, and between the crying and the lack of sleep I felt leathery and dry. But I resisted the urge to crawl back into my bed in favor of being alone for another 30 minutes or so. This kind of freedom was too rare to sleep through.

I took a pee in total privacy. I spent a few minutes experimenting with hairdos in the mirror. I was singing as I brushed my teeth when I heard Milford's heavy tactical boots pounding down the hallway. She was out of breath by the time she got the cell door unlocked. "You're late!" she puffed, bent at the waist to brace her hands on her thighs.

"Me?" I yawned around my toothbrush. "Late for what?"

"Court, you dumb bitch."

I'd almost come to think of Milford's swears as little terms of endearment. "I don't have court today."

"Fine, dipshit, don't go then. Just stay in here in your bare feet like the nut sack you are. *Christ*, Brown! Get your shoes."

Considering I hid my surplus Morpheum packets under the insoles of my slip-ons, I usually wore them with fanatical dedication so Honey would never have reason to scrutinize the gap in the foot beds. But since she was sleeping off the drugs I gave her, I'd left the shoes at the foot of my ladder, which meant that instead of running out the door with Milford, I had to spend a whole five seconds putting them on—seconds Milford used to squawk, "Honey, what's your deal? You too tired to make my life hell or something? Honey? Honey! Why isn't she waking up?"

I scrambled to find a plausible excuse. *She's tired from that mini-marathon. She was out partying. She's been pulling extra hours at the office.* All the reasons one might use to explain sleeping late did not hold up in jail. All I could muster was a very eloquent, "Ummmmmm."

Milford marched to Honey's bed and clapped her hands near her face. When Honey didn't move, she grabbed the radio she kept in an epaulet on her shoulder. "I need a gurney in 482."

"Oh, I don't think that's necessary," I said as I thought: *Shit, shit, shit!* I didn't want Honey going to the infirmary, testing positive for drugs, and getting in trouble or (even worse) getting *me* in trouble. The Morpheum was supposed to *help* her. When was I going to learn that it never helped anything?

"What did she take?" Milford snapped.

"Nothing!" I tried to make this sound casual, like the guard was overacting to my nonresponsive cellmate as she shined a penlight under Honey's eyelids.

Another guard arrived with a stretcher. I had to step into the hallway to avoid getting run over as the two of them hauled Honey onto the bed. Milford was firing off instructions: "Tell the nurse she might need Narcan—maybe methadone after. You know what? Never mind. I'll tell her myself. Take Brown to court." Milford screamed as she almost flattened me in the hall with the gurney, "Brown, you dick-licking dumbass: get out of the way!"

She ran toward the infirmary faster than I thought she could even move, and I wondered if her hustle was for Honey or for her own ass on the line. Maybe both. It didn't have to be one or the other: you could worry about other people and yourself at once.

"Don't worry," said the other guard, as she walked me to the white panel van outside. "Your celly will be alright."

Of course, *I* knew that. I was the one who'd drugged her.

At the courthouse, the bailiff hustled me straight into the same courtroom I had been in before. Janet was already at the defense table wearing a wide-legged olive pantsuit and the relief of a groom whose bride had just shown up to the wedding an hour late.

"Ohmygod," she whispered as I sat down in my chair. "I wasn't sure you were going to make it before the recess ended. They scheduled this pretrial hearing early this morning with zero notice. I'm so fucking annoyed." The sudden cursing made her delightfully more relatable, even as it suggested that she was losing her cool. "Apparently, Dean Jacobs records all his meetings to reference later," she said. "And *suddenly* he has a tape of your confessing to overdosing Sam from April. We're here to get it excluded from evidence."

I thumbed through my back catalog of *Law & Order* knowledge, trying to sound like I knew what I was talking about. "Are they allowed to record me without my consent?" (See, Pete? I could be lawerly.)

"You consented when you took the job. It's in your employment paperwork."

Damn. "Do they have the whole recording?" *Even the part where I accused Malcolm of jerking off in front of me?*

I'd told Janet about that incident weeks ago when she first came to visit me in jail. She thought it was compelling, but not enough to use as her primary defense strategy (maybe as a backup, in case Vitamin D deficiency didn't pan out). *That* was the value of my tale of woe: reports of sexual harassment in the workplace were so easily dismissed as being made up or misunderstood that Janet didn't even think mine was enough of a slam dunk to use as a get-out-of-jail-free card. *Especially since he didn't touch you*, she'd said at the time. *If he didn't touch you, people won't be sympathetic.*

The worst part was: I totally knew what she meant.

"They *said* it's the whole recording, but it's only, like, five minutes' long. So I'm guessing it's edited," Janet told me now. "I haven't heard it yet."

"Where's Pete?"

"He's *supposed* to be getting my witness."

"What witness?"

"All rise!" cried the bailiff.

As I stood, I twisted my head to see who was here. The turnout was better than my last hearing: a few more photographers, even a camera crew. Pretty sure Malcolm was in the back row: I couldn't see him directly, but I saw the reflection from his watch flashing across the ceiling like he was doing it on purpose out of boredom. His presence felt like a broken heater: it made me sweat so hard.

Judge Davis flapped onto her Ikea bookshelf castle at the front of the room. "Ms. Brown, *there* you are," she said with the kind of judgement you reserve for people who show up late to appointments. Didn't she know I didn't even have a clock?

"Counsellor, your defendant is here. Now where is your witness?" Davis said.

"He's coming. Right now. My associate just texted me."

"I do not like to be kept waiting."

"I know, Your Honor. He's on his wa—"

With that, the doors at the back of the room blasted open, and in jogged Altan.

Wearing head-to-toe Snacks Now-branded Spandex.

And those weird bike-riding shoes that clip into the pedals and make a horrible racket when you wear them indoors. He had on fingerless gloves that let him unclip the buckle of his helmet as he trotted up to the witness stand.

Brain-wise, it's strange to fight with someone and then not see them for a month. Without new inputs, your memory hangs on to those last hurled words, those cruelties you'd dragged out of dusty armories, all the shit you heard when you were mad. But resentment, like limestone, is best built in layers: without fresh insults, I felt the weeks' old dust of my anger toward Altan blowing away.

If anyone was impressed by Altan's willingness to appear in Spandex to defend my good name, it was because they didn't know him. Even if he wasn't just coming from work or trying to make a grand gesture of apology, Altan was the kind of person who would do this purely for shock value-derived laughs. (Exhibit A: my picture of him at Père Lachaise Cemetery riding Victor Noir's brass boner like Slim Pickens atop the atom bomb.) The Spandex did not tell me that he loved me: it was his hair, one of the very few trivial things Altan cared about. When he took off his helmet, his hair was sweaty and matted and generally gross—not even *close* to his standard of what he thought was acceptable in public.

I thought he looked great.

"Sorry I'm late," he said taking the witness stand. "I had a delivery in Green Lake."

Judge Davis didn't strike anyone as being someone who cared about small talk or annual incomes that were lower than the price of her car. "Mr. Young, do not make a mockery of my courtroom."

Altan was genuinely confused. "What? I'm not trying—"

"Your outfit, Mister Young."

He looked down like he'd just realized he was wearing a scuba suit. "Well, that's unfair. I didn't have time to change. Not everyone gets to wear suits all day."

Janet visibly cringed as she sat next to me at the defense table. As much as I loved Altan's "fuck it" attitude, even I had to admit this was off to a less-than-awesome start.

"I already held you in contempt once," Davis said, presumably in reference to the time he kissed me at my arraignment. "Don't make me do it again."

"Yes, Your Honor," Altan said sweetly, drawing an X over his chest. "Cross my heart and hope you die." He said it fast enough to swallow the last two words. If Davis heard the change, she didn't let on.

Pete had found his way to the defense table (he must have followed Altan in, but who was paying attention?). Leaning across me, he whispered to Janet, "I had, like, ten minutes to prep him."

"Sweet Jesus," she whispered back as she got to her feet and headed for the front of the court. Pete caught my eye and nodded in greeting. Oh, so *now* he was acknowledging me? Cool. Good to know.

"Mr. Young," Janet began. "Were you present at the meeting where Vanessa Brown allegedly confessed to stealing medication from your employer, WellCorp Pharmaceuticals?"

Altan leaned into the microphone and announced, "I was."

"Do you remember the date?"

"It was April 7 of this year."

Janet paced in front of him. "You're sure?"

"Yes. I keep a diary," said Altan. Here he held up his trusty Moleskine notebook, but where had he pulled it from? The peanut gallery must have wondered, too, because some people started sniggering.

"At that meeting, how long did Ms. Brown say she'd been taking Morpheum?"

"Since the beginning of the trial, which started last September."

"Is that true?"

"No. She first obtained Morpheum from me on March 6 of this year. I know, because I wrote it down."

"So she was lying about being under the influence of the drug for the duration of the trial?"

"Yes."

"So would you say her confession is true?"

"No, I would not."

"How did you obtain the Morpheum that you gave to the defendant?" Janet asked.

Altan recited, like he'd practiced, "I do not want to answer that in accordance with my Fifth Amendment rights."

"Thank you, Mister Young," she said. "That is all."

OK, that didn't seem like much of a to-do. Why were Janet and Pete so stressed about his testimony?

Oh wait—because the prosecutor got a turn next. He was a droopy-faced white man in his sixties named Maurice Nelson, and he was in the wrong profession because his melodic baritone voice was perfect for radio. So this was the guy Malcolm had bribed to offer me the deal? Somehow, I wasn't entirely surprised.

"Mr. Young," he said, walking over to Altan's stand with his hands clasped behind his back. "How do you know the defendant?"

"She and I have worked at WellCorp together for two years."

"Is that the full extent of your relationship?"

"We are also currently romantically involved."

"And when did that happen?"

"A few months ago."

"Around March 6, when she started taking the pills?"

"Yes."

"Was she married at the time?"

"Objection," said Altan.

Janet's mouth fell open. Everyone sitting behind us started giggling again. Altan was probably some of the best courtroom entertainment people had seen all day.

Judge Davis piped up: "Mr. Young, you are not allowed to object."

"But I don't think a woman should ever be judged on her marital status."

"Please answer," she snapped.

Altan rolled his eyes. "She was married."

"So one might surmise that you're not exactly 'neutral' when it comes to this testimony?"

"Objection!" Janet got to say it this time, but Nelson had already proven his point.

"No further questions," he said and took his seat.

OK, seriously: Pete and Janet had been freaking out about nothing. That hadn't been so bad—

"Actually," Altan said into the mic. "I'd like to give a statement."

Janet sprang out of her chair like she knew this would happen. "Mr. Young, that's not necessary."

"I want to, though."

"Your Honor, this isn't how this works—"

"Let him speak," Judge Davis commanded. Her eyes gleamed with the possibility of holding him in contempt.

Altan made a guttural sound into the microphone so his voice would be extra clear—then he decided he needed a drink of water from a nearby pitcher. "By all means, take your time," Judge Davis drawled.

To spite her, Altan downed a second glass of water while staring up at her in her crow's nest. When he was adequately hydrated, he adjusted the microphone and said, "I want to testify that Malcolm Jacobs masturbated in front of Vanessa Brown before the meeting at which she 'confessed' to overdosing Sam Stevens. As such, I don't think what she said can or should be taken seriously due to the trauma incurred."

I've never been so torn in my life. Part of me wanted to pump my arms like *Yes!* The other part wanted to fall to my knees shouting *NOOO!* Obviously, *someone* had to mention the fact that that jerk off had jerked off in front of me, but I wasn't sure this was the time or the place. Or the person. Or the outfit. The optics were horrible: here was my boyfriend trying to get me out of jail by throwing out a sexual harassment charge that was impossible to prove and hard for people to take seriously. God, he was an idiot— a brave, beautiful idiot.

A long and awkward silence followed before Maurice Nelson roared, "Objection!" Suddenly everyone in the peanut gallery felt it was safe to talk amongst themselves. "This is the first the prosecution is hearing of any, ah, masturbatory incidents."

"Of course, it is," Altan said. "You think Malcolm was going to fess up to it when he handed you that edited tape?"

"WellCorp has assured us that the full tape was provided."

"I'm sure that makes it legit," Altan said, rolling his eyes. Everyone started talking at once.

Judge Davis: "Mister Young, that is enough!

Maurice Nelson: "Sir, you are making some very serious allegations."

Janet: "Objection!" (Nobody cared.)

Maurice Nelson (again): "Were you even present at this alleged masturbation incident?"

"No," Altan said. "But I heard Malcolm Jacobs confess to it."
"Where?"

"That's not important!"

"*Where?*"

Altan looked at me for the first time, and I saw the kind of terror you see in the eyes of a climber hanging one-handed from a ledge.

"Answer the question, Mister Young," said the judge.

"In a dream."

Janet covered her face with her hand. Under his breath, I heard Pete swear, *Shit.*

"In a *dream?*" Nelson laughed. (Behind me, there were more than a few who joined him.). "You expect this court to believe this testimony because a bicycle delivery boy saw it in a *dream?*"

"I haven't been a boy in a while," said Altan. "And if you're worried about my current job, focus on my previous: as a former employee of WellCorp, I am testifying that Malcolm Jacobs is up to some shady shit!"

"Mister *Young!*" barked Judge Davis, but it was over: Altan was already on his feet and getting off the stand. The courtroom was filled with the sound of flashbulbs. I swear there were even more journalists before. Had they felt shenanigans happening in the Force or had someone tipped them off? Regardless, Altan walked straight-backed through the crowd in his Spandex, eyes pinned to the end of the room. He lifted his helmet with great dignity and buckled it to his head.

WEDNESDAY, JULY 3

In exchange for my testimony at an emergency hearing, Pete finally agreed to give me five Morpheum. We met up after court at the bar we used to hang out in when we talked about my divorce. I got there first, so I was able to get a beer down to help ease the memory of the black eye Pete gave me the last time I saw him.

Who knew that dude was so mean?

So Pete came in and sat down at the bar next to me, and he was like, Hey. And I was like, Yo. It was very Han Solo vs. Greedo in that both of us were trying to be impossibly chill.

"How have you been?" I asked, as if I didn't know the answer was, *Like complete and utter shit.* Having your marriage fall apart is pretty much the worst.

"Fine," he said. "You?"

Wait: having your girlfriend get arrested for murder was pretty bad too. "Yeah, OK," I lied.

"You still in the same place?"

"Yep." It felt shameful to say that I was, that I had planned to bring his wife to my shitty studio with the laddered bed.

He smiled big at me, like he knew that. "OK, so here's your Morpheum." He handed me an Advil bottle, and I opened it to make sure it was all there. It wasn't. "You said you'd give me five."

"You said you'd do what you were told, but you didn't, so you get three," he said, and I knew I was the Greedo in this cantina.

"We had a deal, Pete."

"Yeah, well, I broke it."

I hated fighting with him. It was awkward enough between us without him being a dick. "I can't believe you wouldn't testify for Ness for free," he said.

"I would have if you'd returned my calls and given me the Morpheum sooner."

"I don't want you dreaming of Ness."

"I don't need Morpheum to do that. I do that for free."

"I don't want you dreaming *with* her."

"She would need to be taking Morpheum for that to happen."

He didn't say anything; he just downed his drink, which was suspicious given the amount he likes to insult me. He slammed the glass on the table, stood, and threw a twenty-dollar bill on the bar, all in one motion. Then he added another. "Buy yourself some pants."

All I could think to yell at his back was, "You can't buy pants for twenty dollars in Seattle!" So take *that*.

I left the bar and met Charlie at the Fairhope, feeling not like my best self. I know we'd been waiting weeks to get the Morpheum we need to catch Malcolm at the Fairhope and hijack his brain, but frankly I was not in the headspace for it.

Fortunately, Malcolm didn't show. Maybe he took the night off dream-torturing people because the Fourth of July is tomorrow? That must be it. Malcolm is, most definitely, a patriot.

Sometime in the evening, we learned that *The Seattle Times* had posted footage of me coming off the witness stand in full-blown Spandex. Subsequently, Seattle's Twitterverse "went nuts." (Pun credit goes to Charlie—har har.)

A huge debate waged between people who thought I was disrespectful to come to court with my dick practically on display and people who thought working-class folks deserved a bit more leeway. People started posting tribute photos of themselves walking their dogs and cooking dinner in bike shorts (#courthousecock).

And then there were, of course, the inevitable Asian-stereotype jokes perpetrated by racist trolls wondering why everyone was getting bent out of shape about my crotch since there wasn't much to see in the first place. (Are we really still saying shit like this in the twenty-first century? People are monsters.)

Having your outfit matter more than the fact you'd outed a millionaire for sexual harassment was the slightest bit disheartening. (How do female celebrities do it every day?) At least Charlie was there. I always do better when there's someone around to convince me that I'm OK.

When we finally gave up on getting into Malcolm's head for the night, Charlie invited me to sleep on her *couch* (emphasis on couch was hers)—like she knew that if I went home alone, I'd do nothing but replay the whole day in my head. She was right, so yeah, I went back to her place. She poured us fists of bourbon and we got lit and she told me her latest plans for her eyewitness "Inside the Mind of a Traitor" article. Then she disappeared into her room for a minute and emerged in the cocktail dress that she's picked out for when she goes to the White House correspondents' dinner. "How do I look?" she asked, twirling in her living room and almost tripping over the coffee table.

Bourbon is like Morpheum: it makes me tell the truth. I told her she's beautiful. And then I curled up on her sofa and went to sleep.

THE GHOST

The evening after Altan's testimony, I had the cell to myself—although I didn't take much pleasure in it. Honey was still in the infirmary under observation, according to Milford. They couldn't tell what she'd taken (if anything) so she wouldn't incur any disciplinary action (thank god). Still, I felt like the biggest jerk, getting her in trouble like that.

Similar feelings for Altan when I saw him on the news that night. The anchors were not kind to him, but he would have known that before testifying. Janet and Pete would have also warned him not to speak out of turn, but of course, he hadn't been able to help himself. And it's not like Malcolm had ever played fair. Maybe someone needed to go off-book to combat a man who didn't obey the rules. Or maybe I was feeling charitable toward Altan because I missed him so much.

As part survival skill and part science experiment with Pete, I'd spent the past thirty days not thinking about Altan. There hadn't been room to process how much it hurt, how stupid I felt, when I discovered he'd kept secrets from me. But when you spend your days locked up with women being defined by their crimes, you develop a knack for looking past the obvious flaws. You have to. Otherwise, who would keep you company?

That's what I thought of as I lay in my bunk alone without Honey's soft snoring. People mess up. People get caught. People say sorry. People show up to court on your behalf and make wild accusations against your personal enemies. Despite their best intentions, people will unfailingly break your heart a thousand different ways, which is bad only if you don't trust them to mend it just as many. Altan could be counted on—not to be perfect, but to make good.

What had he been doing this month—besides delivering snacks? Probably being reckless, sticking his nose into places it didn't belong. Was he making enough to pay his rent? Did he have any left over for takeout? Would he go to Din Tai Fung tomorrow for the Fourth of July in protest like he always did?

Did he miss me? Was he OK? What would happen next?

The next morning at 9 a.m., a guard woke me up to tell me my lawyer was here. I shuffled behind her to the interview room without even brushing my teeth first. There was no happiness or confusion or anger when I found Pete waiting for me at the table. Instead I just felt profoundly tired of being jerked around, sometimes *literally* depending on which guard was leading me that day. Some of them had a tendency toward being a little more forceful than necessary.

Pete looked good, I thought bitterly. He looked clean and reputable and well-rested. *Good for him.* It appeared his vacation from me had been relaxing.

"Good news!" he said brightly—too brightly, like he was trying to trick me into cheering up and maybe forgiving him for ghosting me in the process. "Judge Davis has asked for a review of your 'confession' tape. She wants it checked to make sure it wasn't edited or anything. That's great, right?"

Honestly, I wasn't *trying* to be moody, but I was also fresh out of emotions other than *completely depleted*. "Super," I said.

When Pete saw he wasn't going to be able to sweet talk me into smiling, he took a deep breath and folded his hands in front of him on the table. "I owe you an apology for the other night. I shouldn't have disappeared on you like that."

"You ghosted me, Pete," I said, pausing for effect. "*In jail.*"

"I know. It was rude. But . . ." he trailed off, anticipating how bad the next thing was going to sound. "I needed space."

Oh. Pete needed space. I had a bunk the size of a grave plot to my name, but Pete was the one who needed more room. My tone was extra salty when I asked, "How was dinner with Janet?"

"It was good," he said quickly. "I needed her advice."

"On?"

"On whether or not I should tell you the thing."

So glad he was consulting a third party instead of just listening to my wishes. "What did she say?"

Pete pulled an Opal packet from his pocket and slowly slid it across the table. "Ness, I kept this thing from you for all these years because I was afraid you'd hate me. But if you know, and you decide to hate me, then that's your choice to make. I have no right to take that away from you. That's what she said."

My heart for Pete was still a mean little nugget, and I had fantasies of taking the Morpheum, flushing it down the toilet, and letting him sweat alone in a dream all night. But every now and then the man put words together in the most perfect way. And besides, wasn't this what I wanted?

"Can't you just tell me what it is?"

"I have to show you," he insisted. "I'm sure you understand."

Of its own accord, my hand reached out and took the packet. "One condition. You come see me tomorrow. We talk about whatever this is face to face. Promise?"

He nodded, though honestly, I wasn't sure he'd do it: he looked nervous enough to barf. "Promise me!" I said.

"I promise!" he finally replied. "Sheesh."

"OK, I'll see you tonight."

We stood so we could smell each other (our greetings and departures had started to look like those at a dog park), but instead of a quick sniff, Pete bent to kiss me on the lips. It was light and dry and tender, and even though I'd kissed him a billion times in our dreams, this was different. This was Pete.

We're always too young to know how to love people. That's what I thought standing there in Pete's arms—thinking about all the people I'd cared about and wronged in my own twisted ways. A million things in my heart winged their ways up to the ceiling and scattered around us like moths. They were still hovering in the corners when he left.

THURSDAY, JULY 4

Charlie and I decided to check out the Fairhope tonight since Malcolm missed his usual Wednesday-evening drink spiking. It's a madhouse in here because Amara Kassis is hosting an Independence Day fundraiser for her political campaign. Charlie is *losing her mind* because it's her *greatest dream* to be a White House correspondent for the first female, the first Muslim, and also the youngest president in American history. According to her, Kassis is *totally* going to get the Democratic nomination because her healthcare plan will appease the moderates while still giving coverage to everyone regardless of immigration status—

Honestly, I kind of tune out from my post on the balcony overlooking the lobby chock-full of people swanning around in tuxedos and gowns like it's prom night for Boomers. I'll just stay up here, thanks, listening to Charlie prattle into the phone about reasons to vote for Kassis, like I need convincing—like I might actually prefer that racist asshole we currently have in office.

Charlie's nervous. I'd be able to tell even if she wasn't talking a mile a minute on the phone from her perch at the bar. She's dolled up in what she calls her "thirst-trap outfit": little black dress, heels, a full face of makeup she had done at Nordstrom. The goal is to trick Malcolm into flirting with her again so she can get close enough to smell him. Then, using our own Morpheum (which he doesn't know we have), she can piggyback me into his dreams— assuming she gets her head in the game.

Her hand trembles a little when she takes a sip of her drink (champagne, from a fresh bottle, no way it can be monkeyed with). She spills it on the bar, curses, mops it up with a napkin, wrings her hands. I say into the phone, "Hey, take it easy. You'll get through this." I know she's nervous about dreaming with Malcolm again, but I told her she doesn't have to be. All she has to do is hold the door open to his head long enough to get me in—assuming Malcolm is even going to show.

When he walks in the front door in a tuxedo like he's a casino owner in a Bond movie, that's when I know this is our night.

"He's here," I warn Charlie, and like a pro she puts her phone face down on the bar and swivels on her stool to assume Sharon Stone in *Basic Instinct* pose. At least three Boomers have heart attacks. A waiter with a tray of drinks almost trips as he passes by, but Malcolm walks right past her and up to the bar where he orders a scotch from a different bartender (not Austin. Where's Austin?).

"Hey," Charlie says lightly; I hear her through the phone she placed on the bar. "I've been hoping I'd bump into you again."

"Who are you?" Malcolm asks without even bothering to try and cover up the fact he doesn't remember her.

"Amanda. We met a few weeks ago. You bought me a drink?"

He turns back to the bar. "Oh. Right."

A blow-off like that would have me running for the hills, but Charlie is a champion. "Maybe you can buy me another one later?"

"Not tonight, lady. I got shit to do."

"Aw, come on," says Charlie, grabbing him by the lapel of his tuxedo and leaning in. He recoils, so she only manages to land a kiss on his neck—but it's enough.

"What do you think you're doing?" he practically shrieks.

The same thing he's done to countless women, I think—Ness, Charlie, all the hotel patrons he drugged in in this very lobby. How many times had I watched him touch someone inappropriately while they were too scared to flinch? I want to slit Malcolm's throat right above the lipstick mark Charlie left on his neck.

Her mission accomplished, Charlie falls apart at the bar. "I'm sorry," she whispers, grabbing her phone, passing her fingers over the microphone to make that muffled *shh* noise, but still I hear her say, "Have a good night." It kills me that she feels the need to say that as she lurches for the front door and almost bites it in her heels. It is only then that I realize just how generous she is to have done this for me—and for her future career or whatever, but mostly for me.

Malcolm takes his scotch and adjusts himself as he walks away from the bar looking pleased, like every other privileged piece of shit in here. And then he passes the security checkpoint that will lead him into the ballrooms where I'm not rich enough to follow, so I go find Charlie under the portico of the hotel. She's freaking out. Says she doesn't want to sleep alone if she has to dream with him. She wants me to sleep at her apartment. I tell her I'll walk her back, but I can't stay. *Why not?* she wants to know. *I'm so scared. I need you with me when we crack into Malcolm's brain? Help me, help me, why won't you help?*

She's crying and I hold her to me so I can smell her. If I tell her why I can't sleep at her apartment, she'll never forgive me, and it will ruin the whole plan.

THE THIRD GUY

The dream was taking place in the living room of our old apartment, which had been rendered with Pete's letter-perfect accuracy. Everything from the rip in his leather armchair to the wine stain we could never get out of the kitchen counter—it was all accounted for, and so *real*. Every time I thought that, the dream knitted itself tighter around me, like a living feedback loop that absorbed and confirmed in real time.

I'd shown memories to Altan, but he and I had never lived the same one together—and there was probably a reason for that, because the connection I felt to Pete in this dream was dangerously strong. It was enough to reverse the spin of the Earth Superman-style, taking us back in time to the New Year's Eve we spent home because we both had colds, and my ill-fated month-long yoga phase, and how adult it felt when we replaced the milk crates Pete kept in front of his sofa with a coffee table we'd bought together at the Fremont Market on a rainy Sunday. Here was the nest we'd built, the life we'd amassed, the scene of our flirtations and fights and all the flavors in between.

The bookcase was impeccably, obsessively arranged by Pete in alphabetical order. I ran my fingers across the spines, saying hello to all the titles from our dreams until I found the copy of a Pablo Neruda collection Pete had read to me on our library date and subsequently given to me the morning we got married. I flipped it open to the first page. Beneath the title *Twenty Love Poems and a Song of Despair*, he'd inscribed the phrase: *May we have the same ratio.*

Well, here we were. The song of despair.

"Hey," said Pete from the kitchen. I turned to find him at the counter peeling garlic—a *ton* of it. He had a small mountain of cloves in front of him the approximate size of a sneaker. "How's it look?" he asked, gesturing toward the living room with his paring knife. "Not bad, right?"

I took a tissue from the box on the coffee table and wiped my nose. "You're a vampire. That's the secret, isn't it?"

He looked down at the garlic, like he'd only just seen how much he'd prepared. "No, I'm just nervous."

"Don't be," I sniffed. "I'm sure it'll be fine."

He cleared his throat. "Do you want dinner before we . . .?"

I shook my head.

"I was going to make linguine. You love my linguine."

"Make it for me for real someday."

"After this, you might not want me to, so this is your last chance!" His voice had an electrified edge that betrayed how scared he was as he took his time wiping his hands on a kitchen towel, anything to prolong this feeling of normalcy, of home. "Are you sure you want to know?"

I looked around at the apartment we'd made, the life we'd built. I could say no and remember it all like this. "I don't *want* to know, but I feel like I have to. Does that make sense?"

"More than you know," he said as he came around the kitchen island to stand next to me so that we were facing the door to the hallway together. He reached for the knob, then pulled his hand back, clenched it into a first at his side.

"I love you," he said. "Remember that."

The door of our apartment opened into a house party in full swing. The room stank of CK One and stale beer and pheromones as college kids jostled shoulder to shoulder around a keg in the middle of the room, where someone was doing a stand to chants of *chug, chug, chug.* A cluster of girls in one corner gyrated to Justin Timberlake's "SexyBack" (in their defense, that song was a *jam*) while ten dudes in the opposite corner played flip cup along a folding table despite the obvious mess being made on the carpet. Every now and then a flash of pink or yellow would slash across the room courtesy of a disco light near the "DJ"—who was a kid guarding his first-generation iPod like a mother T. rex—but other than that the room was dark.

Pete went first, and I followed him through the crowd since he knew where he was going. The house was bigger than a normal home, with numerous parlors that had been repurposed for beer pong and games of strip poker. We moved through all of them toward the back of the building, shoving past clumps of screaming teenagers until we found ourselves in an oversize kitchen with stainless steel countertops.

The music was loud enough to bleed through the walls, and in lieu of darkness, someone had hung penis-shaped Christmas lights (undoubtedly bought from Spencer's in the mall) from the upper cabinets to create mood lighting. It was apparently having an effect on two of the female partygoers, who were making out sloppily in a corner. The one facing the room kept peeking at a group of guys lazing along a countertop to see if they watched.

Holding a red plastic Solo cup, a younger version of Pete was among them. He and his friends were shooting the shit about the lameness of the party and where they should go next. They were clearly old enough to drink legally because they lacked the rabid boozy vampirism of the underage. Still, I couldn't get over how *young* Pete looked, unstressed, uncreased, untested. His hairline was lower; I hadn't even noticed it had crept marginally up his forehead in the years of our marriage, but side by side you couldn't ignore that time had passed.

Also, he was taking vodka shots (gross) and chasing them with PBR (what a basic bro), which was so unlike the man he would grow into that I was mortified on his behalf. I looked over at Current Pete to see if he had any regrets about his college beverage choices, but he was watching the door behind his former friends. I saw it open but I didn't see who came in. I *did* see College Pete get ploughed into from the back, spilling his PBR all over the counter.

He spun, shaking his beer-soaked hand, and snarled, "What the—?"

And holy shit, there she was: floral V-neck boho top, bootcut jeans, strappy sandals in a room where all the boys had on winter-appropriate footwear. It was me at nineteen, drunk off my ass, so disoriented I could barely stand.

"What the fuck?" I said in time with my college version.

I'd never been to this party: I'd never met Pete before the night I ran into him tending bar, so what was I doing here wearing the exact outfit I wore the night of my assault?

I rubbed my eyes cartoonishly to make sure I wasn't dreaming within the dream: College Me's eyes bore signs of having been swiped at recently as well, like she'd been too out of it to remember she was wearing mascara. "Getoutmyway!" she shouted at College Pete over the music.

"Um, where are you trying to go?" asked Young Pete, amused, bending slightly to get closer to her ear.

"WhereverthefuckIwant," she answered with an unnecessary attitude that reminded me of the first time I met Honey. College Me shoved past Young Pete toward the counter, whirled around and hoisted herself to sit. (In the process, a bowl of chips fell all over the floor, and one of Pete's friends groused, "Goddammit.")

College Me had the moony look of stoners as she gazed up at Pete, and even though he could tell my affection was chemically manufactured, still he fell for it a little, the way an adult will indulge a child in the middle of a tantrum. "Comfy?"

"Ohyeah. Great." College Me ran a hand through her hair; it got stuck at the elastic where my ponytail was coming down. *Whatever. Big deal. Stop staring.*

For some reason, Pete thought this too-big-for-my-britches act was cute. Also helping was that my top had slipped forward, showing off the red lace of my bra. "How much have you had to drink?" he asked cautiously.

"Notenoughtofuckyou, ifthat'swhatyou'reaskin."

Young Pete's friends quietly backed up to give us some room. It was then that they noticed the two girls making out in the corner, and Current Me was happy their efforts were finally paying off. "Jesus," Young Pete said, amused. "I don't want to sleep with you."

"*Asshole.*"

Young Pete debated between clarifying to try and placate me (it's not that he didn't want to sleep with me *ever*—he just didn't want to do it now) or just moving forward since I didn't seem like I was in the mood to be reasonable. "Are you OK?" he asked.

"Pssshht," I said. "Ihad, like, twobeers."

"No offense, but you seem like you've had a bit more."

"Youdon'tknowme!"

"I'd like to. What's your name?"

College Me frowned, like she couldn't remember. Her gaze was cloudy when she said, "Bananas?"

Pete was entertained by what he thought was my way of playing hard to get. "Fine, don't tell me," he surrendered. "Do you want to go home?"

Poor Bananas. She nodded sloppily.

"Come on, then. I'll get you home—for free! No sex required."

College Me glared. "What'syourname?"

"Pete."

"Writeitdown," said Bananas. She turned to the counter and ripped a flap off a box of Bud Light, then passed a Sharpie someone had been using to label cups. "Nameandnumber."

Pete complied, and as he did, he felt both annoyance and admiration at having to complete this request. Bananas was no nonsense. He hoped she'd call him the next day.

College Me folded the cardboard and stuck it unceremoniously in her bra. Then she hopped off the counter and nearly bit it right there in front of him, but Pete caught her as she came down, clutching her wrists like she was on ice skates. "Lemmegetcoat," Bananas said.

"I'll come with you."

"*IsaidIdon'tneedhelp!*" she bellowed and stumbled off into the house. For the briefest moment, even though he'd been drinking, Young Pete thought of the Little Prince and that bell jar for his rose—and then he returned to his friends, who coagulated the moment I left. "So you gonna get some tonight, Brown?" someone said.

"Don't let her puke on your dick," said someone else.

"Guys, don't be gross," said Pete, but they were gross, and when they'd razzed him about why he couldn't pull any sober chicks, they moved to the topic of how another one of their friends had once puked on a girl because *he* was so drunk—but that's because he was an asshat. Like, remember that one time—?

Fifteen minutes went by while Young Pete eyed the door and only half-listened to his shit-talking friends. *Come on, Bananas,* he thought. *Where are you?* When it was clear that I wasn't coming back, he went to canvass the parlors. He peeked into the bathrooms and poked his head out the back door. When he still couldn't find me, he decided to check upstairs.

I went to follow, but Current Pete grabbed my arm from the bottom of the landing. I'd almost forgotten he was there, but he'd been with me the whole time, moving behind me as quiet as a shadow. "Don't," he said.

It wasn't that he didn't want to relive the memory: I could tell he'd been reliving it for so long that the visuals barely affected him anymore. But he wanted me to stay here, downstairs, like I should have done all those years ago. If he couldn't have it in real life, he wanted it in the dream. Impossible. "Pete, I have to know."

Upstairs, the music was muffled now that it was on the floor beneath us, Shakira telling us how her hips didn't lie. The architecture up here was strange. Like the main floor, there was the feeling of old rooms being repurposed for modern needs: the hallways were very long, with door after door after door—like the prison of the dream I showed Altan. Maybe part of me had remembered after all.

We followed Young Pete at a distance until I heard my voice slur, "Getoffme. Stopit."

Young Pete opened the door to his left a fraction—and just as he did, Current Pete took me in his arms and spun me so that I was facing the stairs we'd come from, my back to the commotion behind me, my heart against his, his arms around me, safe. "Don't look," he whispered. I was more than happy not to as I heard the younger version of him say, "What's going on in here?"

"Shut the goddamn door!" a guy yelled back.

I felt Young Pete jerk at the rebuke. He was about to shut it on pure reflex, but then he said, "Hey, Bananas, you good?"

"She's fine," said another male voice. I recognized them both from years of nightmares.

"She doesn't look fine."

The first guy again: "Look, either come have a turn or go."

"Have a turn?" he repeated, like he couldn't believe it—the gentleman in him was having trouble processing that things like this actually happened in places he went to, to people he knew.

"Rohypnol," the first dude replied, by way of explaining. "She won't know."

"You need to leave *now*," Pete said. His backbone was forming: I felt the memory of his fists clench. "This isn't right."

"Hey, asshole—no one asked you."

"*Get off her.*"

"Goddammit," the second one muttered. "Just wait a sec." There were the rustling sounds of people fumbling in the dark, gathering clothes, banging shins against bedframes, more swearing.

"*Now!*" demanded Young Pete.

"OK! OK!" I heard footsteps approaching from behind me, and I clung to Current Pete tighter, opening my eyes just a bit to watch over his shoulder as two half-naked white guys blurred past. One of them held his jeans to his front like a fig leaf. I was trembling all over.

From farther away, like he'd left the hall and gone into the room, Young Pete's voice said, "Hey, Bananas. Are you OK?"

College Me's voice was so sleepy and small. "Go away. Leave me alone."

"Do you need help?"

"No. I just want to sleep."

"Don't stay here. Not like this."

"I said don't touch me."

"Shit," whispered Pete to himself. "Shit, shit, shit." I felt the memory of his panic, that brain of his for the first time unsure of the answer. No amount of math or literature or academia could have prepared him for a moment like this. "Hey, Bananas? I'm going to go now. When I leave, I'll lock the door so no one will bother you. Call me when you wake up, OK? You have my number. We'll sort this out."

The door closed and I watched Young Pete leave over Current Pete's shoulder. His hands were mashed into his jeans pockets. He was walking so fast.

I followed after him, breaking from Pete's embrace. I chased him through the party and to the front door of the house, which opened and emptied me and Current Pete back into our living room. Young Pete had disappeared at the threshold.

I went down on all fours on the small Persian rug next to our coffee table. It had come from a store in Fremont that had been going out of business for ten years. I'd forgotten how much I liked it. It was important to notice details like this, the beauty around me, and not the way my whole concept of reality was falling apart. I felt like Honey the night she had the DTs. I wanted a Morpheum to escape this Morpheum. I wanted to dig and dig and dig to where no one could find me.

"You were the third guy. Vodka and Irish Spring: it was you." *The one who'd barged in.* I thought he'd joined in with the other dudes, but I must have been confused. Could you blame me, considering I couldn't even remember my own name? "All these years . . ." I trailed off, unable to compute this math. "You knew."

I had no idea where Pete was in the room: it was far enough away to give me space. The rug was so pretty: rust and turquoise. "Yes," he said quietly. "I knew."

I was a well with no bottom: the inside of my body was a tube that led through the earth's core and then straight out whatever Seattle's antipode was in the Indian Ocean before beaming out into space. "What happened after the party?"

I closed my eyes, focused on his voice, pictured Young Pete doing all the things Current Pete was narrating: "The next day, I went to campus security and told them I wanted to report a rape. The security guard said there had to be a victim in order to press charges, but he took my statement anyway, probably to make me feel better. Without your real name, my complaint amounted to 'something bad happened to a girl named Bananas,' so it wasn't very useful."

I laughed once—*ha*—if only to prove I still could, though I'm not sure Pete had intended this to be funny.

"I asked around, tried to find you. I was hoping you'd call, but either my number fell out of your clothes when those guys . . ." He trailed off. "Or you lost it on the walk home. Either way, I never heard from you. You vanished."

His defenses were down then, so I peeked inside his mind. He was blaming himself. He felt stupid for not insisting that he get my real name, for thinking I was playing hard to get. He didn't understand the danger I was in, and it had haunted him ever since—the dumbest he had ever been in his life. He thought all this, but he didn't mention it out loud.

"Two years went by," he said. "I checked in with campus security every now and then, but they never heard from you. I finished undergrad and started law school. I was going to be a defense attorney like Janet, but after that party, I realized I didn't have the stomach for it. And then one day, before finals, you came into the bar."

Blood flooded my brain as I pressed my forehead to the floor. "You recognized me?"

"Of course I did, but what was I going to say? 'Oh, hi! You're the girl who got raped at that party!' When you didn't remember meeting me, I wondered if you remembered anything that happened that night. If you didn't, I wasn't going to remind you. And if you did, maybe you didn't like talking about it with total strangers. I didn't know."

"Your reaction when I told you in Canada—"

"Faked—until you mentioned the baby. And that's when I got upset, because if I'd have known you'd gotten pregnant after that night, I would have never asked about kids. I wouldn't have dared—"

"So you would have just *not* had kids, even though you wanted them?"

"Ness, I would have done whatever you wanted, but it wouldn't have been enough. You can't undo something bad with something good." He blew out a breath; I could picture him hunched in his armchair, tearing out his hair. "I thought you could, but it doesn't work like that."

I sat up from the floor, pulled myself into the sofa to face Pete. "Why didn't you say anything?" I asked.

"Why didn't you?"

"I didn't want you to think I was damaged."

"I already knew you weren't."

"Oh, Pete," I said, my voice cracking pathetically but I had no follow up. There was nothing to say. Pete could only beam me messages on his heartbeats, the way dolphins communicate with sonar. His heart said, *I'm sorry, I'm sorry, I'm sorry.*

And mine replied, *You saved me. You saved me.*

But not in time. But not in time.

Everything was agony: being awake, being asleep, being alone, being in jail, being confused, being in love, being imperfect, being confronted with the fact that you and your husband kept *the same goddamn secret* from each other for years like some fucked-up version of *The Gift of the Magi* wherein I bought him a watch fob after selling my hair and he bought me a comb after selling his watch *only to find out we both knew I'd once been raped.*

"Are you angry?" Pete asked. "Do you want linguine?"

The answer was *no*—to both questions. How could I be angry? Pete had just been trying to protect me, but maybe he'd done too good a job because we'd wasted ten years waffling in an emotional limbo, afraid to push each other (and ourselves) toward something closer to truth.

I wasn't angry as much as I was sad, because I suddenly knew in my bones how ill-suited Pete and I were for each other. Maybe I would have seen this sooner if we'd been more honest. Maybe we could have course corrected early on in our marriage, but now Pete and I were officially incompatible simply because we loved so differently. That sappy romantic saw marriage, like many people do, as a search for your other half. But two halves only make one whole, and I think that's why I was so hungry in our relationship: I was still incomplete. We'd practically grown up together, but Pete and I never grew toward each other. We'd just gotten taller, side-by-side.

I wanted a love that rebuilt who you were, that encouraged you to patch each other's pitted parts and papier-mâché new limbs until both of you were each an entire person, capable of standing on your own two feet. Altan challenged me like that. He'd been pushing me since the moment we started taking Morpheum, charging me to be braver, to tell more truth, to dare greater, reach higher, scooch a little farther out on this thin branch of life to nab the juiciest fruit.

Being with Altan made me stronger—crazier and more prone to getting in trouble, but definitely stronger.

Altan's and my Machu Picchu dream came to me then, the one where he'd learned to Nightcrawl up and down the mountains before I was able to figure it out. Compatibility wasn't a matter of who was the better man but who was the better fit for what I'd become. When I couldn't fly, Altan took the time to teach me. In the same situation, Pete would have loved me until I grew wings.

FRIDAY, JULY 5

PETER MOTHERFUCKING BROWN, PICK UP YOUR GODDAMN PHONE

THE SOBER LIFE

Ever since Honey had gone to the infirmary, Milford had lost some of her spunk—and by "spunk" I meant "tendency toward making death threats," but you know, same thing. "Hey, Brown," she said, leaning in the doorway of my cell at 9 a.m. She sighed as she rubbed a paint scratch on the wall with her finger. "Lawyer's here."

Funny. I was also feeling spunkless.

Sure, I had my shoes on and my teeth brushed, so I was technically "ready" to meet Pete. But what the hell was I going to say? I'd spent the morning sorting out my feelings, replaying Pete's memories, trying to discern how it felt to *know* what had happened, and I still wasn't sure.

When viewing that night through Pete's eyes, I felt sorry for poor Bananas in a way I'd never felt for myself. For so many years, I'd felt guilty, like I'd contributed to this situation by wearing the wrong thing or drinking too much. I should have been smarter, fought harder, said *no* louder. But now I *knew* I'd done nothing wrong: I'd gone to a party like hundreds of kids in that frat house who'd had fun. My only crime was having stupendously bad luck.

And the saddest part was, I'm not sure I ever would have come to that conclusion without seeing it on Morpheum.

There were probably other feelings to sort out, but that was as far as I'd gotten, I thought, as Milford escorted me to the interview room in silence. Inmates around us were squawking as usual, shouting across the tables in the cafeteria, joking too loud. But Milford left them to it. "How's Honey?" I asked.

"They put her on some drug that's supposed to help with opioid cravings," she said. Another sigh. "I hope she stays clean this time."

My head was not in the right place, because I said without thinking, "Cut off her supply, and she might."

Milford whirled on me, her eyes and mouth making two parallel lines running across the middle of her face. "What's that supposed to mean?"

"Nothing!" I said, backpedaling like crazy. "Only that, you know, she wouldn't do drugs if she couldn't get drugs, right?"

Somehow those lines got even closer to each other as she studied me. "Dumbass," she said. (Crisis averted.) "That's not how any of this works. Even if you cut her off pills, Honey would just cook something in a toilet to put in her arm, and then she'd be really screwed." Milford eased off of me and continued walking down the hall. "Only Honey can get her shit together," she said over her shoulder. "No one else can do it for her."

She was right. I couldn't believe I was agreeing with a drug dealer and the female prison guard equivalent to Malcolm, but she was right—about Honey and anyone who used chemicals to escape their own skin. Including me.

People can't make you get sober or stable: you have to want it, and I hadn't wanted it until now. Sure, I wanted to *be* better, but I hadn't been up to the work involved in getting there, not because I was lazy, but because I was so tired of wondering what had happened, if I even deserved to feel good. Events of my past had turned my mind into a desert that I'd been wandering for so damn long, and the exertion was only compounded by the unfairness of it all. I get that some people crash into the Sahara, but why did it have to be me?

Were people like Honey and me within our rights to lie down and take pills and give up? Probably, but that didn't mean we had to. When life's got you down, you don't *have* to let a snake bite you to try and shed some pounds. It's hard to haul your ass across the desert, but no reptile or drug or prince is going to do it for you. I knew that now.

Milford hesitated when we reached the door of the interview room. "Is the lawyer having sex with you?" she whispered in case Pete could hear through walls. Surprisingly, she looked more concerned than mad.

"*What?* No!" *Well, not awake.* "Why would you—?"

"Because I've never seen any lawyer visit a client this often unless they had something going on. And you used to be happy to see him, but lately you're not, so I thought I'd ask."

Honestly? I was touched that she noticed. Jail felt so anonymous with everyone being dressed the same (in orange) and called the same (inmate) and feeling the same (miserable). Considering we were monitored almost constantly, this was the first time I'd felt seen. "No," I told her, and I felt my face go pink because it was like talking to your mom about sex. "It's not like that."

"He's not allowed to do that to you," she said. It was maybe the first time I'd heard her real voice—not her jailhouse growl. "You know that, right?"

"I know that. And he's not. Really. I'm OK."

"Alright." Milford pushed open the door. "Enjoy."

Pete was sitting with his elbows propped on the table, his head hung between them by his fists in his hair, like he was trying to give his neck a break from carrying the weight of *everything*. When he saw me, he sat up, rolled his broad shoulders back, adjusted the weight of my happiness on them, and asked me how I was. "Shitty," I said. "You?"

He snorted a quarter-hearted laugh. "Same."

Maybe I'd gotten used to the prolonged eye contact of Subconscious Pete, but I took a moment just to look at my husband—really *see* him, with my *actual* eyes and my waking brain and my gut and my heart. In honor of the holiday weekend, he was wearing jeans and a T-shirt he slept in and did not usually wear outdoors. He looked paler than usual—which, for Pete, was *pale*— and this made the reddish stubble on his cheek even more pronounced. Even his eyes seemed somehow less blue. I felt sorry for him, for both of us. A decade of secret keeping will really wear you out.

He let me look for a minute before squirming under the silence. "So, how are you?"

"You already asked me that."

"Shit." He licked his lips, stammering for words.

"You don't have to be polite, Pete. I think we're past that. Ask me the thing you need to know."

"Did I do the right thing?" he blurted, and the fear he felt in all our dreams filled the room, smelling of farts and Sulphur. "I've been wondering for years if I should have told you sooner. If I could have helped, but . . . I don't know. And if I did the wrong thing, I'm sorry. Did I?"

To contemplate this is to understand that life is just a crazy game of Plinko. If I'd gone right instead of left, if we'd banked earlier than we did, maybe we would have landed somewhere better than here—or we could have ended up somewhere worse. There are only so many decisions you get to make that don't involve gravity that it's almost ridiculous to even think you have control over anything at all. "I don't know if it was the right thing," I decided. "But it was a good thing. You meant well. And honestly, I wasn't in a place to talk about this sooner."

"But you could have been if I'd forced you—"

"You can't force people to get their shit together, Pete," I said.

I felt strangely calm—not the numbness of shock, but the cool of acceptance, like I knew it was all supposed to end up this way (even though that's a crazy thing to think when you're in jail). A Plinko board is long; I still had room to fall. "I'm ready now," I told him. "I'm ready to deal with shit. Maybe I can work on myself while I wait for my trial in here. Maybe that's why I'm in jail."

"That's . . . like, the most optimistic thing you've ever said," he marveled.

"Right? It feels weird to be this relaxed thinking about everything, but honestly? I'm glad you showed me that night. I don't remember much of it, so knowing how it went down makes me feel . . . complete."

"I don't know if you need to hear this, but it wasn't your fault."

"And it wasn't your fault either, Pete," I said, *clearly*, so he'd stop with whatever guilt he carried. "The only people who deserve to feel shitty are those two guys, so stop it, OK?"

"OK," he said, nodding a little. He was listening. I wasn't sure he was hearing me, but he was listening. Maybe he'd get it in time.

Pete leaned back in his chair, stretched his arms over his head, and yawned. "Um, so, I was thinking I'd go camping this weekend. Get away. Go off grid, or off pill, or something," he said. "Can I see you Monday?"

Why was he asking, like he needed my permission? "Hey, there's no need for both of us to be in jail. Go. Have fun!" Surprisingly, I meant it.

"And you're sure you're alright."

"I have a lot to think about. It'll be good for me to get some alone time."

"But you're always alone," he said.

"Jesus, don't rub it in."

He laughed a little, awkwardly. God, he needed a break. I went over to where he was sitting so I could cradle his poor, tired head against me. "You did good, Pete," I said, in case he needed to hear it again. "Thank you."

He wrapped his arms around my waist and sighed. I felt a weight fall off him, like an actual, physical barbell. It rolled down his back and hit the ground with a clang. Dropping a kiss into the nest of his hair, I smelled my fancy conditioner. For the first time I wondered if he really cared about split ends or if he used it more for sentimental reasons.

I also felt lighter when I said goodbye to Pete. I mean, it wasn't *goodbye*-goodbye, but I was going to be without him for a whole weekend, and that felt like a good next step in distancing myself from him. I'd gotten what I needed from the Morpheum. Everything was coming together.

Why, look! Even Honey was in her bed when I got back to my cell, like I'd never secretly drugged her in the first place. "You're here!" I said, springing into my bunk with an obnoxious amount of energy. I poked my head over the edge so I could look down at her. "I missed you."

"Don't lie, bitch."

"Fine. It was nice to be alone. How was the infirmary?"

"Terrible," she moaned through chattering teeth. "They put me on this drug that's supposed to help you detox, but they didn't give me enough and now I want to die."

"Ouch. That sucks. Look, I was about to get some breakfast. Can I bring you anything?"

"Oxy?"

"Pretty sure they just ran out."

"Fine. Some toast?"

"Sure thing."

I rolled out of my bunk again and made my way to the cafeteria, singing "SexyBack" under my breath. I sat alone with my crappy eggs and pictured my life with Altan in Bali, this time like a mood board to give me #inspo and not like a creepy fetish I obsessed about when I felt like being sad. After I brought Honey her toast, I decided to spend some time in the common room since she was a little crabby from the detox and might like to wallow in peace. Officer Milford intercepted me in the hall.

"Well, look who it is, my favorite sack of shit," she said.

The insult almost warmed my heart: Honey was home, and Milford was back to her gruesome self. "Your visiting privileges have been reinstated," she said. "Someone's here to see you."

The only person on my list was Altan, and it felt fortuitous that he and I should reunite on the same day I got to heal my marriage, start my self-care journey, and help my cellmate recover from her opioid addiction. Getting my shit together never felt so good!

"Brown, I want a clean visit," Milford said as she led me down more featureless halls. "Not like last time. Screw up again and I will wear your skin around my house like that guy in *Silence of the Lambs*. You got me?"

"Yes, officer."

"If you behave, you can have one hug at the end of your visitation."

A hug! "We get hugs?"

"You would have learned that *last* time if you didn't start a fight with your guest!"

Well. I was *not* going to do that again. What was there to fight about, anyway? Everything was working out, I thought, as I scampered through the Plexiglas hall trying to find the booth Altan was in. Everything was going to be OK. Everything was—

Shit.

Altan and I had been through a lot of freaky things together: stumbling upon a medical breakthrough, pushing the boundaries of the human psyche, fighting a Sasquatch, getting arrested. He'd approached each of them with a minimum of panic to the point where I'd started to believe he was incapable of really flipping his lid.

But this assumption was false, because Altan looked like he'd been up all night doing meth and now had a car battery hooked to his nipples: that's the level of freak out he was operating at. He started shouting into the phone the second he saw me, before I even had the chance to pick up the receiver. "—motherfucker needs to call me back," he was raging when I put the phone to my ear. No *Hi* or *How's jail?* or *I'm figuratively dying without you*—all those sweet nothings you like to hear when you're incarcerated and haven't seen someone for a month. "I'm in deep shit, Ness: we both are. Goddammit, this is an *emergency*. I left him like ten messages."

"What are you saying? Altan, I don't understand—"

"He must have blocked my number or something. I've been ringing your doorbell for hours—"

"*Who?*"

"Pete!" he screeched, pounding on the counter in front of him for emphasis. "He needs to call me."

"Hey!" I barked, hoping my voice was hard enough to snap him out of it. Altan looked at me with his mouth hung open. I tried to steady him with my eyes through the window, like I was some kind of human Xanax. "Pete's gone camping. Altan, what's going on? You need to tell me."

"I can't," he said, choking the receiver to remind me (*like I could ever forget*) that our conversations were monitored. "Even if I could . . . I can't. But it's bad. It's, like, *so goddamn* bad. If you see Pete, tell him to call—before tomorrow. I have to go."

"Now? You just got here!"

"*Listen to me*. I have to *go*. I have to *leave Seattle*."

"Wait, what? You can't leave me," I said, feeling (maybe rightfully) abandoned.

"Fuck," he moaned, sinking his head in his hands. "If only you had an *aspirin*."

Ah, our old code word for Morpheum. The Opal packets in my shoe tickled the soles of my feet. *Don't do it*, I thought. Morpheum doesn't help anything: it only makes things worse. But how else was I going to talk to him long enough to know what was going on? "We have *aspirin* in here," I said as casually as I could.

Altan snapped his head up. "You do?"

Anyone listening would have picked up on this weirdness. *Boy, oh boy, I could really go for some blood-thinners*. I nodded vigorously, while at the same time saying into the phone, "Wait. Just kidding. They only have ibuprofen. I get them confused."

"Oh. Right," said Altan. He probably had questions: tons of them, like *How did you get Morpheum?* and *Why am I only hearing about this now?* "But how would we—"

"You're allowed to give me a hug when you go," I said. "If we behave."

The old Altan would have made some kind of quip there, but this Altan didn't. Instead, he suddenly became suspiciously calm. "Cool, so . . . yeah! Well. I just wanted to say hi, but like I said, I have to go now. Can I come back later—at like *nine o'clock tonight?*"

I nodded. "Actually no. They close visiting hours at five."

"Too bad." Altan flashed me an OK sign. "I guess I'll see you some other time!"

Boy, he was a terrible actor. Maybe I'd get to make fun of him about it someday. "Sure," I said carefully. "Let me tell the guard."

Officer Milford led me beyond the Plexiglas wall to Altan for my hug. Have you ever seen the underside of a starfish—thousands of tiny sucking fingers that creep across the ocean floor? That was my body on Altan's. I gripped him with everything I had. After spending three months in jail, I thought I'd gotten used to the fear that came with an uncertain future—but here was a fresh wave of it, cresting over me, to think of Altan in so much danger.

"I'll see you tonight," he whispered in my ear. I locked my arms around his neck like I could keep him from leaving, even as Officer Milford yelled at us to let go: "That's enough, Brown! Back away or I'll revoke privileges again!"

"Let her," said Altan. "I'm not coming back."

And then he kissed me—like he had in Paris, in the courthouse, in all my dreams, and for a moment I tasted the old Altan. He was still in there under all that fear.

"You dumb slut. When are you going to learn?" Officer Milton screeched at me as she took me back to my cell. "That's another month—no visitors. How does that feel?"

Unreal. Unthreatening. Unimportant. Nothing mattered if the future had no Altan. Bedtime couldn't come fast enough.

I arrived back at my cell to find that even after some toast and a few hours to herself, Honey's condition had not improved. Her whining had become louder, almost pornographic. The second she heard the door open, she crawled out of bed—literally—on her hands and knees and caught Milford around the ankle. "Baby, I'm hurting so bad," she said.

"Honey, cut this shit out," Milford barked, shaking her leg free.

"I think I need you to teach me a lesson." Honey dragged herself up the guard's legs to bury her face in the fly of her pants. "I'll do whatever you want."

"You need a good night's sleep and some self-discipline, you wacky bitch. Get back into bed."

It was a long evening filled with Honey's dramatic screaming and punctuated only by the trips I made to the phone to call Janet so she could call Pete and tell him to call Altan. (Oy vey.) Janet didn't pick up: maybe she'd also gone away for the weekend. I tried her again after dinner, and nothing. Maybe Altan had found Pete by now? I could ask him in a few hours when we met up in the dream.

Until then, I paced the hallways, because Honey's moaning had ratcheted up thirty decibels the closer it got to bedtime, which did not help my nerves. Even *with* a Morpheum, I wasn't sure how I was going to sleep through all this. Milford came by twice to tell her to turn it down, but every time Honey realized it was working, she just moaned louder.

If Honey wasn't entirely faking her withdrawals, then she was grossly exaggerating—and I should know considering I'd been holding her hair back as she barfed the last time she didn't get enough drugs. I'd been weighing the idea of giving her the last of my Morpheum (I had squirreled away six packets in my slip-ons) to tide her over until she could get totally clean, but as the afternoon wore on, I understood that she did not need something else to get addicted to. If Altan actually left tomorrow, I'd flush the packets down the toilet. It was a shame to waste them, but enough was enough.

When it was (finally) bedtime, Honey made an elaborate display of cocooning in her covers and curling up against the wall, her eyes gleaming out of a makeshift hood she was using to block out the light. "Can I get you anything?" I asked as I was brushing my teeth—like I had access to a full inventory of teas and essential oils to take the edge off her pain.

Her voice floated out from the blanket. "You could get me some drugs."

Har har. "Would if I could," I said.

"But you can, can't you?"

In the mirror above the sink, I saw my spine stiffen.

Honey said, "I need one of your packets."

Good thing I was standing at a sink and had a completely acceptable reason to gag and spit. "Packets?" I asked my reflection after I finished rinsing my mouth.

"Yeah, I need one those Opals you carry around with you."

I inspected my pores to give myself an excuse not to turn around. "That's just sweetener."

"For what, bitch? I've watched you drink your coffee black every morning at breakfast for *months*."

Oh no.

This was bad. I couldn't have Honey finding out about Morpheum: not ever, but especially not tonight if this was going to be the last time I'd see Altan for a while. If she told Milford about my drugs, I could end up doing time for possession even if I was dismissed for Sam's death—and wouldn't that be poetic? It would be almost as bad as if Honey only *threatened* to tell Milford about the drugs, because then she'd have all kinds of reasons to blackmail me. The only thing worse than either of those scenarios would be if I gave Honey all my leftover Morpheum and she accidentally overdosed. You don't make *that* mistake twice.

But if she was dead, at least she'd be able to keep a secret.

Ugh. Honey finding out about Morpheum did *not* work with my new life goals. This was the last trip, taken only to tie up Altan's loose end, and then I was going to pull myself together, and be generally less shifty, and I would: I would. I would, starting tomorrow.

"Scoot down," I said, crawling into Honey's bunk.

"What are you doing?" she growled.

"Roll over. I'll rub your back."

"I don't need a back rub: I need your drugs!"

"I don't have drugs," I said quietly, without looking at her. It seemed rude to lie any more convincingly than I needed to. After all, Honey wasn't dumb.

She glared at me for a long moment, and then she gingerly rolled over to face the wall. I ran my nails up and down the thin material of her orange top, over the speed bumps of her spine, the xylophone of her ribs. The food in jail was bad, of course. But no one needed to be *this* thin.

When the lights went out, Honey said in the dark, "You're a real bitch, you know that?"

"I know," I replied. "I'm sorry."

THE CAMEO

Altan was waiting for me in his Bali bedroom, pacing back and forth along the foot of the bed in the doorway to the balcony. It was nighttime in his mind, so the air was cooler, the jungle smell wetter, richer, the riot of the frogs and insects almost deafening. In the meager light offered by a trio of citronella candles on a wall shelf, the orange walls looked closer to terra-cotta—or some color you'd only imagine a person having on the inside. The space was small and intimate, like the belly of a beast.

When I popped into the scene, Altan came at me with terror. He put his hands to my face and shoulders like he was making sure I was real. (I wasn't: I was just a chemical in his brain, but there was no need to remind him.) "Is it you?" he said.

"It's me."

"Prove it. Tell me something only you would know."

"You spend too much on hair products."

Even in his franticness, he rolled his eyes. "No good. Everyone knows that. Quick: where did we have breakfast the morning we went to Notre Dame?"

"Café Panis." I made sure to pronounce it like it was phonetically spelled in English (pa-ness) instead of the French *pa-nee*. "You insisted we eat there because—"

"Everyone loves panis for breakfast," we both said at the same time. It was a classic Altan joke: both stupid and crass. In Paris, it had left us in stitches, but nothing seemed funny anymore. When was the last time I'd even laughed?

"Altan, it's me. I swear."

Without warning, he kissed me roughly on the mouth. When he pulled back to study my face, I finally saw his shoulders slump in relief. "OK, you're right."

"You can tell by my kiss?"

"No. I can tell because Malcolm's too much of a homophobe to put his lips on a man—even if he were in disguise." His shadow flickered on the wall behind him when he sank down on the edge of the bed.

"I'm guessing you've been dreaming with Malcolm?"

He nodded, distracted. I was usually pretty good at reading Altan's mind in a Morpheum dream, but for once he had me stumped: his head was a flock of starlings, a formation of scattered thoughts churning randomly through a late-evening sky. "Have you seen the news?" he asked.

Whoever controlled the remote in the common area today had insisted on *Family Feud* instead of the local broadcast. "No. What happened?"

"Amara Kassis died. She had a heart attack after a fundraising dinner at the Fairhope."

"That sucks." I would have like to have voted for her. "Wasn't she young—like thirty-seven years old or something?"

"Malcolm killed her," Altan said. He looked at up at me and I recognized the truth in his eyes, felt the stillness of the air. Even the frogs paused their croaking for a full five seconds so I could register the silence. "He killed her in a dream. I saw it."

My hands flew to my open mouth. Why do people do that when they're shocked? Are they trying to keep the good feelings in or the bad news out? What is it about a barrier between your breath and the world that makes you feel like you're safe for the moment it takes for your heart to start back up? I sank next to Altan on the bed. "Show me."

"Absolutely not. You don't want this memory. It's awful."

"Altan, *show me*."

"*No.* It was— It was the worst thing I've ever seen. I was there in her mind when it happened. I heard her heart stop *from the inside*, Ness." He shook his head, trying to scare off the memories. "I'm not reliving it."

I took his hand with that top-of-the-roller-coaster grip. "Tell me, then."

He took a deep breath. "Malcolm and his Russian friend— who's actually a Ukrainian named Ivan Boyko—have spent the past few weeks drugging women at the Fairhope. The bartender must be in on it, because Malcolm never touches the drinks. I thought Malcolm was just doing it because he's an asshole. I mean, he's definitely the kind of guy who would untraceably date rape someone for fun."

"Yeah, no shit," I chimed in.

"But still, I wanted to know what he was up to in these dreams. I needed Morpheum to heist my way in, but Pete wouldn't give me any. Which was dickish, by the way," he said, sounding briefly like his usual self. "What does he even need it for?"

I didn't dare open my mouth because Altan would know I was lying if I said "I don't know."

"Anyway, Pete finally gave me some pills, and I was able to sneak into Malcolm's dream last night. When I got there, he and Ivan were torturing Kassis in her mind: tailor-made nightmare stuff. They were pretending to kill her over and over—stabbing, burning, hanging, drowning, beheading, gunshots, dog attacks. She couldn't drop out of the dream when she died, so her body was just getting more and more stressed. It was like mental waterboarding—the sensation of dying without the relief." He'd been staring through the wall, but he looked briefly at me. "All the women Malcolm had drugged before? I guess they were target practice."

I wanted to throw up. Could you throw up in a dream? If an idea was so viscerally repulsive that you would only feel better if you purged it from your (chemically realized) specter of a body, wouldn't that be a good thing?

"I tried to stop them," Altan said, getting to his feet. He was pacing again, shaking his fingers out, trying to mitigate all that pent-up energy with fidgeting. "When I figured out that they didn't want anything except for her to die, I jumped out from my hiding place with a flame-thrower—like an idiot. It was a pretty stupid weapon, in retrospect. I guess my subconscious was trying to be a badass."

"Isn't it always?" I said, trying to break the tension. It didn't work.

Altan gripped the balcony and looked into the night, visualizing a horror he could barely describe. "I thought I could kill them, but since they'd taken the new formula, they wouldn't die either, so I gave up my position for nothing. And Kassis, she— I mean, she put up a good fight, but in the end . . ." He trailed off.

My voice was hard when I said, "Altan, look at me."

He wouldn't. He kept staring into the dark.

"Altan Young, you did the best you could. You couldn't have saved her. This isn't your fault." Jeez, I was giving this speech a lot today. "*Malcolm* did this. Not you."

"I know," he said softly, but he didn't believe it. "Oh, you know what else Malcolm did? He killed Sam. He visited him in the hospital, somehow got the Morpheum in him, and then terrified him to death the same way."

Every muscle in my body froze over as my blood turned to ice. Even my heart refused to beat. "Malcolm told you he killed Sam?"

"He didn't have to: I read his mind."

Wow.

Remember that time I promised myself I'd never fall for one of Malcolm's tricks again? Remember those weeks I spent in jail hating myself and wondering if I deserved to get out? Remember that time Altan and I were supposed to be living in an apartment very much like this before I got arrested and blamed for a murder I didn't commit so Malcolm could convince the U.S. government that his pills were safe enough to use for intelligence gathering? Only he ended up turning the pills on another American citizen at the behest of a foreign national, so, really, what the actual fuck was it all for? There was nothing noble here. Not even remotely. What a waste of time and life and resources.

"I know," said Altan, returning from the balcony to his spot next to me on the bed. "I've spent the whole day trying to figure out how and why, but it defies logic. I just can't understand."

He sighed as I continued to spin my wheels in my brain. No traction was being gained: this was all such a muddy mess. "Anyway, once Kassis was gone, Malcolm came after me in a rage. I had the old Morpheum, so I woke myself up. Called his cell. He didn't pick up because he was still in the dream, but I left a message saying he has forty-eight hours to drop the case against you, or I'll spend the rest of my life bringing him down for Kassis's death."

"Did he call you back?" I said.

Altan nodded. "He told me that no one would believe me, and even if they did, he'll find a way to kill me first. Someone will spike my beer or poison my water, and then Malcolm will kill me in my sleep like Kassis. And once that happens, he will have gotten away with the most fucked-up election meddling the world has ever seen."

It was my turn to pace. All these months in a cage, but I'd never felt the urge at all. Now, in the infinite possibility of a Morpheum dream, my mind felt smaller than ever. "So you're leaving," I said.

He stood, tried to catch me in his arms. "Ness, I'm sorry—"

"No. Don't apologize." I twisted away so I could keep pacing. "Believe me, I get it. I'm not happy about it, but you can't *die*, for god's sake. What would I do then?"

No, really. What would I do? It was one thing for him to not be with me—but for him to not be in the world at all? "You have to *go*," I said, more urgently. "*Now*. Don't even tell me where."

"I wasn't going to," he said. "In case Malcolm—"

"No," I spat, shoving my palms into the planes of his chest. "Never say his name again. Now get going."

"My flight's not until morning."

"Well, you have to pack, don't you?"

"Already did."

"Did you pack more than two pairs of underwear?" I sniffed.

"You know I didn't."

The only thing worse than his leaving was prolonging the goodbye. I wanted it over with, like ripping off a Band-Aid. Like a gunshot to the temple. I braced myself against his front, my face to his sternum, my head to his heart. Everyone says they're different, but that's only in a medical sense. Sometimes they are metaphorically the same thing. I looked up into his eyes. "Will I see you again?"

He didn't say *yes* or *no*. An answer that clear-cut would have registered false. "Now that you know what happened, you can tell Pete, and then he can figure out a way to prove it and get you out of jail. Can they run toxicology on Sam? Test for Morpheum? Do some of that *CSI* shit? I don't know. *He's* the lawyer."

"He's a *divorce* lawyer."

"Whatever. He can get it done. I've done the best I could. I'm sorry it's not more."

"It was enough," I said, wrapping my arms around his neck in a hug that was a borderline strangulation. His arms went around my waist, and just like that, I was home. During all the nights with Pete in dreams, I'd tried to recreate this exact feeling of being right where I was supposed to be, and I couldn't. The sensation was unique to Altan. The results could not be replicated with a different person on the same pill. The experiment was over. My heart was made up: he was the one.

I pushed Altan down onto the bed and climbed on top of him, ravenous for his body, for his hands, the braille of his shoulder blades, the scratch of his beard—that wormhole experience of mind/body sex in a Morpheum dream. This would be our last fusion before he jetted off to some undisclosed location, and I had to go back to my regularly scheduled jail life trying to defeat Malcolm, but I was grateful to have it—to have him: awake, asleep, away, whatever. Our relationship so far had been full of endings, but we always found a way to start again. There was no such thing as "the last" of Altan. There would always be a chance to get more.

Or so I thought when I was kissing him—but then I heard a man's voice (not Altan's) say, "Ness?"

I had no words. They were gone, flung from the balcony into the jungle below.

THE
MIDOL TOUCH

"What's going on?" said Pete.

I twisted to face him, inhaling sharply, half in shock, half to stammer something stupid like, "It's not what it looks like"— something along the lines of what Altan probably told June when she came home that day. Instead, I put on the bright, awkward chirp I use when I bump into someone on the street whose name I can't remember: "Oh, hiiiiiiiiiiiii!"

Pete leaned forward, trying to peek at Altan beneath me, as if he caught me wrapping his Christmas gift. "I thought you said you weren't taking Morpheum tonight." For some reason, he looked just as embarrassed as I was. I guess stumbling on your wife straddling another man in a dream will do that. "So, is this what you dream about when you're by yourself?"

"Dude, I'm right here," Altan said, obviously annoyed.

Pete jumped and shielded his eyes with the crook of his arm, like he was looking into a nuclear blast. "Oh my god! Holy shit. I'm sorry. I didn't know."

Altan pushed himself up on one elbow so he could look into my face, which had frozen into the grimace of a week-old jack-o'-lantern. "What's *he* doing here?"

Truthfully, I didn't know. And that's when I heard a woman's voice (not mine) say, "Pete? What's going on?"

I turned again to see that Pete's face was probably mirroring my own in that he was wearing the biggest, dopiest, most shit-eating grin I'd seen from him in a while. "Oh, hi, Janet!" he sang. "What are *you* doing here?"

Great question, considering she was wearing a negligée.

Oh god. I needed to lie down—and I was already lying down because I was asleep! I needed to lie *even more down*. Had Pete been giving *my* Morpheum out to other parties? Was I even allowed to be mad consider I'd gotten caught with my lover as well? What were the rules when it came to intellectual cuckolding, or was I writing them where I stood?

Would a foursome somehow make this all OK?

Wait. *No.*

Janet whipped up a bathrobe to cover herself: not a sexy one, but one in flannel plaid, like it came from L.L.Bean. (Someday I'd get out of the Pacific Northwest and I'd never look at plaid again.) She coughed, awkwardly. "Hey, Ness."

It was a shock, to see her in my place. I felt jealousy that was not warranted but still very much real and sharp and hot.

"Wait," Altan said, his brain finally getting up to speed. He pushed himself up completely so that he was leaning back on both hands. We were practically nose to nose. "Are you *fucking your lawyers*?" His voice was laced with disgust. I'd found the one thing in the whole world he considered gross.

"No?" I squeaked. "Just Pete. I didn't know . . . about Janet."

Like a bubble popping, Altan disappeared beneath me. He'd Nightcrawled somewhere else.

My heart was cramping from squeezing too hard, trying to hold on to two men before letting one go. I looked at Pete, at the decade we'd spent together and where it had led us and all the times I'd loved and hated him. I saw our relationship flash before my eyes like they say happens before you die: the bar we "met" in and his law school graduation and our wedding and my first day at WellCorp when he took me out to dinner and the time we went camping and I thought a raccoon was a bear and all the Sunday mornings I watched him read books with a cup of coffee, thinking I had everything I needed.

It all came and went in a blitz of aquamarine light that flashed between the mirrors of our eyes. "Ness," he said. "You should—"

Only Janet heard the rest. I was already gone.

It was snowing wherever Altan was: total whiteout, blizzard conditions. The snow fell wild and frantic, hurled by a wind that tore across my face. Fat, wet flakes splattered against my cheeks and caught in my eyelashes. The air was so cold it burned to breathe, but still I arrived, screaming, "Altan!"

There was nothing here: no plants or trees. Just a howling, desolate white for miles, the kind of craggy Antarctic bleakness penguins like to winter in. I magicked a full snowsuit to keep me from freezing to death. "*Altan!*"

Through a whorl of snow, Altan's back appeared not twenty feet away. The wind tore through his black hair, making a stark contrast against the white. Pushing against the wind, I circled around to face him. His height allowed him to look over my head, out into the blank.

"I don't want you here!" Altan hollered. "Go away!"

"Turn the storm off so we can talk!" I felt astoundingly, even suspiciously calm considering I'd just gotten caught red-handed cheating on my husband and my lover by both of them at the same time. The night Pete left me, I was so ashamed by what I'd done, but I wasn't now. I'd done what I had to survive long enough to make the choice I made. Altan would see this. I knew he would. There was nothing we couldn't understand in a Morpheum dream.

Altan quieted the wind a fraction so we could speak at a reasonable volume. "Why didn't you tell me?" he said.

"How was I supposed to? The guards listen to the phones during visiting hours. They read all the outgoing mail. I couldn't tell you I was taking Morpheum without telling everyone I was taking Morpheum."

"So that you withheld the fact that you were taking the equivalent of nocturnal ecstasy with your husband *purely* for logistical reasons?"

Altan already knew the answer to that was *no*. He read it on the wind. "I was afraid you wouldn't understand," I said—a weak excuse considering that I was *now* banking on his remembering a time when he'd also been so desperate for comfort that he'd sought it from someone he wasn't supposed to. What was the thing Pete had told me in our *Pride and Prejudice* dream? "Love is like water," I stammered. "You need to drink it. And then you pee it out—"

"What are you talking about?"

"You *need* it, Altan!" I said. *That* was the point Pete had been trying to make. "You need to have it. I couldn't have it with you, so I had to have it with someone else."

Altan barked *Ha!* into the snow. "You think *I'm* not lonely—that there aren't people out here I want to sleep with . . . and pee on . . . or whatever?"

"I don't know," I said, truly taken aback. "Are there?"

He turned his head but not before I caught the other woman flash in his eyes. "Who is she?"

"No one you know."

"Do you love her?"

"You don't need to love people to fuck them."

"Just ask the girl you cheated on June with."

Don't know why I said that. It was irrelevant. But something in me wanted to wound him, to let a little blood out of him so he wouldn't be so strong.

"Don't be cheap," spat Altan.

"Then don't be a hypocrite!"

"Listen to yourself!" he screamed. "You don't get to cheat on me because I made a mistake when I cheated on my wife. Sins aren't transferrable. You can't just do this to people!"

"Altan, I didn't do this *to* you. I just . . . did it."

I saw his temple flare where he gritted his teeth. "How many times? Don't lie: you know I can tell."

"Countless."

He nodded, processing this. "Was it good?"

"Yes."

"Do you still love him?"

"I love him differently. Pete is my past. You are my future."

"But *do you still love him*?"

What was the point of lying? "Yes," I said. "I always will."

Altan turned away from me and I scurried in front of him. I bit into my mittens, ripped them off with my teeth, and tossed them into the snow so I could put my cold hands to his cold face, feel the frost that had gotten caught in his beard.

"Do you know what I dreamed about when I was alone?" I said, looking into his eyes. "Bali. I dreamed about our apartment together, cooking you dinner, growing flowers in your garden. I dreamed of the beach and the sand and the way you would taste when you came home and how you would feel inside me. I dreamed of you in the sun. That's all I wanted. I couldn't have it, and I made do so I wouldn't go crazy."

The wind died, and snowflakes froze mid-fall to hang like baubles from the sky. I heard Altan perfectly as he said, "You wanted to make sure I was the one."

"Of course, I did," I said, taking his hands. *See?* I knew he'd understand. "I was scared that what we had was all a trick of Morpheum. But it wasn't. You and me: it's legit."

"No shit, Sherlock!" he bellowed. His breath puffed great clouds into the cold air as he backed away from me into the blankness of the landscape, shaking his head. "You were right about Morpheum. It's a curse. Or karmic retribution—"

"Altan, no," I begged. This was happening so fast. I couldn't even process. "What we have—"

"What *do* we have?" he said. "Nothing."

"We'll always have Paris."

He stared at me. His gaze was *freezing*.

"Come *on*. Didn't you ever see *Casablanca*?" I smiled like my teeth had the power to induce spontaneous forgiveness.

"You can't movie quote your way out of this."

There I was bleeding out, empty-handed, still smiling for some reason, like I couldn't accept that this wouldn't be OK. "You said it yourself. We're messy, right? That's our thing."

"Not anymore. This mess is too big. I gotta go finish packing."

"No, Altan, wait—"

No one should have their heart broken in a Morpheum dream, because it hurts like hell for everyone involved. Maybe Morpheum *was* a curse, because I finally understood how Pete felt when I crushed him in our apartment all those weeks ago. Everything was my fault. Everything I put my hands on turned into a bloody mess. Me and my Midol touch.

Shit.

THE COLD DISH

My hands were flat on the metal door of our cell before my eyes were even fully open: that's how fast I sprang out of bed to try and bang it down. "Officer Milford!" I screamed, pounding on the door. The hallway outside was dark, cast in the greenish glow from EXIT signs spaced evenly down the hall. A chorus of muffled curses returned—*hey bitch what you doing do you know what fucking time it is shit*—but none were as loud as mine as I shrieked, "Goddammit, Milford! Open this door!"

Officer Milford ambled up without urgency. "Brown, what the shit is your problem?" she asked through the glass, rubbing an eye with her fist.

"I need to make a phone call." I was sweating; I felt it pooling on my upper lip. Altan was leaving, and I had no idea where he was going, and he couldn't—he just couldn't—get on that plane. "Please let me go to the phones. Wait! Better yet! I need to use your cell." I dropped my voice in an attempt to convey the gravity of the situation. "Something happened."

"Nothing happened, Brown." She yawned. "You were dreaming."

"No shit, I was dreaming! That's how I *know*."

The curse was probably ill advised, because Officer Milford rolled her eyes and turned to go. I pounded on the door with the flat of my hand one last time. "I'll do anything."

She came to a full stop, *then* turned to face the window and leered through the chicken wire. *Anything?* she mouthed.

The look on my face must have registered that even in my desperation, I had my limits. Officer Milford flicked her chin up and made a noise like *hmph*. "Go back to bed," she said, and then she went back to wherever she spent the night.

My hands stank of blood when I turned and sat on the cement floor—that penny smell of dirty metal. Honey's eyes were open, but they were glazed in the way of the flu-ridden. I whispered, "Sorry for waking you."

"Fuck you," she replied weakly. I guess I'd feel the same way if someone got me up in the middle of drug withdrawals. She rolled over and faced the wall, curling up like a pill bug.

I leaned against the door and thought about Altan, racking my brain to remember some snippet he might have told me about where he was going. *You should have read his mind, stupid,* I scolded myself. I should have done a lot of things. Apologizing would have been a good place to start, but I'd tried that with Pete, and it doesn't work. That's the thing about knowing something's bad and then doing it anyway: your apology means nothing when you're only sorry you got caught.

Still, I should have given Altan one, just so I would have given him *something*.

Honey spent the rest of the night whining, if only to be obnoxious. Milford didn't come back to tell her to shut up: she'd already given us enough attention for one night, and I didn't feel like I had any right to tell Honey to keep it down, considering my own outburst. So I just had to sit there and endure it, Honey staring at me the whole time, like she was casting a spell. Making eye contact while someone moans in a non-sexual way is definitely not a fun way to spend the night, especially when your boyfriend is literally fleeing the country and you're powerless to stop him.

When the door to my cell unlocked for breakfast, I hauled myself to my feet and sprinted to the phones, thrilled to be rid of Honey, ready to win my man back like they do in the movies. Ripping the phone from its hook, I dialed Altan, praying I'd be connected by some Hollywood miracle.

But the call didn't go through.

It didn't go through seventeen times.

Dropping the phone, I flew back to my cell, frantic for a new plot, refusing to admit defeat. *I can fix this*, I thought, skittering down the hall in my slip-ons. I could get hold of a cell phone—maybe Pete's, if he'd let me!—and text Altan, only Pete wouldn't be here until Monday, and that was too late. A letter! I could write Altan a letter. Maybe Milford could get me a courier if I asked nicely. Sure. Yes. But first, paper! I had some in my—

. . . Bunk.

My stuff had been tossed, the mattress pulled from the bedframe and thrown to the floor with my blanket. My toothbrush was in the toilet. Even the paint samples Altan sent me were scattered everywhere. There wasn't much else to destroy, honestly. Whoever had done this had been thorough in laying waste the few things I had.

Honey's voice came from the corner behind me. "As you can see"—she stepped forward, pushed our door closed—"I couldn't find your drugs anywhere."

"Honey, what the hell?" I said, trying to make myself look tough even as I recognized how untough I was. Not against Honey, who, for all her smallness, came toward me taut, teeth bared, like a weasel. Even her hands made claws at her sides.

"If they're not in your bunk, then they must with you."

There was no persuading her that there were no drugs: we were too far gone to keep playing that game. "OK, you want the drugs?" I said pulling an Opal from my chest pocket and throwing it behind me onto her bunk. I was hoping she'd dive for it so I could get outside and find a guard. "Here. Happy?"

"No. I want *all* the drugs."

"That's all I have." I put my hands in front of me like I was surrendering. My shoulder blades hit the railing of my bunk. Why was I lying? I should have just given the packets to her. I was done with Morpheum—for *real* this time. I know I'd said that before, but now I meant it. "We don't need drugs," I told her.

Honey's lips snarled even higher so I could see her sad, yellow teeth. "Bitch, you have *got* to stop jerking people around."

I only had enough time to whole-heartedly agree before she socked me in the stomach. I wish I could report the moves she used, the kinds of uppercuts and roundhouse kicks or whatever. But I know nothing about fighting: I'd never thrown a punch before, so I didn't even know where to begin defending myself. Even though I had weight on her, she'd known since the day we met that I wasn't a killer.

The only thing I remember clearly was that she managed to cram me into the bottom bunk where I couldn't slink away, and then she focused a lot of her wrath at my face with her fist. The slapping wetness of the sound reminded me of a butcher's cleaver. For some reason, I felt justified in knowing she was overselling her withdrawals: no one could be that sick and still have enough energy to beat me so thoroughly.

My face was messing up her knuckles *so bad*.

Her hands checked me perfunctorily as I lay there moaning: she riffled through the chest pocket of my top and the cuffs of my socks. She even gave a businesslike inspection of my underwear before she figured out the secret compartments in my shoes.

Once she took the Morpheum, she threw me on my mattress on the floor and kicked me in her canvas slip-ons. It would have hurt more if she'd been wearing real shoes—but as it was, it still hurt like hell. Eventually, she must have gotten tired, because the beating stopped. I lay there waiting for something to happen, drifting in a semi-consciousness that at least took the sting out of losing Altan.

#silverlining.

How much time went by? No clue. Eventually, I heard Officer Milford's boots on the cement—and then I felt her hands on my face, a penlight in my eyes. "Brown?" she said. It hurt when she shook me. "What happened here?"

Even as my whole body felt like it was being extruded through a meat grinder, I didn't want Honey to get in trouble. I roofied her, she beat the shit out of me. In the eyes of the universe, we were square. "I put Honey's toothbrush in the toilet," I whispered.

There was the crackle of a radio, and Milford said, "I need a gurney in 482. *Yes, again.* Tell Brown's visitor she's unavailable."

"Who's the visitor?" I whispered. Was it Altan? Maybe he'd woken up and realized he wanted to forgive me. Maybe he was standing outside the jail, hoisting a boom box over his head, blasting "In Your Eyes." Or maybe it was Pete, with a dozen roses, confirming that he wanted me to come home. Or maybe it was Idris Elba, naked, on a silver platter. Was it St. Peter? Or the Devil? Or just some secular version of a personified death itself? Is this what it felt like to die or was I being too dramatic?

"Hang on, Brown." Her voice was nicer to me than it had ever been. "Just stay with me."

But I couldn't.

THE INFIRMARY

The nurse who was taking my blood pressure when I opened my eyes ("opened" being kind of a stretch considering one of them was swollen almost completely closed) startled when I grabbed her hand. "What year is it?" I croaked. "How long have I been here?" *Long enough to sleep through my entire jail sentence?*

She frowned and checked her watch. "You got here ten minutes ago."

Worst. Day. Ever.

The nurse fussed over me, filling out a chart. Everything hurt. Even my toenails. It felt like my entire body was on the first day of its period. "How am I doing?"

"I think you got lucky," she said.

I did not feel lucky. "Can I sleep?"

"Better stay awake in case you have a concussion."

Call The Hague: I was officially being tortured. Having to cope with the loss of my husband, my boyfriend, and my drugs *awake* while alone in a room with a decent bed for the first time in weeks? Cruel.

The nurse pinned my eyes open like they did in *A Clockwork Orange*. I'm kidding: she didn't do that. But somehow even without an ocular speculum, I managed to stay awake for as long as she needed to determine I was OK, and then she let me lie down. I slept like the dead, motionless, timeless, formless—just like my future. There were no dreams: only darkness. A total void.

And then someone was poking me rudely with an index finger in the side of my arm. "Wake up, Brown," said Officer Milford. She was standing over me, undoing the cuffs that attached me to the bed. "It's time for you to go."

I didn't need to inspect my body to know there were bruises big as cabbages all over. I was too weak to cry. "Let me sleep just a few more hours."

"No can do. Nurse says you're fine." She gripped my wrist so I could pull myself up to sitting and put my bare feet on the cold floor.

"Please," I begged into her beady little eyes, looking for whatever compassion she saved for people in the infirmary. Maybe it was reserved just for Honey. "You have to give me another cellmate. I can't go back to sharing with Honey. She'll kill me."

Milford eyed the nurse, who silently walked out the door that led to the hall. I got the feeling that this was something they did often to ensure plausible deniability.

Milford looked out the window one last time before she came back to the bed and grabbed me by the front of my orange top. (Oh *god*, did it hurt.) "You listen the fuck up, Brown," she hissed. "Honey showed me what you had in your shoe, and if you don't want to end up back here with a possession charge, you keep your mouth shut about whatever you think she and I have going on, OK? Tell *anyone* and I will turn you in myself."

I nodded, shallow and quick, because I certainly didn't want any retribution. And then something she said struck me as odd: "What do you mean 'back' here?"

Removing her fist from my top, she smoothed her uniform and eyed me one last time so I'd remember which one of us had the power to screw the other one over. "Charges were dropped," she said. "You're going home."

She opened the door to the hallway and offered me a grand "after you" gesture with her arm as I sat there, dumbfounded, afraid to follow. "Dipshit, I don't have all day!"

I jumped out of bed and limped after her as fast as I could, following her through a half dozen hallways until we ended up at the locker room I remembered from my intake. Milford checked a clipboard and found the locker that held the clothes I'd been arrested in. As she unlocked it, she said, "Honey pretty much messed up all your shit, so I figured you didn't need to go back to your cell."

She said this like it was no big whoop that I was *miraculously going home for no apparent reason.* I was too busy stripping down to complain: surely there was a clerical error. They would figure it out any minute now, so I dressed in haste.

When Officer Milford handed me my backpack, I realized that I still had my passport. If I could just get through that door before they figured out I wasn't supposed to, I'd Uber straight to the Canadian border. "Check the contents," Milford said. "Make sure it's all there."

It was all there: my phone, my wallet, my camera (hello, lover), the stack of sepia pictures Altan had given me, secured by its velvet ribbon—like the airline had lost my bag and was only just returning it to me now: three months later.

Milford handed me a pen. "Sign here, and here—initial here. And here. Name and date here." I couldn't tell if I was being released or applying for a mortgage. But finally, it was done. My boots felt foreign after not wearing them for so long, but by the time I headed for the door, I was starting to feel like a person—a person who owned things like underwear and a camera and personal dignity. Probably, I was dead. Honey had likely killed me. This was what Heaven felt like.

Or this was a really sick joke. But when Milford swiped her ID to get me through the last checkpoint, the card reader beeped, and I heard a click, and Milford turned the handle and pulled to show me a waiting room identical to any government waiting room known to man: linoleum flooring and molded plastic chairs, phones ringing off the hook. More officers shuffling more papers. Small kids chasing each other, their moms rolling their eyes. It looked so normal and real. I'd never seen anything so beautiful.

"Take care of yourself, Ms. Brown," Milford said.

Oh. So I was *Ms.* Brown now that I was a civilian. Fine. I didn't care. Hopefully, we'd never see each other again. In the doorway, before I turned to go, I said, "Take care of Honey."

"I will," she said seriously, holding out her hand. I didn't want to shake it; she didn't deserve my esteem. She deserved to have the shit reported out of her for abusing her position, but I had enough battles to fight, and I wanted Honey looked after, so I shook.

"Wait—what's her real name?" I asked as Milford started to shut the door behind me.

She stuck her foot in the crack as the alarm squealed in protest. "Why do you want to know?"

"I want to put some money in her canteen account to say sorry."

"Pretty generous of you considering she beat you senseless."

"I had it coming. Can I please have her name?"

She gave it to me as the door alarm kicked the volume up a notch, and then her foot disappeared and the door hissed shut.

In the lobby, Pete was waiting for me, no suit. He had on jeans, a button-front, and his Pumas, and it was then that I realized I had no idea if it was still the weekend or if he'd taken the day off. I didn't know what dimension this was, if it was real, or what was in the white Coffee Talk cup he was holding in a cardboard sleeve.

Compelled by nerves, I rushed toward him, stumbling as I did because I was trembling so hard. He caught me before I went down and held me to him, one-armed. Had I ever stopped to feel how strong and warm he was?

He pulled back to look at me, horrified. "What happened to your face?"

"Cellmate jumped me for the Opals."

"Are you OK?" he muttered, sweeping my hair behind my ear. It felt matted with something—probably blood.

"Depends. Is that for me?" I pointed to the cup.

"Here. Americano. Still hot." He pressed the drink into my hands. It *was* still hot, hot enough to burn the roof of mouth, but it was the pain that let me know I was very much awake, and I was getting out of here with a real cup of coffee.

That's when I started to cry.

THE
SADDEST LINES

As much as I whine about the weather in Seattle, nowhere is there a summer more spectacular: skies are blue for a full two months and the temperature rarely cracks eighty. Shuffling after Pete to our car, I felt like a mole person squinting against the light. He handed me his sunglasses, because he was a gentleman.

The smells were the best: even better than a Pete dream. Never mind the briny seaweed scent of Puget Sound: layered on top were the piroshkies and flowers on sale at Pike's Place. There was coffee and weed and the fug of bus exhaust. I wanted all of it. I wanted to stand there like someone addled and just huff the air and squint at the sky, but Pete insisted I get in the car, which smelled best of all: road trips to Portland and burnt coffee. Pete and I climbed in and clicked on our seat belts, like we were going to Costco.

"Well." He was grinning. "Happy Independence Day."

"Is it really?"

"No. It's July 7." He started the car and pulled into traffic. No one threw on a siren and followed us. We were just . . . leaving.

If it was July 7, that meant Altan had already left yesterday. I must have slept in the infirmary. I noted this scientifically, knowing I would be more upset about it later once I got past the shock.

Frankly, I was grateful to be keeping it together as much as I was. "So that's it? It's over?" I asked.

"Yeah. The prosecutor dropped the case."

"But *why?*"

Pete shrugged. "It doesn't matter. Maybe they realized there wasn't enough evidence. Janet says it happens all the time."

I wanted to ask about Janet—just as soon as I figured out if Pete had finally gotten ahold of Altan. Either option involved opening the door to a very awkward conversation.

"Speaking of *awkward*," Pete said—even though we hadn't been—"how about the other night, eh? Boy, *that* was weird."

I nearly spat my coffee across the dashboard. "Smooth segue."

"Well, I thought one of us should bring it up. Did you and Altan get to talk?"

"Um, yeah, it . . . didn't go well." I loved feeling numb from shock! Shock was my friend! "Did you get to have sex with Janet?"

Pete's face turned the color of salmon. "I can't believe we're having this conversation."

"Add that under *getting out of jail* on the list of things I didn't think I'd be doing today. But seriously, did you?"

"Um, yeah," he said, blushing even more crimson. "We worked it out."

Well, at least one of us was in for a happy ending. "So how did you two . . . ?"

". . . end up taking drugs together? Probably the same way you and Altan did." Pete was grinning again, and I couldn't tell if he was happy or embarrassed or both. I listened as I dug in my backpack for my phone. "Janet and I have been spending a lot of time together strategizing your defense. She was getting pretty upset that you wouldn't just take the deal, because it made so much sense, so

I took a pill with her the other night so I could show her what it did, and things kind of escalated quickly."

Once I found my phone, I plugged it into the charger Pete kept in the car. "The other day when you said you weren't going to take your Opal, I thought she and I could meet up again," he said. "But I should have maybe anticipated that you'd change your mind. That was stupid. I'm sorry I didn't think of it."

"Honest mistake," I said. Most mistakes were, but that didn't stop them for being any less devastating.

When my phone finally turned on, there was a text from Altan at the top of a list of dozens of unread messages. Attached to it was a screenshot of a text exchange between him and Malcolm:

Malcolm: *I got everything sorted. It'll be done tomorrow. Are we good?*

Altan: *As long as you leave her alone, we're good. I'm leaving the country tonight. Anything you need to say before I disappear?*

Malcolm: *No. Have a shitty life.*

Altan: *Fuck you, too.*

So Altan's bribe had worked: he'd traded his silence for my freedom. He'd gotten me out of jail at tremendous personal expense, only to find out I'd cheated on him in a dream with Pete.

I punched in a reply—*Hey*—as in "Hey, I'm out of jail" or "Hey, I love you" or "Hey, don't leave me. Not now. Not when my life is finally on track and I owe you ten thousand apologies and we owe it to ourselves to try again: for real, awake." But the message bounced back. The number was invalid. Altan had not only left but was *gone*.

"So you and Altan are . . ."

"Done, apparently." I sighed. "Did you talk to him by chance?"

"No. He left me, like, three hundred emails the other day. When I tried to call him back, his phone was disconnected. Is he OK?"

"I'm sure he's fine," I said, debating whether or not I should tell Pete what Altan had seen Malcolm do to Amara Kassis. Justice would at some point need to be served, but I could handle that on my own without dragging Pete into it or putting Altan at even more risk. Pete was ignorant, and Altan was far away, and I was keeping a border between their well-being and mine. This was the most rational decision I'd made in months.

"So, I have a surprise," Pete said, pulling into the portico of a large hotel. "I hope it goes over better than my anniversary present."

Some kind of footman opened my door. The mat on the polished marble floor read THE FAIRHOPE. Maybe it was because I wasn't used to drinking coffee, but suddenly I wanted to throw up.

Pete handed his keys to the valet. "I thought you deserved some luxury after jail. Grab your backpack. Let's have a drink to celebrate your release."

"No!" I said a little too quickly as we shuffled through the revolving doors. What if we ran into Malcolm or Ivan or whatever bartender was spiking the drinks? "No, I don't need a drink. I have my coffee. Just take me home."

"Well, we came all this way." (Ten minutes in traffic wasn't exactly the Oregon Trail.) "So let's sit a minute." Pete gestured to a velvet fainting couch that was situated just inside the entry—appropriate, because I felt like I was going to pass out. Two tremendous staircases arced upward into what I assumed was the main lobby. They weren't that tall, but still the idea of climbing them alone gave me vertigo.

"What are we doing?" I asked, even though I already knew. I knew with the instinct of dogs as they are ferried to the vet.

Pete took my hand. I swear his voice broke as if to tell me his heart was doing the same when he said, "Ness, you can't come home."

This was it: the *coup de grace*. We both knew it needed to be done, and still I panicked to see the sword in his hands. "I already got you a room," he added, pulling a key card from his pocket as I registered his use of pronouns (Seattle is all about pronouns): he got *me* a room. Not *us*. "It's super nice. I saw it when I brought your bag up. Top floor. Great view. Your eyes deserve a treat."

Oh, no! My stupid, insatiable eyes! "Come up with me," I begged. "We can have a drink upstairs."

He shook his head and kissed my knuckles just as he had when he was Mister Darcy. "It's not me you want." His voice was so gentle. "I felt it in the dream."

"No," I said. "Just . . . no." Even though he was right, that didn't mean I had to believe it. I could pretend he was wrong—just like people who maintained the earth was flat. I could overcome my mind. I could love him again. If I asked him to let me, he would. I knew he would. But even so, I felt, in a way that was stronger than knowing, if we didn't die now, our marriage would only kill us slower.

Pete drew me into him and held me close. *Keep squeezing*, I thought. *Just put me out of my misery.* "You can have the apartment if you want it, OK? I can move out."

"No," I said. "It'll take you forever to move your books. Besides, it's better if I get a new place."

"No offense, but can you afford a new place?"

Oh, right. I blew all my savings in Paris. "Aren't I supposed to get like a hundred bucks or something when I get out of jail?"

"That's only if you're convicted," said Pete, taking out his wallet. He had cash in there, lots of it, like the Boy Scout in him had been expecting this. (*Be prepared.*) He handed me a stack of bills. "Call me tomorrow. We'll figure something out."

I nodded, wiping my nose on the back of my hand. "OK." This was the second time we'd talked divorce. The first time I'd had Altan to soften the blow, but now I was alone.

"OK," said Pete. He stood to go. He was always standing to go. I was always wishing he wouldn't. My voice was rubbery as I tried to joke. "I can't believe we're ending in a hotel lobby. It feels cheap."

"Nothing's cheap at the Fairhope," he quipped. "And besides, it's only our marriage that's ending. We still love each other. Do you know how *rare* that is?"

Funny how he hadn't asked if I still loved him. He knew—just like I knew that this was the way we were meant to be. All that Morpheum was good for something in the end.

He leaned down and kissed me for what I knew would be the last time. It was like blowing out a candle, soft and quick, a whisper and then an end, the flame gone, a thin ghost of smoke in the place where it used to be warm. "I've seen a lot of marriages end," he told me, the knuckle of his index finger lingering under my chin. "This isn't a bad way to go."

I don't know how long I sat there after he left—long enough for me to finish my coffee. Long enough for me to forget I'd finished the coffee and had to endure the embarrassment of drinking from an empty cup: three times. Long enough for the doorman to ask me, "Miss, are you alright?"

Oh, don't worry, I said, showing him my keycard. *I'm a guest.*

"You should go up then," he replied delicately. "You look like you've had a hard day."

This was code for, *You look like you just got beaten up in jail—and you need a proper shower.* Part of me wanted to get offended, but the other part of me knew he was right. And considering I'd just gotten my heart broken twice and my ass handed to me by someone who weighed a hundred pounds less than he did, I wasn't in the mood to fight.

SUNDAY, JULY 7

Dear Charlie,

This feels like a Dear John letter, and it doesn't help that you have a dude's name, but whatever. By the time you read this, I'll be gone. I broke my lease. Packed my bag. Dumped all my shit on the curb for the homeless guys to fight over. It was so tempting to set it all on fire, but the last thing I need is to be arrested for arson when I just spent the last of my savings on a plane ticket.

This is the diary I kept when I was on Morpheum. It has everything I know about the drug—all my notes and details. You could probably contact some of my old patients in here and see if they'd be interviewed for your story. I mean, the ones that you didn't already try to talk to. Maybe when you tell them what you know, they'll be more anxious to talk.

I only ask that you please don't reveal me as a source. Believe me when I tell you that my life would be at stake if you did. After what I did, I wouldn't blame you if you didn't care. But please care. You're too good to break bad, and the White House needs someone of your integrity.

I'm sorry I ruined your plan for "Inside the Mind of a Traitor." I know you wanted to report the Morpheum dream firsthand, and it was shitty that I shot you in the face the minute you got me into Malcolm's brain—especially considering all the work you put in to help me get there in the first place. I don't blame you for being pissed, and yes, I got all fifty-seven of your hate texts. But I don't regret protecting you from what happened in there. Now you know why I couldn't sleep at your apartment: I didn't want you waking me up. I didn't want you coming back in the dream. I didn't want both of us to get screwed.

For reasons that I can't explain, I am unable to tell you what happened in the dream. All I can do is *strongly encourage you* to make sure someone does a thorough toxicology test on Kassis. Compare it to Sam Stevens's autopsy. Find out bartender Austin's last name. See if you can get footage of Kassis getting a drink from Malcolm, or being close enough to smell him. I think you'll figure out the rest.

I'm leaving you with a pretty crappy to-do list. That's sort of what I'm famous for: when shit gets too hard I bounce harder. Just so you know, I'm leaving the country and treating myself to a life that doesn't completely revolve around women and drugs—even though there are some women in my life who aren't awful. You, for example, are pretty damn cool.

(In fact, you'll read how cool I think you are in this journal. I left it unredacted, so you could maybe take pleasure in knowing I had a massive and borderline-pathetic crush on you.)

In addition to the epic instructions, I'm sorry for leaving without a proper face-to-face goodbye, but it's for the best. I should say, it's the best for me. If I had come to you in person, I'm not sure I would have left. Maybe we'll see each other again someday. But if we don't, good luck bringing down Malcolm; that dickhead deserves all the worst things. And all the best to you. I hope you have a really nice life.

A

FOUR
MONTHS
LATER

THE CHANCE MEETING

After weeks of brilliant, climatic orgasms that constitute a Pacific Northwest summer, autumn rolls in like a cold, gross fart. The foliage is spectacular for about two weeks, but once it all comes down, leaves the size of bear paws papier-mâché the sidewalk, making it squish when you walk. The city smells like damp cardboard, and the sun starts dipping out at four. Sure, it wasn't jail, but Seattle in the fall is just about as cheerful.

It was November, and I was at a party on Capitol Hill with Daryl, formerly known as Coffeehouse Crush. In my WellCorp days when I went to Coffee Talk in the mornings to avoid my desk, I used to get a kick out of Daryl's Irish accent as he rang up my Americano. Now that we worked together as baristas, I was learning the hard way that Daryl was deeply, profoundly boring.

Why? I couldn't put my finger on it. Maybe it was because he was in his twenties, or he was stupid, or he'd never been to jail. Maybe it was because I didn't have the drugs I needed to detect the secret magic of his mind. Regardless, Daryl had no life skills and even less imagination—but he did have friends who threw parties in expensive, cramped apartments, so there I was standing in front of someone's couch with a lukewarm La Croix, wedged into a clump of people prattling on about obscure bands. It was . . . fine.

Sure, I could have gone home to my crappy apartment a forty-five-minute bus ride away. But my Craig's List roommate had a boyfriend who liked to scream racial slurs during sex. Which was wholly unenjoyable: for her mostly (I imagined), but also for me. It was better to wait for them to fall asleep before I went home.

It had been four months since I'd been released from jail, and I confess I hadn't landed as elegantly into life as I'd hoped I would. Coffee Talk wasn't awful considering I had unlimited access to espresso, but the pay wasn't as good as the corporate world. I can't believe I used to hate my desk job: now, I'd give anything to sit on my butt all day and take bathroom breaks whenever I wanted. Alas, the arrest record on my background check makes me *persona non grata* at any company that offers dental benefits, so I take what I can get.

At least at Coffee Talk, I didn't have to say the words "pivot table"—and they let me display my photos on the walls: in *frames*. I'd even sold a few, which was enough to keep the dream of travel photography alive, even as I went home every night to scrub coffee grounds out of my nails in the shared hall bathroom.

When I got out of jail, I spent a few nights at the Fairhope, trying to figure out what the hell I was going to do. The room Pete had procured for me was stately and boringly decorated to be some rich white dude's wet dream. I loved it. I loved it *so* much. The toilet was in its own little room, and the shower was private and pre-stocked with my conditioner, courtesy of Pete.

There was also an assortment of my favorite junk foods imported from Bartell's, and next to that was a white paper sandwich bag placed upside down over something. When I lifted it, I found a single blood-red rose in full bloom, cut short and placed in a water glass—one last gift from Pete. I put the paper bag back over the flower, marveling at his final communique: my soon-to-be ex-husband would still protect me if I needed it. He really was marvelous.

I spent the night crying and getting drunk off the bottles in the minibar (I didn't trust anything that came in a glass), emailing Altan and telling him all the things I should have said before—like how sorry I was and how much I loved him. I showered (twice) and took a long hot bath which didn't do much to cure all the aches Honey had inflicted on me, but it still felt good.

After one of the greatest nights of sleep in my life, I woke the next morning and went immediately to Bartell's, where I bought a box of legal-size envelopes, a ream of computer paper, and a hundred stamps with the cash Pete gave me. In my room, I spent the next three hours writing "Malcolm Jacobs poisoned Amara Kassis and Sam Stevens with a WellCorp drug called Morpheum" on separate sheets of paper. I stuffed them in envelopes and addressed them to the medical examiner's office—all by hand, so they'd know I meant it.

Then, I found Honey on Facebook using her real name. A few Google searches later, I had her uncle's address, and I dispatched Child Protective Services over there immediately. I told them I'd call every day to follow up until they could guarantee Honey's daughter was being taken care of. Anonymous tips were my jam.

I met Pete for coffee; we found me my Craig's List apartment. The divorce was quick, and he deducted Janet's fees from my alimony at my request. Between the support from him and my meager Coffee Talk paycheck, I was getting by. Not enough to get a therapist (honestly!) but I'd started going to Narcotics Anonymous meetings, and that helped me get my head on straight.

A month after I got out of jail, *The New York Times* released an intimately reported story by a woman named Charlotte Goodman, which detailed Malcolm's very stupid #ginception dealings: how he was courting governments and arms dealers on Instagram and meeting with them at the Fairhope to drug random people and demonstrate how Morpheum worked.

The story was pretty controversial, first because it was generally outrageous (footage of Altan's testimony at my pretrial hearing resurfaced on the evening news, which broke my heart), and second because it couldn't be corroborated with traditional fact-checking. But when the medical examiner found a Sam Stevens-size Morpheum dosage in Amara Kassis's toxicology report (thanks to seventy-four mailed-in tips from a single anonymous source), people started paying attention.

Investigations were opened, the bartender at the Fairhope got arrested and confessed to taking *one hundred thousand dollars* (!!!) to make ice with Morpheum-laced water before turning on Malcolm, who is now in jail. (Ironically, the judge used me as precedent to refuse bail.) The courts are *super* backed up, so it looks like he has a long wait until his trial.

I hope Malcolm cellmate is *insufferable*.

I hope his coffee is *awful*.

I hope he really *hates* pooping in front of people.

I honestly wish him every loneliness and dehumanization that comes from being incarcerated. People say you should forgive and forget—but why do that when the very thought of your enemy getting his comeuppance fills you with so much pleasure? I think about Malcolm in jail at least once an hour, and I smile every time.

It's ridiculous that the scandal went unbelieved for so long simply because it was so unbelievable: why would the CEO of a major pharmaceutical company sell lethal drugs to foreign governments to meddle in U.S. elections—on *Instagram*? What was Malcolm thinking? Of course, the answer was: he wasn't. Malcolm never thought, because he never had to. He'd spent his entire life under the assumption that his money and his privilege made him both reputable and untouchable. In *The New York Times* story, Charlie Goodman coined the word dubris—a portmanteau of douchebag and hubris, the excessive pride of rich, white guys. I couldn't be happier that this exists now.

WellCorp offered me a very, *very* large sum of money both for my pain and suffering at Malcolm's hands, and to agree I'd never talk about Morpheum in public again. I happily took it. After all, the facts were out, Malcolm was in jail—no one needed me chirping on about WellCorp in order to sink it. (WellCorp was sinking itself.) I needed the money more than I needed the attention, so now I was waiting for my check, which would arrive by Christmas in order for the deal to be valid. If the money didn't come through, I had three book publishers fighting for rights to my story, so either way, I'd be rich enough to blow Seattle in the New Year.

What was I going to do with the money? I dreamed about that on the daily. First, I'd pay Pete back for all the alimony he gave me. (When we met for coffee last week so he could tell me he and Janet were engaged, he told me not to worry about it. But according to my steps, I'm supposed to be making amends, so I'll at least buy them a nice wedding present—like a house.)

Next, I was going to pay my debts, including my student loans, and make a sizeable donation to Honey's bank account (she was getting out of jail in time for Thanksgiving). The amount would be enough to send her to college without having to work simultaneously, and then I'd set up a fund for her daughter so she could do the same in ten years.

Then I would arm myself to the teeth with premium, grade-A, uncut health insurance, the kind that will allow me unlimited psychiatry visits, which I would conduct via Skype once I get out of Seattle. And finally, I would treat myself to a stupidly good camera. Then I'd go travel.

Where? I wasn't sure yet. Part of me foolishly wondered where Altan was, if we could casually bump into each other on the Ponte Vecchio or in Angkor Wat. But Altan had made it clear he wasn't looking for me. After I'd emailed him a dozen times when I got out of jail, my messages started bouncing back with the warning that his address was no longer valid. His Facebook had gone dark; even his LinkedIn went down. His Instagram remained up, but he switched it to private and wouldn't accept my request, a specialized cruelty designed just for me: I would have given anything to see pictures of where he was.

Even though I had no right to mourn him, I did: on the bus, in the shower, on my lunch break, when I thought of Malcolm, when I planned my future—all of it was bleak, not because I was alone but because I was without *Altan*. Even the guys I'd begrudgingly met on Tinder (for distraction purposes only) didn't have Altan's brand of danger and humor and magic. And so, I grieved. Every night in my bed. Every shift at work. Every heart I poured in latte foam, I poured it out for him.

While Daryl and friends argued over the stack ranking of Sigur Ros albums, I cashed my La Croix and went to the kitchen to get another, unnoticed. A broody-looking couple was pressed against the fridge like a particularly suggestive magnet. I was in no mood to watch them suck face. "Sorry to interrupt," I muttered, pulling the door open to get another drink.

The guy was in his twenties and had a tattoo of a snake crawling up his neck. "No problem," he said as he hoisted his lady friend on the kitchen counter next to the fridge. She was wearing a flowy boho dress, the kind favored by festivalgoers, unseasonable in this weather—which was how I knew she was high.

She said in a far-off voice, "You're pretty. Wanna zed with us?"

"Um, no thanks," I said. Didn't know what zedding was. Didn't care. My sponsor wouldn't like it, and I was probably too old for it anyway. But the guy with the snake tattoo was unable to detect this, because he pried a pill bottle from the pocket of his skinny jeans.

"C'mon," he said, tipping a few tablets into his palm. "It's supposed to be amazing."

The motion was enough to send me back in time, to that moment on the street corner across from WellCorp when Altan offered me my first Morpheum from an aspirin bottle he kept in his desk. I felt the chill of that distant spring, the warmth of Altan's hand as he closed my fingers around the pill so that I would keep it safe. The slowing of my heartbeat, the uncharacteristic kindness in his eyes, the voltage that leapt from his skin to mine when I realized, oh my god, Altan Young cared about me enough to hope I slept well. It was so quick, that moment, so easily forgotten in the deluge of misadventures that followed, and yet here it was, standing in front of me, so close, like I could relive it all again.

I asked, "What's in the bottle?" Even though I already, inexplicably, *knew*.

The dude said, "Remember a few months ago when that lady was accused of murdering some guy in the drug trial?" The pills in his hand weren't pink capsules, but tablets, white and chalky, with flecks of color throughout like funfetti cake. "This is the drug."

It wasn't. This was a bathtub gin version someone had made in a basement and cut with Comet. *How?* Maybe Honey had smuggled the packets she stole from me out of jail, and some meth doctor had reverse engineered the formula to be close. Who knew if he'd gotten it right?

I would know. I was the only person who would.

"So," said Boho Dress, taking the pill from her man friend and holding it out to me. "You want to try it?"

No. Not at all. I couldn't watch these two make love in their minds like I had once done, then scatter themselves on some rocky shore alongside the brittle wreckage of drug-fueled dreams turned "good" ideas. This medicine that had ruined my life and also made me the purest version of myself was out on the street. People were taking it for fun. At parties.

Seattle had just constricted to the size of a beer can. "I gotta go," I said.

"OK," the girl replied, like she didn't care. I saw her toss the pill into her mouth, and then I turned away.

Daryl was still debating albums right where I'd left him; he didn't notice as I ran out the door, down the stairs, and into the dark, wet night of Capitol Hill. Even in the drizzle, my old neighborhood was still colorful and gay—literally *and* metaphorically. There were rainbows painted at the crosswalks in honor of Pride, and sometimes after a drink or three they could make you feel like you were going someplace magical. But I wasn't going anywhere good. I wasn't even going home: I was just heading to the place I slept in with my Craig's List roommate and her noisy, racist lover. I didn't know where home was anymore. I didn't have one.

There is a joke that Seattleites don't own umbrellas because everything they have is already waterproof, but I always keep one in my bag in case the weather decides to suck extra hard. That night it was sleeting at a slant, fat, icy drops zooming through the headlights of passing cars—the kind of precipitation you had to squint against. I carried my umbrella almost perpendicular, like a jousting lance, so I didn't see the guy I nearly shish-kebabed in the middle of the sidewalk. "Jesus, look where you're going!" he shouted from the inside of a parka with the hood pulled up.

At one point not too long ago, the thought of antagonizing a male stranger in the middle of the night would have frozen me to the spot. But the last thing I needed now was to be hassled by some random dude during an existential crisis. "*You* watch where you're going," I fired back without turning to address him as we passed. "Use your damn eyes!"

The dude said, "Ness?"

I stopped. Everything stopped. My heart? Stopped. Even the sleet paused its dive-bombing as my name in that voice found its way to my brain through my ears. It turned to smoke and infiltrated all the boarded-up rooms in which I kept the memories that cracked me open.

The man pulled his hood back, and there he was: unshaven, dark haired, eyes gleaming. "It's you," Altan breathed, his breath fogging as he reversed direction on the sidewalk and stooped beneath my umbrella. Our fingers brushed when he took the handle so he could hold it above us both. It happened so fast, I couldn't tell if he wanted to get close to me or if he wanted to get out of the rain. Either way, he was so near I could swear I felt his heart beating through his parka.

"Hi," he said. His teeth sparkled against his tan.

I craned my neck to look into his face. He looked relaxed, good natured—happy, like he'd spent these past four months practicing yoga, drinking beer, seducing beautiful women, and doing whatever he wanted to the point where *stress* was just a word he'd forgotten along with all the French he'd learned in high school.

"Hi," I said back. *So* smooth. "What are you doing here?"

"Ummm . . ." He looked like he was trying to think of something plausible before deciding he couldn't. He twitched his shoulders in his coat. "Just hanging out."

"Sounds legit."

"Long story. I can tell you over a drink—unless you're busy right now?"

"Yes—I mean, no. No: not busy. Yes, let's drink. I don't drink though. Not liquor. Liquids are OK." I reached up and goofily touched his face. His cheek was warm against my chilly hand.

Altan knit his brows together. "What are you doing?"

"Making sure you're real."

"Are you high?"

"I hope not."

This made him laugh, and oh god, I missed the sound. "Come on. Follow me."

THE HOLLYWOOD ENDING

Altan took my cold hand in his and led me up the street. No idea where we were going: I'd lived in that neighborhood for years but I saw nothing as I followed him blindly into someplace that was decorated by hipsters to look like an old library: mahogany walls, oil paintings, dim. It was sparsely populated on a Thursday night, so we didn't have to sit at the bar. Instead, we got a booth lit by a brass lamp with a green glass shade like the one I gave Pete to keep on his bedside. (Maybe he still had it, for all I knew.)

The waitress came; I ordered a mocktail. Altan got something from the bottle menu—"And would you bring me an opener so I can uncap it myself?" It was an odd request, but the waitress didn't flinch (after all, she was used to dealing with hipsters, who are, by reputation, persnickety) as she bustled off to get our drinks.

My nose was running from being outside; I wiped it on a napkin and sniffed, a quick clean-and-jerk of an inhale. But when I blew out, it felt like the first time I'd breathed since July. My blood was flooded with oxygen. My pupils were dilated, my mind galloping as fast as my heart. Altan Young was in the flesh, and he was making me so high I didn't even know what to say, where to start, how to tell him about those latte hearts I'd been making at work just for him.

"So, you're here," I began, using that famous wit of mine that had attracted Altan in the first place.

"Yes, but not permanently. Just visiting."

"Oh? From where?"

"Bali."

A little sound escaped my mouth, a bittersweet "oh" made of equal parts surprise and jealousy and regret. "I thought you might have gone there, but then I also thought it was too obvious."

"That's why I went there," he said. "To throw you off."

"How is it?"

"Almost as good as I thought it would be."

Why almost? *Because I'm not there?* I wanted to say, but I wasn't sure I had the strength to make it sound like a joke—and even if I did, would Altan laugh? *Could* he laugh with me anymore? I'd dicked him over pretty hard, and while Altan had a good sense of humor, I wouldn't blame him if I'd found its limit last summer when he left me cold. Depending on how willing he'd be to forgive me, maybe we could be . . . something. Anything. Maybe we could go back to that pre-Morpheum state where we emailed dumb jokes to each other over the cube wall, only the cube wall was the ocean. I'd be OK with that.

The waitress arrived with the drinks, and Altan gratefully took his, happy to have something to fidget with.

"What's with the bottle opener?" I asked as he snapped the cap off his drink.

"Force of habit. After the Fairhope, I'm nervous about drinking anything I don't open myself."

I held up my glass to toast. "Welcome to the joys of being afraid that your drink will get messed with."

"Dude, you weren't kidding: being a woman *sucks*," he groused.

I snorted as we clinked. Maybe it was the sleet trickling from my jeans into my socks, but did I detect a thawing between Altan and me? If I could open up even the smallest crack in the ice, maybe I could slip an Instagram friend request through.

"OK, so tell me: what are you doing in Seattle?" I asked.

Altan spun his bottle on the table absent-mindedly. "WellCorp flew me in to offer me a shit-ton of money to never talk about Morpheum again. I guess the new CEO didn't know I already promised to do that for free, so here I am."

"That promise to Malcolm wasn't free," I corrected. "That promise made you leave the country."

"Actually, *you* made me leave the country," he said lightly.

Ouch. "That's because I got the Midol touch: I turn everything into bloody mess."

"How long have you been waiting to say that?"

"*Ages.*"

The laughter was short, followed by silence that felt awkward. The mood was—brisk. Like one of the three nice fall days you get in Seattle: cool, but not unpleasant. Probably appropriate considering the circumstances. "WellCorp made me an offer, too," I said.

He glanced up. "How many figures?"

"Seven. Almost eight."

"Aw, man! I only got six."

"Well, *I'm* the one who got my face pummeled in jail."

"Big deal: you're still beautiful." He trailed off at the end, like the baldness of the statement took him by surprise. He shook his head and recovered while I tried (and failed) not to get my hopes up. "I got *two* shiners as a result of your incarceration. *Two.*"

"Your eyes look fine. They look . . . good."

I felt that dopamine hit I only achieved when I made Altan fumble with his cool. "You think so?" he said.

"I always thought so. Your hair, too. Looks nice."

"Well, shucks." He leaned back into the corner of his side of the booth and put his long legs on the bench seat next to him. I liked that he was making himself comfortable: maybe it meant he'd stay for another drink. Maybe I could charm him some more—enough to get his new email.

"So, what are you doing in Bali? Surf instructing?" I asked. (OK, this was not charming, but I hadn't glimmered for anyone in so long I was forgetting how to do anything but make small talk. *C'mon, Ness! Get your wit together.*)

He sighed dramatically. "Apparently, I'm not the hot, young thing I was when I was last in Bali. They have harder bodies teaching the tourists now, so I'm a landscaper at a fancy resort."

"Which one?"

He waggled his eyebrows. "The Fairhope."

"I'm surprised they let you in."

"You and me both. What have you been up to workwise?"

"I'm at Coffee Talk, if you can believe it."

"I'm surprised they let *you* in. Do you drink all the profits?"

"Most of them." I shrugged. "Once an addict, always an addict. But they let me show my photos there, which is cool. I've actually sold a few."

"Of course you have," said Altan, completely unimpressed. "Your photos are good. Are they up now? I'll have to buy one."

"Don't waste your money. You can have one for free."

"It's impossible to waste money on art. Besides, I'm going to need a few. Got a lot of wall space to fill."

"Mango wall space?" I teased.

"No, not this time."

"What color *is* your bedroom, anyway?" I asked, like I wasn't more than just a little curious. Like I hadn't painted it a hundred times in my dreams.

Altan's mouth twitched up a fraction in a cautious smirk. "Have you been thinking of my bedroom?"

"In jail, I thought a *lot* about your bedroom."

"What about since jail?"

"I still wonder about it sometimes," I said, trying to sound coy.

"Don't lie."

Fine. "OK, more often than sometimes."

If this made him happy, he was too cool to be obvious about it. "It's white."

Of all the paints I'd tested in my fantasies, white had never made it to my color scheme. But it suited him. It was clean, uncomplicated, borderline lazy. It hid nothing and scratched like all get-out. I tried to imagine my photos on Altan's white walls. "Lots of sunlight?"

"Tons."

"White sheets on the bed?"

"Stolen from the Fairhope."

"Haven't you had enough of stealing stuff from work?"

He grinned over his beer, and it literally took my breath away. "Once a bandit, always a bandit."

Goddammit. We would have been so good together.

"What color is *your* bedroom?" he asked. Was he flirting? Wait: of course, he was. Altan's default mode was flirty. The real question was: did he mean it?

"Pink." I rolled my eyes. "I'm renting and I can't repaint it."

"You must hate it."

"You have no idea."

301

"I do actually," he said, tapping his temple, reminding me how he used to vacation in my mind. I remembered him in there, sprawled out on the beaches of my subconscious. I wanted to send him a postcard of my cortex that said *Wish you were here.*

"Speaking of Morpheum—"

"I thought we weren't allowed."

"I think we can. Just this once." I took a sip of my drink and secretly wished it had booze so I could be brave. "Do you ever wonder what we'd be doing if we never took it?" I asked.

"All the time," he said, without missing a beat. "I'd be dating some girl on Tinder. You'd be pregnant. We'd still be at WellCorp. Malcolm would be perving at your ass. Diana would be perving on her plants. Our lives would be boring as fuck."

Ugh. When he put it like that, it sounded kind of dismal. "But would we be happy?"

"Sure, we'd be happy. Why not? People talk about happiness like there's only one way to get it, but as long as you have food and shelter and good health, the rest is just details."

I rolled my eyes. Of course, Altan would say that. Some people had a concept of destiny, of one path you are meant to find and follow, like contentment is the prize at the center of a maze. But Altan lived for the nooks and crannies, the twists and tight squeezes, the surprises around every corner. Without an endgame, it was all just a game, and for all his devil-may-care cool, Altan was probably the cockiest cock-eyed optimist I knew.

As scientifically as I could muster, I asked, "Do you think we would have been happy together?"

Here Altan wrinkled his nose and looked up, like he was considering it for the first time. (This performance was how I knew he'd thought of it dozens of times before.) "I think we would have been very happy together."

"Yeah." I sighed. "Me, too."

I thought of all the wine we'd had in Paris, side by side in those lovely sidewalk cafes. Back then, I'd thought the world was the most interesting thing to look at. But seeing Altan again—the angle of his cheekbones, the mahogany of his eyes, the fall of his hair in his face and the toss of his head as he tried to coax it back—it occurred to me that maybe I'd had no idea what I was talking about back then.

We sat drinking in that Sunday-morning silence I loved with Pete, that comfort that only comes from being with someone you don't feel the need to impress. After all, I couldn't impress Altan: he knew what I was. We both did, only I hadn't admitted it out loud in a while.

Or, you know, ever.

"For what it's worth, I owe you an apology," I said.

"For sleeping with Pete?"

I shook my head. "That was something I had to do—for my own sanity, and as a fairness to him."

Altan narrowed his eyes across the table. "This is the worst apology ever."

"That wasn't the apology, dumbass!"

"So now you're calling me names?"

"Would you please *shut up* so I can tell you I'm sorry?"

He flashed me that wicked smile of his before he mimed pulling a zipper across his mouth.

"I'm sorry," I said, and suddenly I didn't feel like joking anymore. His hand had a gravitational pull: the urge to hold it across the table was so strong, but I laced my fingers in my lap instead. For his sake. "I'm sorry for hiding the fact that I took Morpheum with Pete, and for expecting you to forgive me because you felt guilty about June. It was dishonest, and I tried to exploit your most shameful moment. Both were cruel, and you deserved better."

For a moment I saw his eyes flash with the memory. Altan was cool, but he wasn't cool enough to pretend he didn't have a heart that still bore a scar from the time I took an axe to it. He pulled from his beer and set the bottle roughly on the table. "That sounded like you practiced it a few times."

"I did. You know, in case I ever got the chance."

"I'm glad you did."

Fuck it. I placed my hand on the table, close enough for him to reach, if he wanted to. "Altan, I miss you so much."

He didn't move except to clench his jaw: he stared at the table, refusing to meet my eyes. It was hard to see Altan hurt, first because I loved him, but also because pain was baggage. I hated that I weighed him down, that I deserved his anger and suspicion, that I had no way to convince him I could do better, try harder, be truer.

"I still dream about you," he said after a long silence, centering his bottle on its coaster to give himself something to do. "A lot. Sometimes I'm not even asleep."

He didn't say this like it brought him comfort. "I dream about you, too. All the time."

My hand was between us, begging, the table tacky beneath my palm. If I could have wormed my way into his brain then, I would have told him to believe me, please believe me. *Even though this sounds stupid and sappy, it's true.* "You changed me," I said. "You changed the way I saw the world. I thought it was the Morpheum that did it, and sure, it helped. But the drug was you."

This had all been welling inside me for the past four months. I was babbling, trying to get it all out before he shut me down. "When I love you, I feel more alive than I ever have. And even if you don't love me back, I'm so grateful that you did once—because if you hadn't, I'd still be at WellCorp and getting perved on by Malcolm. *And* I'd be pregnant. Which would suck. Oh, and you got me out of jail, so . . . thanks for that, too."

He shook his head: what was he saying *No* to? "Never a dull moment with you, is there, Ness?" he said to the coasters. Then he drained his beer and signaled the waitress for the check.

Slowly, I retracted my hand back to my side of the table. Hot, angry tears pricked the corners of my eyes. I'd failed. Oh shit, I'd failed. And now I was going to cry while Altan fished his wallet out of his back pocket; he was going to pay, and then he was going to leave, and I'd spend the rest of my life trying (*and failing*) to find him in another man. I'd search the whole world, and every picture I took, every vista I saw would be drab without him.

He was talking, but I couldn't hear him over my private hyperventilation: I had a hard time understanding when he said, "So look, I'll come into Coffee Talk tomorrow and check out your pictures"—my heart was in tatters, falling into my stomach, through the floor, down into the core of the earth, a stone seeking the bottom of the sea—"but you know I have no eye for this shit. It really would be best if you could just bring your photos to Bali and tell me which ones to hang up where."

I heaved a shaky breath, and I said, "*What?*"

"I mean, if you do that sort of thing. I don't know what services you offer as a professional travel photographer-slash-millionaire, but I think in-home consultations would be a unique selling point."

"In-home consultations," I repeated, dumbly. He was taking this poker-face thing between us a little too far. "You mean, like *your* home. In Bali?"

"When you get around there, yeah. Not sure what your travel plans are."

What the hell was he saying? "You're inviting me to Bali?"

"Only if you want to come."

I blinked. Four times. Then six more times. "This isn't some revenge plot, is it? Like, I fly to Bali and it turns out you've never lived there, and I'm running around looking for you . . ."

"No!" Altan laughed: rich, glorious music. "But even if it was, you'd be able to afford the airfare, so who cares?"

My hand flew back to the table, palm up, seeking confirmation. "But what do we do with Morpheum and jail and Pete and June and Malcolm and Sam—just pretend none of it ever happened?"

"Yeah." Altan shrugged. "It'll be like every movie where the main character wakes up at the end and realizes it was all a dream."

"I hate those endings. They're so cheap."

"I know," he said, taking my hand across the table. His palms were calloused from gardening, but his long fingers were the same, and that's how I knew this was real. "But Hollywood does it all the time," he said. "So, fuck it."

Altan's mantra fell somewhere between a joke and a philosophy, kind of like the rest of him. The waitress arrived with the check, and Altan tossed his head toward me. "She's paying," he said to her, haughtily. "She's a millionaire because she got beat up in jail."

"That's not true," I muttered to the waitress as I handed her cash. I mean, I *did* get my face pummeled in jail, but "I'm a millionaire because Malcolm is awful," I told Altan as we shrugged on our still-damp coats. "And I'm not going to Bali with you if you're going to tell everyone I was once accused of murder."

"But you *are* coming to Bali?" he said as we made for the door. When he opened it, a sheet of sleet blew straight into my face. Over the course of one drink, the night had become even more miserable, as if it were conspiring with Altan to reinforce how nice and warm and sexy Bali would be.

I'd made my mind up before I'd even paid the check, but still I pretended to be blasé about this decision—because that's what we did. "Sure," I said, and then I sighed to really sell the idea that I didn't give a shit either way. Even so, I felt the heat of the moment zing up my spine. "I guess I'll come to Bali."

"Yeah?" Altan pulled his hood up, but not before I caught the gigantic Cheshire cat smile that split his face.

"Once I get the WellCorp check, I'll book a room at the Fairhope."

"Will you be able to afford it?"

I snapped my umbrella open. "I'll be able to afford ten."

"Still, maybe you should stay with me after a few nights instead. Just to save some money."

"And what if your white apartment doesn't meet my standards?"

He held out his hand to get me to shake. "I guarantee it'll be better than jail."

I shook. I shook! Like this was a professional arrangement—this thing where we agreed not to be turds to one another after we'd weathered the most ridiculous psychic adventure known to man. Just before I let go, Altan took my umbrella from me so he could hold it high above us both. He leaned in and kissed me on the cheek, at the corner of my mouth, right on the border of friends and lovers, where we'd found ourselves in Paris all those months ago. We were there again now, like no time had passed, like the rest of this year had just been a nightmare, a long and aggravating layover on the way to somewhere good.

When Altan pulled away, I put my hand to my face as if to press the memory of his lips into my skin. The sandpaper of his stubble gave the slightest after burn, like a tactile shot of tequila.

"So, I'll see you in a few weeks?" he said, handing me my umbrella.

"Yeah," I answered dreamily.

"Do you need someone to get you home? I know you don't like being alone at night."

"Yeah, well, then I went to jail, so everything is slightly less scary now."

"That logic is questionable."

"Tell yourself that the next time you want to cut through an alley."

"Are you sure?"

"Yes, I'm sure."

"Last chance!"

"You're ridiculous."

"The worst."

He backed up the sidewalk four steps and stood, watching me. I yelled, "Go already!"

"*You* go."

"Ugh. Fine. OK. Bye."

"Bye."

"*Bye!*"

Altan finally sauntered off—not that I was *really* in a hurry to see him go. Before he turned the corner, he looked back to see if I was still watching.

You know I was.

MALCOLM JACOBS DEAD IN JAIL

Charlie Goodman, January 23

SEATTLE—Malcolm Jacobs, son of WellCorp CEO Dean Jacobs and former WellCorp executive, was found dead in his jail cell yesterday morning. He was 46 years old.

Jacobs was awaiting trial for his alleged participation in a plot to kill presidential candidate Amara Kassis at a Fourth of July fundraiser last year. A bartender at the event confessed to taking money from Jacobs to add a WellCorp drug called "Morpheum" to Kassis's drink, though Jacobs's lawyers have maintained that the presence of Morpheum on Kassis's toxicology report did not conclusively prove the drug caused her death.

Jacobs was being housed at King County Correctional Facility in a private cell for his own safety. But despite extra precautions and increased guard detail, it is reported that Jacobs was able to use his uniform pants as a noose. "He was found naked," says a King County correctional officer who refused to be named. She added, "It wasn't pretty."

The coroner is ruling Jacobs's death a suicide, but reports that his underwear was found over his face like a hood have fueled suspicions that Jacobs was executed. Those who worked with him are similarly skeptical that he would have taken his own life.

"Malcolm Jacobs never displayed shame or remorse for any of his actions in all the years I worked with him," says Diana Wilson, who oversaw medical trials at WellCorp's Urban Campus. "For him to start feeling bad about things now is unimaginable. It's fairly obvious to anyone with a brain that Malcolm did not kill himself."

HOW'S MY DRIVING?

Please leave a review for *Poison Dream* at
https://www.amazon.com/kittycookbooks
https://www.goodreads.com/kittycookbooks

WHAT'S
KITTY COOKING
NEXT?

Stay up to date on giveaways and new releases.

Instagram: @kittycookbooks
Facebook: @kittycookbooks
http://www.kittycookbooks.com/newsletter

ACKNOWLEDGMENTS

You! Yes, *you*. I am acknowledging you. Whoever you are, that you picked this book up means a lot to me, and that you've gotten to the end means even more. Thanks for coming with me on this ridiculous adventure about love and sleeping pills. I hope your own life is considerably less dramatic.

Cheers to my always-wonderful editor, Brian Colella, for ensuring I don't sound like an idiot. Let it be known that all typos found in this book were introduced by me after the final edit.

Let it also be known that Scott Howard is the greatest designer I could ever hope to work with. The covers for both *Sleeping Together* and *Poison Dream* are perfect. Thank you for your artistry and patience through a thousand revisions—and for being my buddy for life.

Thank you to JD for taking a chance on these books. I'm so honored you chose me.

Unspecifiable kudos to Jess, Carissa, Nicole P, Nicole BA, Alison, Maria, Lauren, Amanda, Mariette, Lisa, Allie, Mr. Darcy's, Sando, Marcus, Mom, Dad, and everyone else I forgot to mention for their enthusiasm and vibes.

To my biggest (and littlest) fans, Matilda and Scott: you inspire me every day with your humor, cleverness, determination, and imagination. Thanks for being you.

And finally, to Brady: thank you for encouraging me to follow my dreams (poison or otherwise)—and for ensuring that our own love story isn't nearly as gnarly as the ones I write about. You're the best.

ABOUT THE AUTHOR

Photo ©2018 by Nicole Pomeroy

Kitty Cook is a book chef based out of Seattle, specializing in salty heroines, spicy plotlines, and semisweet endings that hit the spot. With two energetic kids and a very patient husband, Kitty spends her free time exploring the Pacific Northwest in the sun and curled up with a book in the rain. Her first novel, *Sleeping Together*, won a silver 2019 IPPY for best first book and a 2019 IndieReader Discovery Award for best romance. Her writing has appeared in *The New York Times* and Salon.com under a different, less ridiculous name.

CPSIA information can be obtained
at www.ICGtesting.com
Printed in the USA
LVHW111628031122
732209LV00007B/269

9 781732 998421